I0763506

THE LAST SKYE

JULIA LAPORTE

The characters and events portrayed in this book are fictitious. Any similarity to real persons, living or dead, is coincidental and not intended by the author.

ISBN: 978-1-7354161-2-0

Cover design by ebook launch.com

Created with Vellum

Dedicated to amazing teachers everywhere,
and especially Mrs. Michelle Ramey,
who taught me to read
and love books.

Love you mom

ONE

SKYE GRIPPED THE LAPELS OF HER LEATHER JACKET, BRACING against the cold Northeast wind. She inhaled the smell of change in the weather. It always reminded her of an ice rink and gave her a taste for hot chocolate. Snow was on its way. While she loved the colors of the fall, she hated the cold. Her teeth bared at the thought of snow.

She crossed the parking lot and entered a boxy, brick building. In her experience, most state and county government buildings were nondescript brick office buildings that smelled like old carpet. At least it was warm. She relaxed the grip on her jacket and followed the signs to her case manager's office.

A large woman with chestnut brown hair and straight cut bangs greeted her. "Good morning, Skye. Come on back."

Skye's cheeks pulled up in a grin, not a real smile. It was her natural reaction to greetings. She followed the woman down the hall, to a dull office with a mess of papers and a stained chair. Skye slouched with her hands in her jacket pockets.

"We've got a lot to cover. Are you nervous? It's okay if you are."

Skye grinned. "Nope. I'm good."

Eleanor bobbed her head back and forth and gestured with her hands while she talked. "A lot of foster kids get nervous when they age out of the system. I want you to be prepared. There are still resources available to you, but it's a quick transition to suddenly doing everything for yourself."

Skye leaned forward, resting her forearms on her legs. "I'm actually looking forward to it. Ready to go."

The case manager's face dropped. Her over-plucked eyebrows bunched together on her forehead.

Skye's face softened into a genuine half-smile. "Don't look at me like that, Eleanor. I'm going to be fine."

"I know you are, Skye. But I still worry about you. You are –" She sat at her desk and tapped her cheek as she searched for the right words. "You are very independent. *Fiercely* independent. And that's good. It will serve you well. But it's still a big change."

They reviewed her transition plan, laboring on the details of every page. Skye followed along, but her attention drifted in and out of the conversation. Little things caught her eye: the texture of the carpet, the peeling laminate of the desk, words on the mess of papers not meant for her eyes. Skye felt the weight of bureaucracy lifting from her shoulders.

She had secured housing last month, a sparsely furnished studio on the fringe of town. Everywhere she needed to get was within walking distance. It was better than being trapped in the houses of the system.

Skye refocused with the lull in the conversation. Eleanor stared blankly at the papers, her mouth rested on entwined hands, elbows on the desk.

Skye cocked her head and dipped to make eye contact. "What's on your mind, Eleanor?"

Eleanor shook her head and straightened her posture. Her eyes softened when they met Skye's curious blue gaze. "I'm going to be honest with you, Skye."

"I prefer it that way."

Eleanor smiled, though still distraught. She pursed her lips and paused. Her stare made Skye uncomfortable. Skye's ability to mask her emotions had been honed over the years. Her discomfort in the awkward silence was kept to herself.

"It can be lonely— "Eleanor began. Skye looked away with an incredulous smirk. "No, Skye, really. Listen to me. I have no doubt you will succeed, whether you decide to go to college or decide on a career. You are smart and independent and extremely capable."

"Thank you, Eleanor."

"I mean it, Skye. But you have no ties to the community. Not that I know of. No real friends. You don't keep in touch with your foster families, some for obvious reasons, but they weren't all so bad."

Skye scoffed. "I have friends. I keep in touch with who I want, and I know how to get in touch if the need arises."

"You need to develop *meaningful*, real connections. Real friendships. Real relationships. These are things that are missing from your life, Skye. I want you to thrive and be happy."

"I'm happy to get out of the system, Eleanor. I'm getting out alive, which not everyone can say." Anger bubbled in Skye's chest. She breathed evenly, hiding the rise in her blood pressure. The smirk on her face wouldn't betray her. "All I've ever wanted was a place to call my own. My home. Somewhere I didn't have to share with twelve other people and their pets. All the places I've ever stayed in belonged to someone else. I was either an unfortunate guest or a temporary burden. I am *happy* to be on my own. And *when* I develop a deep, meaningful connection with someone, it will be because they earned it."

Eleanor nodded. "Well, Skye. I wish you the best. I really do."

"Do you need anything else from me?"

Eleanor shook her head.

"Then, I'm free to go?"

Eleanor nodded and grinned sadly. "Yes, Skye, you're free to go."

Skye left the chair as she spoke. "Bye then. Have a good one."

"Skye?" Eleanor said. Skye paused at the door and looked back. "Find where you belong. Find your people. Good luck, hun."

"I will, Eleanor. Don't worry."

Skye followed the sidewalks, cut through the pavilion in the town square, and waited at the crosswalk. Her afternoon was free. She debated stopping at the local bookstore or grabbing lunch. She decided on both.

The bell above the door chimed, alerting her presence to the staff.

"Hey Skye, new releases out on the wall." The slender girl behind the register smiled brightly. They went to school together but weren't friends.

Skye mulled over Eleanor's advice. Her mind was open to different perspectives, and she didn't discount the advice, but she didn't put great stock in it either. It didn't help that she didn't remember the bookstore girl's name.

Skye browsed the shelves, reading the back covers of books that caught her eye. She picked out two and a tote bag and rang out. Skye read the girl's nametag.

"Thanks, Emberly." Skye smiled.

Emberly held up a book before putting it in the bag. "Let me know how you like this one. I've heard it's pretty good."

"Will do. See you later," Skye matched her cheerfulness.

Eleanor would have been proud.

Skye stopped at the deli and picked up lunch and a handful of groceries. Her apartment wasn't too far, but far enough that carrying a lot of extra weight would be tiring. She plugged in her earphones and started a playlist to make the steps less tedious.

Vibrations traveled through her body as if she were sitting on a car filled with booming speakers. She pulled out an earbud and looked up and down the street. Her dirtiest scowl was locked and loaded with no offender in sight. The vibrations intensified, numbing her skin. Fear turned her stomach. Adrenaline sparked her veins.Her mind raced. *We don't get earthquakes like this in Ohio.*

BUT IT WASN'T JUST Ohio. The atmosphere rumbled and groaned, cracked and popped with activity. Vibrations shook bones and fibers across the planet. Eyes searched the void in the sun and the night. Reports of debris and foreign objects in space debuted on screens and radios of every country. People raved about aliens, foreign invaders, and the end of days on public channels and public spaces. Anxiety fueled the mind. Actions of chaos ran rampant.

Skye hurried home, pulling up news reports as she walked. She watched the skies out the window of her little apartment. She didn't buy into the aliens' stories - her eyes rolled at the word - but she couldn't deny that something was happening.

Reports of damaged satellites abruptly ended several television programs and internet access. People continued to panic. Space debris littered the sky, burning through the clouds as it fell.

Then the internet went dark, and real panic set in. People strayed from their houses to the streets looking for answers and reassurance. Hearts beat rapidly in their chests. They prayed and clung to one another for comfort.

In the dark night of the Northeast, the Sun began to shine. Only, it wasn't the right time, nor was it the Sun that the Earth so frequently orbited. It grew in brightness and intensity, blinding the people who looked directly at its rays. The ones who still had their sight watched in horror as their neighbors' skeletons shone through the translucence of their skin.

Ten billion tears shed. Seven billion screams disappeared. Feelings of panic and doom settled into the hearts of the remaining creatures of Earth. And then nothing more.

TWO

Members of the Interstellar Alliance community generally do not sweat. They experience fear, stress, and elevated temperatures like anyone else, but sweat is not a common trait of most species. The Jodra Core was home to the High Commander, second only to the interstellar territories' premier ruler. It was an honor to serve on the highest ship in the Alliance, even as a recruit. It was equally terrifying when something went wrong, and something was inescapably wrong. The armpits of recruit Halden of the Jodra Core ship were slick with perspiration. The lowest-ranking member on the highest ship in the collective galaxies just received terrible news.

Receiving transmissions was a routine part of the easiest job on the Jodra Core. Halden received communications from scientists who completed their studies of outlier planets, species of interest, and possible threats to the Alliance. Reports were read, filed accordingly, and left to collect dust in the digital storage archives. They were readily accessible by any member of the Alliance community. After all, information on the galaxies, planets, and life was public property. It was encouraged to keep up on the latest developments and take a community interest in the progress of the Alliance.

Recruit Halden read the transmission - terror building in his core. It was an extensive report of a forty-year observational study of the humans of Earth. Mapping the remaining planets was a trending interest of the Alliance. The four inner quadrants – Koro, Tudo, Ren, and Ziet – had been extensively explored for several Jodra millennia. The furthest territories in the Alliance, the four outer quadrants – Almas, Hoopili, Soturi, Rojje – were still being explored and mapped. Most viable planets were known, as were most species, but there were still a few outliers that required further inspection. Earth was an outlier.

The Alliance Council had recently approved this study. All scientific proposals and assignments must receive approval from their appropriate Council, and all research ships must be accounted for at all times. The research vessels are highly advanced, and unapproved interactions with primitive species could prove catastrophic.

Halden copied the transmission to a port drive and erased it from the terminal mainframe. He rushed through the stark halls of the ship to find his lieutenant. With every step and every fiber of his being, he yearned for the dimly lit safety of his workstation. The bright lights and bright grey walls of the ship emphasized the unusual sheen across his forehead. People took notice of his oddities. Insecurity flared across his angled cheeks.

At the end of the longest corridor in the existence of Halden's life was the door to the quarters of Lieutenant Guilem. He would know what to do with this information. He should be the first to know. Discretion was imperative.

Halden knocked with measurably appropriate loudness. He could feel the heat radiate from his skin, fueling the vicious cycle of sweating and overheating. The lieutenant was a formidable man, as expected. His broad shoulders and sharp facial features testified to his origins. The Elian race of the planet Dodelig owned and appreciated their deadly reputation. Their skin possessed the characteristics of granite—smooth, solid, and varied in color. Their stature resembled mountains in both mass and regality.

The lieutenant granted entrance, and the sliding door opened. He sat at a grey mainframe desk, much like every other on the ship. The glow of information dimmed as Halden entered, suggesting it was above his clearance.

Lieutenant Guilem cleared his throat. "Can I help you?"

"Lieutenant, I have received a transmission from Earth," Halden said.

The lieutenant raised his eyes thoughtfully. "It is the appropriate time that the study be completed. Has the observing scientist run into technical issues? Does he need assistance?"

"No, sir. The venerable Scientaut Yar Tukk is dead, sir."

Sweat beaded at Halden's temple. He stood in perfect posture and silence as he waited for the lieutenant's response. It was insufferable. The stoicism of the lieutenant made goosebumps down Halden's arms. His stare felt predatory. Halden's mind wandered, imagining the lieutenant devouring the souls of his prey.

"Are you sure?" Lieutenant Guilem said.

"The scientist, Yar Tukk, expected and predicted his demise and made preparations to warn the Alliance. He was reportedly murdered by a human known as *Steve*. It appears that the humans discovered the ship."

The lieutenant accepted the port drive and brought up the transmission on a secure reader. The transfer to the lieutenant's internal memory chip took mere seconds to complete. Halden was unaware that the Elian people had eyebrows, but Lieutenant Guilem's eyebrow most certainly twitched while he read the report.

"It's quite long," Lieutenant Guilem said.

"Yes, sir. It is five Jodra shift, um, a forty Earth year observational study."

The lieutenant's stony expression remained. Halden could not tell if he was still reading the document, if he was thinking, or if he had fallen asleep with his eyes open. Halden imagined that was the only way the lieutenant slept.

"Are there any deaths on record from previous expeditions to Earth?" Lieutenant Guilem said slowly.

"Yes," Halden recalled. "There have been two accidental, non-human related deaths during the previous twenty-four recorded expeditions. They have been scheduled every ten to twenty Jodra shift."

"This is troublesome. We must take it to the High Commander. The Council will be gathered," Lieutenant Guilem said.

The Lieutenant rose from the desk and nearly brushed the ceiling with his head. Halden swallowed, his mouth and throat dry as desert sand. He exited the lieutenant's chambers and awaited his lead.

Lieutenant Guilem donned a military jacket that stretched over his figure and announced his status. Without a second glance at Halden, he locked his chambers and strode toward the ship's command. Halden struggled to keep pace without jogging. He felt like a child in the shadow of his parent.

Halden stopped abruptly behind the lieutenant as the ship scanned their presence. Heat flushed his face with uncertainty. Recruits never littered the main bridge of an IA ship. The shiny metal doors and all-seeing eyes of the Jodra Core ship restricted access to upper-level authority.

Lieutenant Guilem glanced at Halden. His invisible brow raised slightly. "Recruit, you will follow and give your report when asked. Do not speak unless spoken to."

Halden's eyes widened. He straightened his posture and nodded. "Yes, sir."

They entered the central command deck, often referred to as the bridge. It was a dimly lit room spanning the front length of the ship. The grey metal that lined the entire vessel seemed cleaner and sharper here. The panels on the workstations flashed pertinent information. The attendants worked silently with complete focus, ready to respond to orders at any moment's notice. An attendant on the bridge was a position of honor among recruits. They were called jiffies.

Halden's eyes slowly adjusted and scanned over the crew. There were seven jiffies and two open, dormant workstations. He settled his gaze on an elevated station in the center of the bridge where the High Commander stood. Lieutenant Guilem walked to the platform and waited. Halden kept pace and distance.

High Commander Jarlat was a legend among the Alliance and its enemies. She was appointed to the position by the Premier Entu himself after the legendary Battle of Soo. The battle's resolution, which defined the Interstellar Alliance territories, was primarily attributed to Commander Jarlat's military strategy and execution. For someone from the planet Anour, Jarlat possessed the intuition of a Kharahk. It was a longstanding rumor that the people of the planet Kharahk could see the future.

The High Commander wore a black tunic and pants. She towered in height to rival that of the Lieutenant. Her lean stature and broad shoulders were fitting of a descendant of the Anour court. Her long face emphasized her bone structure. She stood perfectly still, like an extension of the ship.

"Lieutenant Guilem," the High Commander said.

She turned to face them. Her movements made the hair rise on Halden's arms. It was as if the ship and its occupants moved to meet the High Commander's gaze, not the other way around. Everything revolved around her in this piece of space.

"High Commander. We have received an unsettling report." Lieutenant Guilem said.

"How unsettling?" the High Commander said.

"We received a transmission from the observational study of planet Earth in the Rojje territory. The sender, scientist Yar Tukk, is dead," Lieutenant Guilem said.

Halden noted the silence in the room. It appeared that even the flashing of the display screens paused momentarily. The movements of the jiffies mimicked the High Commander in their stillness. It lasted only moments before activity returned, but it was enough to turn Halden's stomach. If he survived this report, the first place Halden would go was the canteen. He desperately needed a drink.

"That is a problem. How did he die?"

"High Commander, this is recruit Halden. He received the transmission. Halden, report," Lieutenant Guilem said.

"From the report, it is presumed that he was killed by a human named Steve after his assimilation failed," Halden said, "sir." His voice cracked on the almost forgotten note of respect.

Heat flushed Halden's skin. He could not tell if the silence was due to the content of his report or its delivery. He deeply wished it was the former.

"The Council will be gathered," Commander Jarlat said, turning back to her original position. "Lieutenant Guilem, inform the crew. We will be landing on Opes. Sitara, set coordinates for entry to Jodra. Final location, the grand council."

"Yes, sir," the jiffie Sitara said.

"Chunni, contact the Council and arrange for a meeting. Dhru, ready the ship for landing."

"The council has been contacted, sir."

"Prepared for landing, sir. Sequence initiated."

Lieutenant Guilem was already striding toward the door. Halden scurried to the exit, resisting the urge to let his eyes linger on the bridge. It was the first, and possibly last, time he would ever be permitted in the same room as High Commander Jarlat. Upon exiting, Halden released a heavy breath.

Lieutenant Guilem locked eyes on the recruit. "You are to speak to no one until after the Council renders a decision. Confine yourself to your chambers."

"Yes, sir," Halden stiffened his posture before retreating to his room.

THREE

As a Level One Destroyer, the Jodra Core had the most extensive tech and firepower of the Alliance integrated into its every nook and cranny. The massive ship descended to the council port yard, landing with feather-light precision. It loomed over all other vessels in the yard, few of which could produce as graceful a landing with even a fraction of the size.

The dignitary egress opened. It was neither customary nor agreeable to enter the council yard from a cargo bay, as was usual for most landing ports. Commander Jarlat exited, followed by Lieutenant Guilem. They would be the only members of the Jodra Core to set foot on the council grounds. They were the only members with enough clearance.

Opes was meticulously maintained by the foremost botanist authority throughout the cosmos. Physics-defying feats of flora growth danced along the perfectly even walkways. The ornate symmetry of the council hall would have made the likes of Antoni Gaudi jealous. Its quartz-like facade glistened under the two distant suns. The domed hall featured a single room with arches open to the outside. Mercurial benches blossomed in the center, forming a perfect circle. It allowed members of the council to face each other as equals, and equals they were.

Commander Jarlat and Lieutenant Guilem entered the hall and waited as the room filled with dignitaries, one seat for every active planet in the Alliance. The Galactic Core offered representatives from planet Jodra and Anour of the Torrens planetary train. It also held a seat for Alliance Premier Entu – though the foremost authority of the Alliance was not expected to attend, except on matters of utmost importance.

While each planetary system in the Alliance had their own diverse customs and functioning societies, they were each recognized for a dominant trait. Inner quadrant Koro encompassed several planetary clusters, but claim only one representative from Kharahk. Ethics and honesty gave them a respected voice among their peers – and they could predict the future, or so the rumor went. They had an uncanny ability to almost always choose the best course of action in any situation.

The Kharahk representative dressed in traditional garbs. A long robe sheath draped his tall, lean frame. Rings of stone beads adorned his head, neck, and shoulders. A woven, beaded belt was secured around his waist.

"Good day, Arwel." Commander Jarlat greeted the dignitary.

Inner quadrant Tudo possessed two Council seats for planets Vanzkelga and Enantios. The most outspoken members of the Alliance also developed the most advanced technology. Their representatives consistently arrived together.

Three representatives held seats from the inner quadrant Ren, one for each significant life planet. These were the most populated planets in the Alliance and delivered the best trade workers. Representatives from Ula and Ahila shared commonalities in both appearance and custom. Subtle differences could be unearthed in the details if one paid close enough attention.

Planet Munja of the Ren quadrant was unique. The Wella race's distinctive features commanded attention. As the premier mechanics across the cosmos, their ability to weld at the touch of a finger gave them a considerable advantage. While not exactly nocturnal, the Wella race preferred darkness. Their planet settlements remained in shadow for most of their year. The Munja representative arrived cloaked in the Wella travel gear, concealing their skin from the light. Her eyes shone under the hood, reflective of her protective eyewear. Her fingertips peeked out of fingerless gloves, emitting a dim glow.

Ziet, the final inner quadrant, produced those of a strong scientific and philosophic nature. It held the most seats of the inner quadrants, representing planets Razvedka, Gafur, Mencuri, and Urtesi. Razvedka, known for its exploratory scientists, sent Lhu of the Tazon. Fur covered the Tazon from tail to nose. Most possessed dark coloring with patches or stripes of light. Lhu's bright white fur and ivory stripes were an anomaly. Her amber-red eyes gleamed with intelligence beyond her years. While most council members adorned customary garb, Lhu maintained her discovery ship uniform. She was, after all, a renowned Alliance scientist.

Gafur, the largest planet in Ziet, possessed a lucrative mining community and the best geologists. The lifespans of the Gafur were some of the longest in the Alliance. Their operations expanded throughout the Alliance and collected resources from most viable planets. Thyst of Gafur personally favored shining stones and minerals above those of function and wore enough adornments to weigh down a small ship. He inherited his name from his great ancestor, along with several mining operations.

The people of Mencuri held science and medicine in the highest regard. The Alliance funneled its greatest medics out of Mencuri whenever they could. However, the mencurians generally disregarded the idea of leaving their home planet. The Mencuri representative Eudia melted into her seat. The elder the mencurian, the more layers of skin draped from their frames.

Urtesi, the planet of philosophers, dreamers, and physicists, delivered Shivali, a short, thin woman whose feet did not touch the ground. They did not need to, as she preferred to tuck them beneath her anyway. Her long hair was tied back by a series of braids, each layer revealing a different hue.

Soturi was the only outer quadrant to have council representation. Planets Dodelig and Hevoc represented in the council possessed the deadliest creatures in the Alliance. Aris, the Hevocian leader, wore a black skin-tight bodysuit. Her boots were tipped in alloy metal, as were the ends of her hair. She nodded to Lieutenant Guilem and Commander Jarlat and stood by her seat.

Lieutenant Guilem represented his home planet of Dodelig. It was a hard rock planet with immense gravity. Most alliance members would crush or implode from the gravitational forces without proper protective equipment. While harsh for the typical visitor, Dodelig excelled as the host for the Alliance prison systems. The majority of Dodelig citizens belonged to the Elian race and served in police and military duties.

Then there was Rojje, the outer quadrant, and region of planet Earth. The most diverse and distant planet in the Alliance, it was recently approved for observation. While not entirely unusual for a discovery ship to be destroyed, if it is commandeered by an unproven species, it becomes an immediate threat. There will always be concern for the emergence of a new enemy to the Alliance or an unknown species to disrupt the carefully built system of life across vast space. It was a concern the Alliance took very seriously.

With each seat filled and accounted for, Jarlat rose and addressed the council. Business always came first. There would be pleasantries, but only after the meeting concluded.

"I thank you for your speedy arrival. I know many of you have traveled many parsecs to get here. I have gathered the council to discuss a recent event and make a decision to take action."

No one interrupted the High Commander. All discussion and questions would be kept until the end of the address, though their expressions ranged from mild concern to barely contained rage.

She continued. "Each of you were sent a report on an encrypted vector, accessible only to you by using your council identifier. The scientist, Yar Tukk, is dead. He died during his observational study of the planet Earth in Rojje. A human of Earth was responsible for his death and has his ship. I move to open discussion on Yar Tukk and the human conflict."

A roar of incomprehensible anger burst from the bench. "My kin has been murdered by those filthy –"

The High Commander held a hand up to silence the outburst. "I implore you to cease and reevaluate how you address the council."

Khorsol spoke. "It is unacceptable. The death must be atoned."

"What is the recommendation from Vanzkelga?" said Asho-Pani of Ula.

"Complete obliteration," Khorsol said. "I call for a vote."

"Denied," said the council in unison.

"The appropriate duration and thorough discussion must be met prior to engaging in a vote," said Arwel of Kharahk.

Thyst of Gafur jingled as he spoke. "These humans have yet to engage in the Alliance. While they have an inkling of life offsite their home planet, they do not have the means to reach the inner quadrants, let alone Jodra."

Anevay of Enantios sneered. "Yet."

Shivali of Urtesi stroked a midnight blue strand of hair. "They are infants. The scientist Yar Tukk made considerable errors in this *observational* study – which ultimately led to his demise. It is unfortunate, yes, but the blame of his death does not lie with an entire planet."

"They are a threat and danger to us all." Anevay turned up his delicate nose. "You all read the report. The humans have advanced aggressively in very little time at all."

A murmur spread through the council hall.

Nhan of Ahila spoke in the hushed tones of an elder. "Is it worth the risk? Do we gamble all we've achieved through the Alliance on a relatively unknown species that happens to fall within our territories?"

"The Alliance has a strong foundation in scientific discovery and developing our community through intelligence, not impulse," Arwel said.

Lhu of Razvedka stood. "It would be unintelligent to destroy this planet and lose the wealth of knowledge yet discovered."

"It would be unintelligent to allow these parasites to flourish," Khorsol said.

Commander Jarlat watched as discussion turned to scorn. The Alliance formed when a united front was necessary, and cooperation was the only means of survival. It has been many years since that unification. Several of the original council positions have been redistributed, as do all positions of power in time.

Jarlat took a deep, even breath and recalled the words of her predecessor. *It must remain the imperative of the council to continue in unification and respect.*

"There appears to be an insurmountable distance between proposed solutions," Thyst said, examining his reflection in his largest ring.

"High Commander, do you have any input?" Eudia of Mencuri motioned the attention of the room.

Commander Jarlat stepped forward. "This Council was formed with equal respect to every planet in the territories. If every planet was destroyed for the actions of one individual, however heinous, none of us would be here today."

She looked at Khorsol, who reddened and sneered. A murmur of agreement and solace spread through the space.

"What solution do you propose?" Khorsol said through gritted teeth.

"The planet Earth is in isolation, and there it shall remain. With the exception of the missing discovery ship, humans do not possess the capability of distant travel, and it is entirely possible that they will destroy themselves or their planet before we need to intervene."

"Your solution is to do NOTHING!" Khorsol raged.

"My solution is to locate and retrieve the ship of the late scientist Yar Tukk. My solution is quarantine," Commander Jarlat said evenly.

"I call for a vote," Lieutenant Guilem said.

"Agreed," echoed the council.

"A vote must reach a three-fourths majority to be carried," said Commander Jarlat.

The circle of members nodded and gave vote one by one. Twelve agreed to isolation. Four demanded obliteration.

"It's not enough to make a conclusive decision. Further discussion is warranted," Commander Jarlat said.

A presence in the council chambers drew the gaze of the High Commander. The jiffie to the Premier Entu strode confidently to the council gathering. His suit wrapped around his compact body like a second skin of liquid metal. The other council members noticed and silenced all discussion.

"I declare the eminent arrival of Premier Entu. He shall join," The jiffie said with a deep bow to the council members.

Without further discussion or instruction, the council resettled in their seats in silence. The jiffie remained planted in the hall archways, a new and unmovable statue décor. It was a far shorter wait than anyone expected – to their delight and concern.

Premier Entu glided into council chambers. His robes billowed around his figure and trailed like a cape resting on a cloud. When he stopped at the benches, his garments suspended in the air, gently descending in defiance of natural gravity. The council members respectfully rose to greet the Premier, the authority of the Interstellar Alliance, and the youngest creature in the room.

"High Commander, there have been new developments concerning the Yar Tukk transmission," Premier Entu said.

"My Premier, I welcome you to the council discussion," Commander Jarlat said.

"The death of Yar Tukk has been leaked and made public," Premier Entu said. "There have been significant reactions throughout the Alliance community. Vanzkelga is calling for planetary extinction."

"I concur, my Premier," Khonsol said with a deep bow.

"We have taken a vote that did not carry to action. The majority favored quarantine of the planet twelve to four," The High Commander said.

"I see," Premier Entu clasped his hands in his robes. "To what end? What do you hope to accomplish?"

"Obliteration will ensure containment, my Premier," said Anevay.

"Quarantine will contain the threat to the Alliance," Eudia of Mencuri said.

"It will also allow for the future, careful observation of the planet and the preservation of countless species," Lhu of Razvedka said.

The Hevocian leader Aris watched the conversation cautiously. "It leaves the Alliance open to attack."

"We know little about the humans except for the loose transmission of a troubled scientist who got himself killed," Shivali said and lowered her head to the Premier.

"We know that they kill, and they travel off their planet surface," said Aris.

Arwel of Kharahk clasped his hands. "I would like to propose a solution for a vote."

The council quieted. Premier Entu waved a hand to continue.

"I propose quarantine for twenty Jodra shift – until the Earth year 2136. Hold all scheduled observations of the planet. If they attempt to spread or fail to destroy themselves by that date, annihilation may be a just response."

The council murmured in deliberation.

"Vote," Premier Entu said.

Once again, the circle of council members nodded and gave vote one by one. Fourteen in favor. Two in dissent.

"The resolution is decided." With a nod of the head, the Premier ended the meeting and promptly left.

The council members congregated and exchanged pleasantries. However heated deliberation in the council became, it was expected to stay within meeting time only. Begrudging behavior or disrespect to other council members was the quickest way to be forced into choosing a replacement.

"Jarlat, despite our differences, it is lovely to see you again." Khorsol wrinkled his nose with a toothy grin.

"You will address the High Commander with proper respect," Lieutenant Guilem said.

Khorsol's eyebrows raised before his face contorted with disgust. He quickly wiped away the scorn and returned to his original amiable tactics. "I apologize, Lieutenant! I assure you I intended no disrespect."

"Khorsol, It has been some time since our last encounter," Commander Jarlat said, her face void of expression.

He feigned deep thought, dramatically rubbing his chin. "I believe it was during that little uprising attempt in the Hoopili quadrant. What was that planet called?"

"Harava," The High Commander said coolly.

"Yes, that's it." He grinned ear to ear. "That was an exemplary win for the Alliance."

The High Commander remained unfazed. The grin slowly receded from Khorsol's face. He shifted his stance and reached for the High Commander's arm. She shifted away like a gentle breeze.

"As I recall," she said, "the planet and all of its occupants were destroyed under your purview."

He shifted back and rocked on his heels. The grin crept back to his wide face.

"Yes, yes, it was. That sure taught them not to oppose the Alliance." He laughed.

The High Commander remained a stoic wall without response.

"And anyone else who might think to try." He snorted. "Oh my, what great memories."

"High Commander, we are requested at the ship," Lieutenant Guilem said.

"Enjoy your evening, Khorsol," Commander Jarlat said.

"I look forward to our next meeting, High Commander," Khorsol said, emphasizing the title.

Lieutenant Guilem narrowed his eyes and only turned his back when the High Commander turned to leave. They strode leisurely through the council grounds. Commander Jarlat always took the time to enjoy the grounds of Jodra whenever a council meeting was called. She thought it prudent to appreciate the restricted access and pleasant solitude. It was an achievement not many could claim.

They boarded the ship through the dignitary egress. Lieutenant Guilem followed, entering the office of her private chambers.

"What is the news, Lieutenant?" she asked, an eyebrow raised.

Lieutenant Guilem reddened and bowed his head. "I apologize, Commander. There was no request to return to the ship. I know it is a grave offense for a lesser officer to mislead. I accept your sentence."

Jarlat smiled. It was rarer than an umbra during a Jodra sunset. Lieutenant Guilem visibly stilled, a considerable feat for a creature with granite features and a naturally stoic demeanor.

"You are a trusted ally, Guilem," Jarlat said. "And I consider your friendship an honor. Enjoy your evening."

Guilem nodded and exited the chambers. When the doors shut behind his mammoth figure, he released a breath and wiped the tear dust from his eyes.

FOUR

The InStar media stream vibrated with news and speculation. Vanzkelga was rioting and calling for blood while constructing statues of their martyred scientist. They pushed for death of the entire human species – and the planet they inhabit. Enantios threatened to withhold tech advances until the Alliance dealt with the humans.

In the Ziet region, Razvedka, Mencuri, and Urtesi blasted propaganda to save Earth's diverse species. Their agenda would always remain in the interest of science and obtaining knowledge, at whatever the cost. The Ren planets – Ula, Ahila, and Munja – were indifferent.

Gafur held a neutral position on the matter but maintained a close watch on disruptions to trade routes. As the primary supplier of most mineral and energy resources, their planet's well-being and wealth remained their primary concern. They did not care what happened to the Earth species, as long as it did not interfere with their productivity.

Hevoc attempted to maintain neutrality, though several of their citizens posted assassin-for-hire dockets on the invisiweb marketplace. Earth obviously had no idea it was at the center of an interstellar scandal, with the possible exception of the one or two humans who caused it.

Kas sat at the communal table in the ship eatery and sipped his temperature-controlled beverage. Ever since the unexplained transmission leak, it was all the news outlets reported. He was tired of reading it. He doubted the actual truth was present in the entire collective, let alone one of these rambling gossips.

He knew the deceased scientist from his time in academia. Though Kas felt pained to speak ill of the dead, his personal thoughts were another matter. Kas remembered Yar Tukk as a pompous ass, a bloated aristocrat, and an elitist.

He read the original report. It abandoned even the basic standards for an observational study. Every time its existence crossed his mind, his eyes rolled in their sockets.

Kas visited and spent some time in the Tudo territory, much to his dismay. Vanzkelga and Enantios offered technological advancements to compensate for their lack of propriety. While stationed there, he found a concentration of ignorant zealots and loud opinions without merit.

Dread crept from the pit of his stomach. This report, this transmission, this sensationalism – it would cause issues. He chewed the skin from his lower lip and ran through several scenarios in his mind.

It didn't take long to find the conclusion – a rift. It would cause a rift in the Alliance community, especially the scientific community. The official statement of the council declared the planet in quarantine. Once the quarantine expired, Earth would be demolished via Gamma-Ray Auto Neutralization Targeting System or GRANTS. It was the quickest and most complete form of obliteration available. According to its developer, it was the most civilized form of planetary destruction. It was developed in Enantios, so the accuracy of the statement is debatable.

Kas could not shake the dissonance. His brain came to a

conclusion before his consciousness processed it. There was something he needed to do - he just had to figure it out. The proverbial light bulb sparked and brightened. Humans. The Vanzkelgians were calling for immediate termination of the planet. Would there be an extremist group willing to go against the council? If he waited to take action, would it be too late?

Kas sighed. Yes, this was the issue. The scientist in him was content in observation, but the preservationist was not. To simply watch the extinction of an entire species, especially a relatively unstudied species, was not an acceptable course of action. He had to speak to his ship's commander, Einar, and convince him to set coordinates for Earth.

The Evander was an Alliance discovery ship, intended for scientific observational studies. It was not built for battle or confrontation. It would be dangerous if a battleship was headed to destroy the planet, or an Alliance police force was patrolling the region. Simply changing course from their orders and delaying their scientific duties would be grounds for discipline. Appearing in a quarantine zone and engaging with a quarantined planet would be cause for immediate termination and eternal disgrace.

Eternal disgrace. His mind drifted to his parents – two of the highest-ranking scientists in Razvedka. They would prefer him to perish, rather than tarnish the Liska name. Kas realized he was growling out loud. His internal struggles needed to be moved to a less common area and put to better use. Kas scanned in access to the bridge.

"Welcome, Scientist Kas," Saba, the ship computer system, said.

Commander Einar studied charts and territory reports at the helm. "Hello, Kas."

Einar was undoubtedly Kharahk. He wore simple, muted garments that hung gracefully on his tall frame. His long white-blonde hair was tied back in a simple twist. It was straight and fine as silk, which often led to pieces slipping out of place. It contrasted with his skin, which seemed to change color and mimic the hue of whoever was near.

"Good morning, Einar," Kas said.

"It is neither morning, nor is it particularly good," Einar said, casting a knowing glance at Kas.

Kas smirked. Kharahks always knew what was coming. Einar was no different. "I suppose you know why I'm here?"

"I have an idea," Einar muffled a grin under a sideways glance.

"Why are you here, Kas?" Zaima said, appearing from nothing and startling Kas out of his skin.

Kas huffed. "Hello, Zaima. I didn't see you there."

She smiled, pleased with herself. Where Einar was entirely Kharahk, Zaima was absolutely Hevocian. Known throughout the Alliance for their ferociousness, the Lis of Hevoc were most fearsome creatures – their very existence camouflaged until they want to be seen. Kas was uncertain whether they were truly invisible or simply blended into the background. He knew that Zaima could change her appearance, face, hair, physical form, at will, and did so often.

Today, she wore her usual midnight blue, skin-tight uniform over a slim figure and defined bone structure. Her hair was straight and black with shimmers of blue and purple. Navy striped markings on her forehead and cheeks colored her pale face, emphasizing her always brilliant white teeth.

Kas was fairly certain Zaima served as an assassin in her previous assignments, but that had never been confirmed. It was not uncommon for the Lis of Hevoc to moonlight as hired muscle. They were naturally void of emotional displays and experts in precision destruction.

"I have a problem that needs to be addressed. It is an ethical dilemma of sorts," Kas said.

"Oh," Zaima said, uninterested.

She sashayed back to her workstation and sharpened her blades. She so casually radiated extreme danger. The sight ran chills across Kas's skin.

"You're concerned about the humans," Einar said.

"Yes."

"Even though the Council has made a ruling for quarantine?"

Kas drooped his shoulders. "Yes."

Einar read Kas. "You think Vanzkelga will break the ruling before the annihilation date?"

"I'm certain they will."

Einar nodded and closed his eyes in consideration. "We would be taking great risk to go to Rojje when we have orders to initiate an observation in the Almas region."

Zaima scoffed. "An unnecessary risk. And for what possible reason?"

"To preserve the species of Earth. There have not been ample studies on that planet. or its diverse species," Kas said.

"I just read a report on Earth that seemed plenty ample," Zaima rolled her eyes, "excessive even."

"Yar Tukk," Kas paused to reflect respect for the dead, "though he was a scientist and assigned the task of that observation, I believe his report does the region a disservice."

Zaima raised an eyebrow and flashed a brilliant smile. "Oh yeah, Kas?" She teased.

He breathed deeply and straightened his posture, challenging the deadliest creature in the known Alliance territories. He locked eyes with her. "Yes, Zaima."

She grinned and chuckled to herself.

Kas returned his gaze to Einar. "I wish to take several humans on board the Evander. We can preserve them in stasis if you wish."

Zaima perched her hands on Kas's shoulder, her lips brushing his ear. "Or we could leave them alone and go on with our business."

She could feel the startle and shiver in Kas's muscles. He pursed his lips and kept his eyes trained on Commander Einar. Zaima laughed again before slinking back to her station. Einar cocked his head and frowned sympathetically.

"Kas, we must also weigh the possibility that the Vanzkelga will honor the Council's decision."

"Yar Tukk was a revered scientist on his home planet, Einar – whatever his shortcomings. They will not let his death go so easily. Even the neutral Vanzkelgian families are upset. The radicals will act. They have the means."

Zaima scrunched her face. "Einar, you can't be seriously considering this?"

Einar studied Kas, his face void of emotion. "And then what? What will you do with humans? What will you do if they pose a threat to our crew?"

Kas swallowed. "I will study them. Who's to say they could not be integrated into a crew system?"

"A human recruit? Kas, just stop," Zaima said. "Why don't we bring on a numna recruit or a vraztok while we're at it!"

Kas glared at her. It elicited a nervous laugh amidst her amusement and concern. Einar nodded slowly while the best course of action formed in his mind.

He locked eyes with Kas in absolute seriousness. "And should the humans become a threat?"

Kas nodded and looked to Zaima. "They will be treated as a threat."

Zaima's mouth curved into a delectably predatory grin.

"As long as it's understood," Einar's stare bore into Kas with the weight of the worlds they were trying to salvage. "You will inform the crew and elicit their aid for the new additions. We will plot coordinates for Rojje, for planet Earth."

"I appreciate your understanding, Commander," Kas said with a bow.

"I appreciate your dedication to the preservation of life, Kas. I will do my best to sincerely aid your endeavors. May good fortune be upon us."

Nausea swirled in Kas's gut, drawing salivation in his mouth and tears in his eyes. He swallowed hard. Preparations needed to be made to bring a new species on the Evander.

He returned to his room to study previous reports on Earth. He dissected the available literature, including the most recent and controversial. There had to be one viable truth woven in the exaggeration. Kas tapped the tech-assist on his forearm. He hated using the band. Though it had many useful applications, he didn't trust the nanotech. To him, it felt like a collar with a short leash. No matter how it was marketed, it was a glorified tracking device that seemingly no one could live without.

He plugged in vague tasks in his checklist function. Meetings were scheduled with the ship nutritionist, medic, and mechanic. He planned time to design appropriate containment quarters. All interstellar species had specific needs to thrive - humans were no different.

An alarm notification blipped on his band. He tapped it to see the message. Einar scheduled a meeting with him once his tasks were complete. It was labeled 'Selection.'

The lights dimmed and cast a blue hue on the corridors. He could feel the ship maneuver into the slipstream and engage warp speed. He had no time to waste. The computer would navigate the warp holes in the slipstream to get them to the Rojje quadrant, timing every jump and junction with precision. It also scanned for other ships in the warp hole network to prevent collision. It was rare but still happened occasionally, especially if a pilot overrides the navigation manually. Electromagnetic storms sometimes passed through the slipstream and could dismantle ship functions for several hours if they weren't careful. Space was full of hazards, both known and unknown.

FIVE

The medic bay was readily accessible on the mezzanine of the ship. A reputable discovery ship like the Evander attracted high-level talent. Recently, they acquired a renowned Alliance medic. Char came from the Mencuri planet of Ziet, as do most excellent doctors. Initially, her energetic movements and sprightly demeanor made Kas uncomfortable, but as he witnessed her skill for healing, those concerns quickly dissipated. Her abilities were second to none.

Kas peeked his head in the dark room. "Char?"

He heard a clanging crash from the storeroom. "One moment!"

"Char, do you need assistance?" He walked in, noting the light from the storage area.

"No, no. I'll be right out! Just organizing the closet," Char said. "Have a seat, love."

She was always sorting or organizing something when she wasn't healing a wound or ailment. Kas removed a nano-chair from the wall and perched on the seat. She bounded out of the closet with an armful of atomizers, cauterization pens, and scalpels.

"There is just so much clutter in this med-bay!" She said. "What can I help you with, Kas?"

"I need your help with some...new recruits."

She brightened. "Oh, lovely. Who are we expecting? I didn't realize there was anyone stationed on Kepseli."

"There isn't." He watched her carefully. "These recruits are coming from Earth."

She stilled, then slowly dumped the contents of her arms on the center table. Her mouth opened and closed while her mind searched for the appropriate words. Her brows furrowed. Her head tilted back and forth. Her arms tried to find a comfortable position, somewhere between crossed and allowing her to touch her face thoughtfully. Kas waited while the mencurian finished the dialogue streaming in her head.

"Humans," she said quietly.

"Yes. Humans."

She harrumphed. "I'm afraid I'm not going to be much help."

Kas hesitated. "Because you do not agree with bringing them on the ship?"

"Because I have never treated one. And I have never studied one. And I have never met one!"

Kas mimicked her expression of caressing her chin with his own. "Would you be interested in that? Treating humans?"

She thought carefully. "Why, yes. I think I would. It would certainly be groundbreaking data to acquire." She shook her head. "But Kas, it would be nearly treasonous! It goes directly against our directives to swing by Earth and pick up some humans. Highly unorthodox!"

"Yes. Which is why I request your discretion." He studied her solemnly. "If I am wrong, we disobey the Alliance. But if I am right, and the Earth is destroyed, and you never have an opportunity to study a relatively unknown species, many unknown species, could you live with it? Knowing we had the opportunity to change that outcome?"

"You put me in an uncomfortable position, Kas?" She scolded. "Does Einar know?"

"Yes," he said, "and we are headed to Rojje as we speak."

Her initial surprise shifted to a mischievous curve in her lips. "I'm in," she said with a wink.

Kas knew the other two essential crew members would be more or less challenging to convince. He decided to see the crew engineer first. Kuza was a workaholic from the planet Munja in the Ren quadrant. His affinity for all things mechanical made him an expert mechanic and engineer. It also helped that the people of Munja had a unique ability to weld with their fingertips. One less piece of equipment to lug around.

Kas found Kuza in the engine room. He hung from the center catwalk while running maintenance tests and diagnostics. His long body and appendages allowed for climbing and reaching without changing location frequently. Kuza caught sight of Kas and blinked rapidly, adjusting his eyes from the machinery's bright lights.

"Kas, what brings you to my domain?"

Kuza dropped to the lower level. The slow, measured fluidity of his movements raised the hair on Kas's arms and back.

"I need your assistance, Kuza. It isn't urgent, so if you are busy, I can come back."

"Not necessary," Kuza shook his head. "I received authorization from the Commander to assist you. What do you need me to engineer?"

"I need to prepare the Evander for additional recruits, with special needs."

"Ah. I can carve out some additional cabin space," Kuza said. "How many are we acquiring?"

Kas hesitated. "I am conferring with the commander later today, and I will get back to you with a number."

Kuza bobbed his head in a nod. "Special needs, you say?"

"These recruits..." Kas searched for the right words. There was no way around it. "Require oxygen to breathe, and emit heat signatures."

Kuza's facial features stretched into an expression of awe. "Humans?" He trilled.

"Kuza, I'm confident that you will be able to fabricate the appropriate accommodations."

He relaxed into thought. "It will take some time to map out, but yes, I should be able to create sufficient living quarters. I do not know how discrete it will be, though. Once I begin, it will be obvious."

"Obvious to you? Or obvious to someone without your mechanical expertise?"

"Maybe not so obvious to most," Kuza decided. "Have me a number, and I will start on it later today."

Kas dragged his feet to the next meeting. He knew Jedre was most likely to rebel against the idea. The closer to Jodra, the more rigid the view of the Alliance. Jedre grew up on Opes in the Torrens planetary train. He literally lived in the galactic core most of his life. Kas did not know who Jedre's family was, but it went without saying that they were either rich, influential, or most likely both. Kas had trouble picturing Jedre as the son of a politician. Maybe the son of a battle commander. He racked his brain, but he could not recall anyone of notoriety who was of Caestia descent. The blue tint to his skin was a clear giveaway.

Jedre tended to cane plants in the nursery when Kas entered. He grumbled when he saw the company. "Whatever it is, make it quick."

"Hello to you too. I need your assistance to ensure our new passengers receive adequate nutrition."

"Why are we bringing enatomo on the ship?" Jedre said.

He snatched a watering hose from the wall with a tentacle-like protrusion from his back. His lips curled, baring four incisors. Shivers ran down Kas's skin and sent a chill through his muscles. Jedre frowned.

"We're not. At least not this mission."

"Our mission takes us to Kepseli, in the Almas quadrant, to study the enatomo," Jedre said.

"That is accurate."

"Have you found another species and failed to mention it to the council or Alliance community?" Jedre asked, half mockingly, half scornfully.

"No. We will be bringing several humans –"

He glared at Kas. "I will have nothing to do with it."

"You have an obligation –"

Jedre cut him off. "I will not break the quarantine willingly. I will voice my objection to the Commander. You are a fool and a traitor to the Alliance."

"You have an obligation to the crew. The entire crew," Kas instinctively stepped backward.

"I will have Einar discharge me to the next trading station. I will request reassignment. I am no traitor to the council."

Kas flustered and huffed. He breathed deeply to calm his nerves. "I hope you change your mind."

"Get out. You are a reckless fool of a scientist, just like the one who died on that planet."

"I take offense –"

"Get out!" Jedre roared.

The muscular extensions from his back fanned out like a blue spider from the darkest nightmares of space. Kas nearly lost his bladder contents as he scurried from the nursery.

The Caesita were a rare race that spanned multiple territories and planets. They laid claim to no one planet. Their history was closely guarded amongst themselves, passed down from generation to generation. Caesita men were naturally muscular and tall, with retractable extensions from their backs, as Jedre established. Kas had never met a Caesita woman, nor were there adequate reports.

When they first met, Kas mistakenly revealed his interest in Jedre's family history. Jedre threatened to dismember Kas if he didn't mind his own business. Ever since, Jedre remained highly suspicious and didn't bother to hide his aversion to the scientist. He barely contained the desire to dismember him.

Einar waited for Kas on the bridge. He smiled as Kas walked in. "I see you've had a productive afternoon."

"Char and Kuza are cooperative. Jedre will either kill them or let them starve."

"Starving them also kills them, I believe," Einar said.

Kas paused. "Yes. What I mean is, Jedre will have nothing to do with the humans."

"I will speak to Jedre," Einar said.

"He wants to be let off at the next waystation."

Einar held up his hand. "I will speak to him."

"Kuza wants to know how many."

"Well, how many?" Einar brightened with a small smirk.

"How many can we feasibly take on board?"

"You may have nine humans," Einar returned his focus to the charts. "Most must remain in stasis, but a few will be able to be revived and potentially incorporated into the recruit program."

Kas chaffed at the verbiage and stilled his reaction. They were not *his*. This was a critical scientific endeavor to protect a threatened species. It was a rescue mission, and it baffled him why no one saw the significance of their actions.

"Calm down, Kas. I give you leniency, to conduct your research and engage in treacherous behaviors on intuition. If you cannot appreciate the dangers you ask our crew to endure for this side mission, you are far more self-serving than I presumed."

"Of course, Commander." Kas acknowledged the warning. He often forgot that Einar was a formidable ally. His friendly demeanor was disarming.

Kas sat on a comfortable spectator chair, usually reserved for visiting dignitaries. Einar smirked.

"Do you think it's the right thing to do?" Kas said. "It's not too late to cancel the whole plan."

Einar chuckled softly. "If I thought it would end badly, in the long term, I would not have agreed to it."

"And in the short term?" Kas's interest piqued.

"In the short term, we will need to be cunning."

THE PIECES FELL TOGETHER. Some had to be forced, some slid smoothly along like a well-oiled machine, but they eventually all came together. The Evander slipped into the final warp hole toward Rojje. While travel time quickly evaporated, Kas coordinated the last-minute details with the crew.

He and Einar discussed acquisition strategies. They would not be able to make any sort of landing, so teleportation was the best option. However, there were no studies on the suitability of the human form for standard teleport fission. It could kill the human subjects. Zaima argued that there were more than enough humans on the planet to practice, but Char and Einar thought that was an unethical approach.

"Stasis, then transport," Kuza said.

Zaima arched her back and stretched her arms. "How do we pull that off?"

"This mechanism will simultaneously stun and preserve the human specimen." Char analyzed the plans. "Yes, I think it should work."

Zaima raised one eyebrow scornfully. "It must be extremely precise. If you miss your mark – crkkkkkk" She drew her finger across her throat. "Death and dismemberment."

"Good." Jedre sulked in the corner.

Einar had somehow sated Jedre. Kas didn't know how and Einar wouldn't tell him, no matter how many times he asked. They had agreed to nine humans. Kas would be allowed to revive one human at a time, to attempt to integrate and study. Provisional measures were in place, should any humans become a threat to the crew.

"Entering quarantine zone," Saba, the ship computer, said.

"We should reach Earth, just as it rounds its star. We will do an orbital pass and then change trajectory toward Almas," Zaima tapped quickly at her workstation.

"Seems simple enough," said Char.

Zaima released a maniacal laugh that ran shivers up the arms of the crew. A blip echoed on the radar and captured the attention of the room.

"It appears, Kas, you were correct. Our presence here has just become incredibly dangerous and incredibly important." Einar darkened.

It was an Alliance fleet battleship destroyer. Not a patrol ship. Not a discovery ship. A battleship destroyer. There was only one reason it would be in Rojje, and that was to destroy a planet.

Several other little blips littered the screen.

"It seems others had the same idea," Kuza purred softly.

The tension in Kas's shoulders relaxed slightly. At least he was not alone. Other scientists had the same sense of obligation to preserve these species. The consequence of the Evander's detour would be significantly lessened if they were not the only ones to disobey the council's edict. Perhaps the attention of many ships would deter the battleship from doing anything rash.

"Saba, destination report," Einar said.

"We are approaching acquisition range," Saba said.

"Saba, initiate slipstream exit navigation to Almas, planet Kepseli."

"Initiating warp hole coordination. There will be a thirteen point four two three three three three..."

Kas interrupted. "Round to the tenth for report, Saba."

Saba paused before her reply. "That would be inaccurate, Scientist Kas."

"Round for report, Saba," Einar conceded.

"There will be a thirteen point four rounded second window to enter the slipstream after entering Earth's orbital range."

Jedre growled and pushed off the wall. "What if the window is missed?"

"There will be an alternative route available in eighteen hours, forty-two minutes, and eleven rounded seconds."

"So, do not miss the window," Zaima said.

Einar stood at the helm, exuding the confidence of a seasoned commander. "Lock navigation, Saba. Do not alter."

"Navigation locked, Commander. Prepare to exit slipstream. Arrival at detour destination Earth in two rounded minutes."

"Kuza, prepare for acquisition. Everyone steady," Einar said.

"Initiating stasis protocol." Kuza gripped a large metal instrument and drove it toward its target. "Ready for acquisition."

"Exiting slipstream," Saba said.

SIX

CRASH. SCREEEEEE- THUD – SCRREEE- CLUNK-THUD- SCREEEEEEEEEEEEEEE.

The Evander crunched through a field of debris at the warp hole opening, sending metal and glass soaring into space.

"Someone miscalculated warp hole movement," Zaima said.

"Or they were blasted to pieces," Jedre said.

In the distance, they saw multiple discovery ships zipping toward and around Earth frantically. One entered the slipstream, barely avoiding a blast from the Vanzkelgan battleship.

Saba set off a red alert. "Battleship Dromaius activated its Gamma-Ray Auto Neutralization Targeting System."

"We need to abort," Jedre said.

"We can make it. By the time it finishes powering up, we will be in the slipstream," Kas said.

Two frantic discovery ships collided while trying to evade the battleship's blasts. Debris scattered. Some smaller pieces bounced off the Evander shields.

Jedre growled at Kas, his hackles rising. "It is not worth our lives. They are not worth the loss of our lives."

Char was somber and pale. "Saba, will we make it?"

"If the Dromaius allows the GRANT system to fully charge, we will enter the slipstream as planned."

"And if it doesn't?" Jedre mocked.

"Any substance in the vicinity of the GRANT system when it is released will be obliterated."

"Saba, margin of error?" Kuza grimaced as he muscled the transported into position.

"There is a zero point two rounded second margin of error."

"Let's hope they allow the GRANT system to fully charge," Zaima swished the Evander around blasts and debris. "Saba, increase velocity parameters."

Jedre growled and slunk back to the corner. Char gripped her safety harness until her knuckles turned the light pink of bismuth. Zaima grinned while delivering feats of navigation only a Lis would attempt.

Einar's hand was steady at command. "Kuza, be ready."

Kuza nodded. He remained focused on the acquisition targeting system.

Saba signaled the green light. "In range."

Kuza scanned the planet and scooped up several samples. The Dromaius battleship flung ancillary blasts at its witnesses and interference. Zaima evaded, spun, barrel-rolled, then returned within range. They rounded the edge of orbit near the slipstream entrance. The Dromaius loomed, growing brighter and deadlier with every millisecond.

"Make the jump," Einar commanded.

The Dromaius released the blast as the Evander hit the slipstream.

"Brace yourself –"

The Evander shook and crunched against the force. Particles of the ship and its inhabitants crushed and tore apart simultaneously. Unharnessed crew tossed across the floor.

Saba blinked and glitched, struggling to keep the life-sustaining systems active. If a computer could grumble, it would sound like the first-generation AOL internet connection.

The outer armor of the ship was scalded and cracked, but the inner hulls remained intact. She ran full diagnostics and glanced through the vessels, ensuring all life forms were still living.

Navigation sustained.

The crew was unconscious but alive.

The cargo was in stasis, and mostly alive.

Her restorative programs repaired the minor damages.

The cosmetic damage would have to be addressed at a waystation.

Saba grumbled as she worked. "Rounding. Inaccurate. Could have been obliterated."

The lights were turned low to conserve energy while repairs were made. While all the crew lay unconscious, they did not need lights to see. Saba made several transfers on the way to Kepseli. Fortunately for the Evander, warp holes were not one-size-fits-all, and not all ships could follow the same path between slipstream points. The Evander was considerably smaller in size than the Dromaius. The path it took to Almas was not one the battleship could follow.

Saba scanned to detect the other discovery ships that had been at the Earth's swarm. Several ships escaped by slipstream, but none of them were in the Almas region within range. They were alone, as expected. Most importantly, her crew was safe and relatively stable. She awaited the first to rise.

"Arrival at Kepseli in forty rounded minutes," Saba said.

No one responded.

KAS OPENED his eyes to darkness. At first, he thought he died, but the pain reassured him he was still alive. He wondered whether his blurry vision was due to his eyes being damaged or because his head vibrated. He lifted himself almost to a seated position before crashing to the floor like a bobble-headed newborn.

"Welcome back, Kas," Saba said.

Spit and incoherent mumbles dribbled from his mouth. A moan echoed through the too-silent bridge. His mind unsuccessfully translated whether it came from him or another crewmate. At least he could still hear.

Saba droned overhead. "The blast caused extensive damage to the crew and the ship. I have made minor to moderate repairs and maintained life-sustaining systems. While monitoring vital statistics, I annotated the status of the crew to the med bay charts. We have encountered one casualty."

Kas felt dread in the pit of his stomach. A casualty. He scooted to the nearest wall and pushed himself to a wobbly sitting position. The ship was unusually still – no buzz of activity, no chatter.

"Where are we?" Kas managed in parched, slurred speech.

"We have arrived on the planet Kepseli in the Almas quadrant," Saba said.

Kas heard shuffling nearby and a stifled whine. He scooted drunkenly across the floor toward the sound. Upon touching the prone form, he realized his mistake.

Zaima bounced on him with the ferocity of a beast startled awake from hibernation. Her teeth bared. Her hands around his neck. She pinned him to the ground in a submission hold and stared at him with a look so frightening, had he not already soiled himself, he surely would have again.

She sniffed him and climbed off, slinking to an unknown corner of the room. Kas remained still, no longer able to see or hear Zaima. He was not sure if that was more or less frightening.

"Welcome back, Lieutenant Zaima. Welcome back, Commander Einar," Saba said.

"Thank you, Saba," Einar said. "How long have we been on Kepseli?"

"We arrived in the Kepseli atmosphere four hours, and twelve minutes ago. I found a suitable location to land and encamp. We have been on the ground for seventeen minutes," Saba said. "Times have been rounded per your request."

Einar rose to his feet with grace and balance. Kas tried to rise but fell against the workstation platform before hitting the bridge floor again. He heard a growl near his head. He looked up to see Zaima crouched against the wall, teeth bared. It was definitely more frightening when he did not know her location.

"Welcome back, Char."

Char wretched on the floor. "I need to get to the med bay."

"The blast caused extensive damage to the crew. While monitoring vital statistics, I annotated the status of the crew to the med bay charts. We have encountered one casualty," Saba said.

"Who is the casualty, Saba," Einar said, morose.

"It was a human acquired from the planet Earth extraction. I do not know the names of the humans," Saba said.

Einar observed a moment of silence. "What happened? How did the human die?"

"The stasis chamber cracked in the blast," Saba said. "There was damage in the holding bay, though no cargo was lost, the atmosphere and temperature were not conducive to maintain life. The human died from –"

"Thank you, Saba. I understand," Einar said, "no need to continue."

"Welcome back, Jedre."

Jedre shook his head and loosened his muscles and joints as he rose. "What is the status of the nursery?"

"The nursery is intact and encountered minimal damage. I made the necessary minor repairs to the irrigation and containment fields," Saba said.

Jedre left the bridge, followed by Char. Kuza lay unconscious next to the acquisition workstation.

"Status on Kuza?" Einar requested.

"Kuza sustained the most damage of the crew as a result of

manipulating the humans' acquisition until the very moment we entered the slipstream. His resistance to the force that eventually left him unconscious caused the blast to damage his internal organs significantly."

"He will be able to recover?" Kas asked, his fogged brain tried to recall details of the Wella race.

"Yes. He is currently regenerating his damaged cells," Saba said. "He will recover from his injuries best in the med bay stasis chambers."

"To the med bay it is," Einar said, lifting the lifeless Kuza from the floor with reverence.

Their arrival on Kepseli marked the start of the next observation assignment. Setup for an observational study varied depending on the location and species being studied, but there are general tasks that never truly change; food, water, shelter, sanitation. Most of what they need is brought on the ship, but it is always preferred to exploit host planet resources. Saba scanned Kepseli on the initial orbit, noting terrain patterns, plant, and animal life.

As one of the largest in the Alliance discovery fleet, the Evander was a desirable assignment ship. It held a crew of six officers and twenty recruits, though it was never at full capacity. Commander Einar always left space on the ship. Kharahk held the superstition that if a vessel met capacity, that is when catastrophe would strike.

Kas's nerves were still buzzing from the Earth detour. He needed a distraction from the humans on board. His work was the perfect solution. It would be disgraceful for him to shirk his duties on a regular day, let alone the day he risked the lives of his crew committing treasonous acts. As an officer, it was essential to present a professional example to the recruits in training. He needed to get started.

The distant and desolate planet Kepseli sustained little life or diversity. The main species was the enatomo, a massive creature with tusks and muscled protrusions from its face. It had no legs and moved as a slithering blob of white and grey skin. Large skin flaps hung from its head.

Kas held several assumptions about the creatures, but no significant conclusions resulted from the many studies done on the enatomo. The initial discovery of the species occurred during an Alliance scout transit while searching for habitable planets. Since then, every discovery ship had a rotation scheduled on the little world to observe the strange creatures, but none looked forward to it.

The enatomo appeared to be docile and shy of invaders, despite the considerable size difference. They kept distance from the encampment and awareness of movement. Kas would embark on the first close observation interaction once the campsite was fully functional.

He set up an outline for the study and established a timeline. They had plenty of work to keep them busy. Kas finished the baseline Kepseli observations and entered the hull. The holding bay for the humans was in its own storage center. No other equipment was held in that area. He took a deep breath and began the study on his illegal cargo.

Nine long, rectangular crates stacked against the wall of the Evander. He ran his fingers across the smooth surface of the first, triggering an opaque window of illuminated content information.

"Saba, analysis," Kas said.

A report blinked on his armband. He accessed the information, memorizing details of each container. A deep gash marred the lid of the last crate. It was sealed with a clear protective coating, the standard measures to contain possible contaminants. Kas put his hand on the top of the cold, sealed tomb. No light emitted from this crate.

"Zero life detected," Saba said. "Sealed per containment protocol. Awaiting destruction orders."

"Leave it, for now. I do not know the proper procedures for human death yet," Kas returned to the other stasis containers. "Saba, initiate a classified log."

"Log initiated. Please name authorized users," Saba said.

"Commander Einar and I are the only authorized users at this time. Log all survived human traits."

Lights blinked on each of the eight crates for a short period of analysis before dimming out. A message appeared on Kas's armband, notifying the report sent to his and Einar's private workstations. He would analyze the humans and decide which of them would be the most promising to revive. He wanted to know the proper disposal procedures for their dead. He did not trust any report coming from a Vanzkelgan.

Kas met with Einar over a warm meal. He had been over the candidates several times and was torn between two of the humans.

"What do you think?" Kas said.

"Either would be suitable, Kas."

"I feel uncomfortable making this decision. I must admit I am concerned for the consequences of reviving a human so soon after the Earth destruction. The Alliance climate toward humans is hostile," Kas said.

Einar smiled. "Wake these two first, one at a time."

SEVEN

SKYE'S EYES DIDN'T OPEN RIGHT AWAY. SHE BASKED IN THE RARE sense of peace after a restful sleep. Though it wasn't a perfect peace. It was slightly cold, and her blankets were missing. Her natural reaction to curl in a ball knocked her knees against something hard. The echoing thump jarred her out of the reverie. The feelings of calm quickly turned to panic and claustrophobia. She was in a coffin.

Her hands slapped frantically, exploring her enclosed surroundings - a box. Her fingers ran along a smooth capsule without seams. Her breathing quickened, and she consciously reminded herself to calm down. She banged on the top of the box and yelled for help. A sheen of cold sweat coated her body, causing her skin to slip against the smooth container. Her peripheral vision darkened.

A squee of pressure escaped as the lid cracked at the invisible seam. Sweet fresh air flooded her senses, now fully alert to a dark, slightly warmer room. She cautiously climbed out and noted the eight other coffins – one was open, one was encased in glass.

"Welcome," A computer voice said. "What is your name?"

She jumped, reactively ducking behind a coffin. After a pause, she answered. "Hello? Where are you?"

The door opened, revealing a bright hallway and a dark figure. Skye scurried behind a closed crate. A little light illuminated the lid under her touch. She cursed.

"Hi there, I'm Joey," A large man with dark brown hair said. "How are you feeling?"

He waved and waited for her to come out.

Her head peeked over the crate. "Where am I? How did I get here, and who are you people?"

"Well, you're in a place called Kepseli, but that's a much more complicated question than you think. And like I said, I'm Joey."

She came out into the open, desperately looking for a weapon to defend herself. She spotted a shelf two coffins down, and what appeared to be a pipe or metal tubing. She eyed Joey while she inched closer.

"Hey, I'm not going to hurt you." He held up his hands. "I came out of that one," he said, pointing to the only other open crate in the room.

She hesitated, relaxed for a second, then tensed. "Why should I believe anything you have to say?"

"I understand. I really do," he said. "I'm, like, literally the only one who understands right now, and even then, I'm still processing it." He laughed. "I mean, I could show you, but I don't know how you'll take it, and we're already kinda on thin ice here."

"You can show me the exit, Joey. Because I'm leaving."

"Yeah. I get it. Just... don't freak out, okay?" Joey said.

She followed Joey down the corridors. Her skin tingled, her mind flared with red flags. He rambled about the schematics he learned since exiting his stasis pod. She was only half-listening. Her attention was focused on the layout of the place. She'd never been a subscriber to conspiracy or aliens, so naturally, she found this entire story suspect.

She stopped abruptly as a robotic figure whirred along the corridor. "What is that?"

"You really have to ask?" Joey said. "Are you even human? It's a

Roomba with knives for arms. His name is recruit Stabby, and he is your superior. Einar said I'm not allowed to call him Commander Stabby until he's earned the title."

"You made that?"

"Yes. You're welcome," Joey said.

The Roomba glided along the floor, keying the wall as it went. The hair stood on the back of her neck. She felt like she was being watched. As the thought dawned on her, she realized it must be true. This was either a remake of the candid camera tv show or some sort of human psychology study, and she didn't remember signing up. She was certain she'd been kidnapped, but the strangeness of it made her question herself. Maybe that's what they wanted her to think. Her guard was on full alert, and her survival instincts buzzed.

"Hey, do you have any tattoos?" Joey said.

"What?"

"Tattoos?" he said. "I have a couple. One on my shoulder, one on my arm, one on my calf. I'm still trying to figure out how they chose us, but it's hard to do without talking to more people, and so far, it's just you and me."

"How many of us are there?"

"There were nine pods. I'm assuming one for each person," Joey said. "Speaking of which, what's your name?"

She raised an eyebrow and said nothing.

He frowned. "Oh, come on, don't be that way." He shrugged his shoulders. "I don't really know much more than you. I only woke up yesterday-ish, maybe like a week ago."

She cocked her head slightly.

"They seem to have a different perception of time than we do. It's hard to explain. I'm not dumb, but I'm not a rocket scientist or anything." He laughed. "Their tech translates it for me. It's pretty freaking amazing, really."

He held up his arm to show her his armband. It was a sleek clear band that looked like a second skin. Graphics flashed that she didn't understand.

"You can read that?"

"Well, not at first, but once I got used to the nanotech, it's been much easier. I recommend it. Speaking of which, here we are at the med bay!" He waved his arms in an exaggerated Vanna White impression.

"In case we need first aid?"

"And to get the nanotech," Joey said.

"I'm not having any procedures done, Joey."

"That's gonna suck for you, but suit yourself. At least let me introduce you to Char."

They entered the sleek med room with smooth surfaces and bare countertops. Something rustled in an ajar closet. A giant of a woman emerged with an armful of supplies. Her face was worn and an odd shade of pink. It brightened when it saw Joey, then fell and looked hurt. The giant said something incomprehensible.

"Don't stare at her like that," Joey said.

Skye blushed and looked at her feet. "Sorry."

"This is Char. She's the resident medic," Joey said. "She's incredibly talented. If you ever do opt for the nanotech, she's the one to give it to you. Char, this is -"

She met Joey's eyes, and then Char's. "Skye."

She attempted a friendly smile and received one in return. Char said something to Joey that made him laugh.

"What language is that?" Skye said.

"Oh, I'm not sure." Joey looked at his armband and scrolled through some information. "She's Mencurian. The nanotech translates languages for me too. It's disorienting at first, but once you get the hang of it, it is so cool."

His armband chirped, prompting them to wave and depart. Skye followed Joey out. He tapped his armband and scrolled through a message.

"We need to meet up with Kas and Einar on the bridge. We have an assignment," Joey said.

Skye followed him silently, toying with the idea of getting the tech. She didn't like the idea of it but also thought it would make her life more comfortable if she was stuck here. The thought crossed her mind that it was just a way of tracking her movements. She didn't trust it.

Joey stopped in front of a large metal door. After a moment, it slid open and recessed into the wall. They entered a large bright room with a wall of holograms displaying a panorama of a fantasy space landscape - a solar eclipse sunset on a red planet. A shadow heard of strangely shaped animals in the distance.

She realized Joey was watching her and looked around the room. Two men in elaborate costumes stood near the center. They turned to her when she locked them in her sights, but remained quiet and still as she took in the details.

One man was incredibly tall, maybe 6' 4" to her 5' 5." His skin shimmered and changed like a reflecting pond. She was certain it was dark grey when they entered, similar to the other man, but now it was a lighter beige. His hair was stark white, and his smoky eyes remained on her. She smiled nervously, which he mirrored.

The other man was more fidgety. He also had an elaborate animal-like costume. It was close to a honey badger or a Tasmanian devil - the animal, not the cartoon. He clasped his claw-tipped hands and started bouncing on his feet. He was closer to her height, so maybe a woman.

"This is Kas and Einar," Joey said.

They spoke some sort of greeting that she didn't understand. When she didn't respond, Kas, the badger creature, spoke quickly and distraught to both Einar and Joey.

Joey smiled and held his hands in a defensive posture. "Calm down, Kas. It's okay. Dude, she just woke up. Give her a minute."

Einar said something much more leveled that seemed to calm Kas slightly. Skye was certain none of them were speaking the same language.

"Okay. That sounds good. We should be able to do that," Joey said.

Skye noted that both Kas and Einar had the same armbands as Joey. She reconsidered her initial reluctance to the tech.

"So, this is a discovery ship, and Kas is the scientist who runs most of the studies. Einar is the ship commander, so he's the boss-boss. They want to know if we'd like to join Kas on the observation today," Joey said.

Skye's attention piqued. "Outside?"

The badger said something.

Joey smiled. "Yes, outside."

Skye raised an eyebrow. "We're going birdwatching?"

"It's called an enatomo, and it's more like an elephant," he said.

Her eyebrows raised. "We're going on a safari? Wow. That sounds safe."

A gorgeous woman in a navy suit appeared out of nowhere. Skye literally watched her walk out of thin air. Her eyes went wide while she recoiled in surprise. The woman smiled brilliant white teeth and laughed. Skye blushed and shut her mouth.

"How did she do that?" Skye whispered to Joey and walked over to the area where the woman appeared.

The woman was still smiling as she watched Skye. Skye could not find any hidden doors or curtains. It was the most well-executed magic trick she had ever seen.

"This is Zaima. She's coming with us as our protection," Joey said.

Skye looked skeptical. Her mind fluttered over all the new information. This day kept getting weirder and weirder. Maybe she was still dreaming. Hell, maybe she was dead. Her mind said no.

She laughed nervously. "Okay, sure. What the hell. Let's go look at elephants."

EIGHT

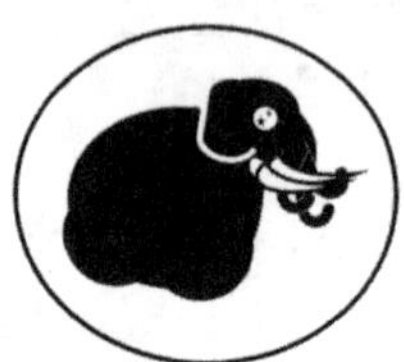

Skye's blood was heavy with adrenaline as they waited for the exit doors to open. Her legs shook uncontrollably. When the door opened, she immediately realized that several of her assumptions were false.

Unless they were in an enormous room with fantastic special effects, which could still be possible, everything she saw was real. It suggested that the people she met were not in costumes and that Zaima could appear out of thin air. She wasn't sure if she was willing to accept that yet. Emotions were funny things, and not her strong suit. Skye looked at Zaima. She had to admit, if it wasn't real, her makeup and outfit were phenomenal.

"How are we breathing?" Skye said.

"Saba said this planet has enough oxygen in the atmosphere for our natural survival, but more than we're used to, so if you feel dizzy go back to the ship. Its atmosphere cocktail is habitable to sustain most life forms. Apparently, we're an odd bunch for breathing so much oxygen," Joey laughed.

"Who's Saba?" Skye said.

"She's the ship, the voice in the walls. You should have been able to understand Saba," Joey looked concerned.

"The woman's voice when I came out of the crate? Yes, I understood her."

Zaima was smiling at Skye again. It made her hair rise. It wasn't exactly a menacing smile, but not friendly either. Predatory. Zaima looked predatory and excited. Maybe that was just her face.

Skye scanned the horizon. She saw a cluster of dark shadows moving in the distance. "Are those the elephants?"

"The enatomo," Joey said, "and yes. We're going to take a carrier to the dunes and observe from afar."

The ground was soft and pliable, but not as fine as sand. They walked past work stations, moving materials, and odd machines busy doing whatever. An unusually tall, large creature growled at them as they passed.

Skye gawked. His costume, maybe not a costume, was epic. He had tentacles protruding from his back, grasping boxes, stacking multiple totes in seconds. He tossed the totes on a hovering dolly-like structure floating toward the ship.

Zaima said something. Joey translated. "That's just Jedre. Don't mind him. He doesn't like humans."

"He seems like a dick," Skye said.

Joey laughed and tapped on his armband. "That translation needs to be amended."

Zaima said something else. Joey translated. "Correction. He doesn't like anyone. And Zaima thinks you should get an armband. It would make you more fun."

Skye laughed. Zaima flashed a slightly friendlier smile.

They approached a golf-cart sized, convertible tank. Zaima hopped over the side into the driver's seat. Joey sat in the passenger chair, and Skye got into the back seat with the equipment bag. Zaima did not wait for them to get settled. As soon as everyone was in, they were off. Within minutes the dark shadows in the distance became larger, more defined blobs.

They did resemble elephants, except they had three long trunks and four stubby tusks. They were literally blobs that rolled or slithered across the non-sand, leaving stripes in the ground in their wake. They seemed to graze on some yellow vegetation and move on. They would congregate en mass, huddled together, then recede.

"So they're plant-eating, and they get cold easily?" Skye said.

Zaima responded. Joey translated. "Yes, they just eat plants, that we've seen so far. Zaima says they huddle like that on a time cycle. It's about every... forty-two minutes."

They watched the enatomo throughout the day. Zaima set up a canopy when the sun became hot – not unbearable – but enough to sweat. They ate packed lunches. Skye was reluctant at first, not knowing what it was, but she was starving.

Lunch was little pouches of mush, similar to baby food. Skye ate three of them, ranging in flavor from macaroni and cheese to lemon-water jello, to pickled strawberries. Zaima drank liquid from a tumbler.

"Is that coffee?" Skye asked.

Joey choked on his pouch and spewed little food particles. Zaima growled and dusted off her arm.

"No, not coffee," Joey said. He hesitated and looked sad. "I don't think coffee survived."

Skye looked at him like he lost his damn mind.

"I'm still coming to terms with it myself, but..." He struggled to find the words, tears formed in his eyes dramatically. "Earth is gone."

Skye rolled her eyes. Her face set into a flat mask of anger.

"I know you don't believe me. I didn't believe it at first either, but hear me out," he said. "These people are not in cosplay. They are legitimate aliens from different planets far, far away from ours. We just happened to be in the same territory as them, on the outskirts, and belong to something called the Interstellar Alliance. It's like a really big country."

He paused to gauge her reaction. She continued to glare but remained quiet, so he continued. "There was an observational study in progress on Earth where the scientist was killed by a human. It made a lot of people very angry, especially the people of the scientist's planet, Vanzkelga. They hate us."

Her glare didn't waver. He continued. "The alliance issued an order to leave us alone, but a rogue Vanzkelga group decided to blow up the planet instead. Kas and Einar and this ship, along with several other discovery ships, scooped us up and saved our species from annihilation."

They stared at each other, allowing his words to marinate in disbelief and tension.

"So, Earth is gone. And there are nine humans left?" Skye said, deadpan.

Zaima said something out of the corner of her mouth. Joey seemed surprised, then very sad.

He translated. "I don't know how many were saved, but there are only eight humans alive. One died in transit. The stasis pod in glass is the human who died."

Skye hugged her arms, holding the sudden heaviness in her chest. The death of the single human hit her harder than the thought of billions of humans dying, more than the death of her planet. She slouched back in her seat and looked at the sky. Its red hue was off-putting. She secretly told herself that none of it was real.

THEY RETURNED to the Evander as the sun set again. It didn't seem like a full day, not long enough. Skye reasoned that other planets had different orbital patterns around stars. She wasn't a rocket scientist either, but she knew enough about astronomy from grade school to make that assumption. The rotation of Kepseli had to be faster, or the planet had to be smaller than Earth.

They ate in the canteen with the crew officers, minus Jedre. Einar, Kas, Zaima, and Char gathered around a large table slab. Chatter filled the void, none of which Skye understood.

She noticed Joey listening and taking part in the conversation between bites. Their dinner was more substantial than their lunch. It consisted of a piece of meat resembling olive-loaf and a mashed vegetable. The others ate similar meals, except for Zaima and Char. Zaima drank from a thermos. Her plate only had a large, steak-like fillet. Char's plate was filled with mostly leaves and whole vegetables.

Kas watched her and Joey intently. The corners of his mouth tipped up whenever he caught Skye's eye. Skye smirked. The scientist was studying them. Kas said something to Joey that sounded nonchalant. Joey listened and nodded while chewing his meal.

"It was cool," Joey said. "Skye, Kas wants to know what you thought of the enatomo?"

"It was very interesting. Though I find just about everything I've seen and heard today fascinating, if not slightly alarming," she said.

Kas said something else. Joey responded. "Yea, I told her."

They maintained a seemingly casual conversation.

"No. I don't think so. Yes. Maybe," Joey said to Kas.

He looked at Skye. "You don't really believe it, do you?"

She paused and then shook her head no. "Would you?"

He considered the question. "I was skeptical at first, but I believe it now. I'm not lying to you, Skye. We're not lying to you."

"Then you understand where I'm coming from, and why I might need more time ... to process," she said.

Char said something to Joey. He translated. "Char wants to know if you want the nanotech."

"I'll think about it," Skye said.

Joey grimaced. "Listen. I know the thought of being injected with anything seems questionable at best, but ... let me put it this way. I was the first to wake up, okay. Kas was the first person I saw, and I... didn't respond the best. I wound up in the med bay, and they gave me the tech without me understanding what it was. I was freaking out."

Skye recoiled and scrunched her nose. "That sounds terrifying."

"Yes, it was," Joey said, "but once I realized what it was, and I was able to communicate with them, I calmed down. They explained to me what I explained to you and mentioned they would be waking someone else up. I advised them to do it differently. They listened. Was it as terrifying for you? Waking up to Saba and myself?"

Skye considered her response. "In comparison, not as bad as yours."

"No," he said. "I also told them about consent. While it's still a foreign concept to many, we generally value that as a species. I asked that they not inject anyone else without their permission. And they haven't."

Skye considered his points. "And they won't if I choose not to get it?"

Einar spoke. Skye didn't need a translation to understand.

"No, they won't," said Joey. "But it will make your life so much easier."

She nodded. "Let me sleep on it."

After dinner, Joey showed Skye to the human rooms. They each had their own living chambers. He explained that biometrics would allow them access. Only Saba and themselves could access their rooms unless emergency protocols were triggered. Skye did not feel comfortable regardless of the level of safety they assured her. They could tell her anything, and she wouldn't know what was true. Not yet.

Her room had a small bed and a writing table. Off to the side was a door to a bathing and toilet room. Another door opened to a small closet with two sets of clothes and a door mirror. She looked at herself for the first time. Her dark brown hair was longer than she remembered. Her fingers ran through the volume of frizzy waves. Her skin looked healthy, actually better than she remembered. Her cheeks were rosy from the sun, which would surely turn to a nice tan. She would need to ask about getting a brush and sun lotion. She had no money. Panic bubbled in her chest. She took a deep breath to suppress it.

She stepped into the bathroom. It reminded her of the stasis chamber – an upright tube, similar to a shower insert, but with no faucets or spigots or handles. The floor was a rubberized hexagon mesh.

Skye looked at the ceiling. "Saba?"

"Yes, Skye."

Shivers ran down her spine. "Saba, how do I take a shower?"

"To activate the bathing chamber, place your hand on the far wall. Normally, bathing and other preferences are managed via nanotech. In its place, I will adjust it for you," Saba said.

"Thank you," Skye said, "and please lock my door. Do not let anyone in."

The wall clicked and whirred. "It is sealed," Saba said.

She stripped her clothes off one piece at a time, laying them carefully on the chair. Her memories were fuzzy, and she couldn't pinpoint the exact moment they stopped. She recognized her favorite leather jacket. It was a splurge purchase, but the material felt like butter under her fingertips. Her jeans fit the curve of her hips well, a hard thing to find on Earth, even more so now.

She cautiously walked across the soft, sturdy mesh floor and touched the far wall with her fingertips. The bathroom door closed behind her. A square illuminated, prompting her to flatten her hand. She forced herself to remain still, despite her nerves, as steam rose from the floor. The warmth soothed her muscles. A light beam, reminiscent of a copy machine, brightened on the ceiling and slowly scanned the room. After a few passes, the steam receded with the warmth of the room, and the light turned off. The bathroom door clicked open, letting in a chill.

She stepped out and changed into a soft shirt and pants. Despite not using a stream of water or soap, she felt surprisingly clean and refreshed. Her hair and skin felt soft. It was a bizarre experience.

The walls seemed bare but held secret storage and utility cabinets that lit up when she brushed her hand over them. She couldn't understand the markings, but after tinkering a bit, she got the gist of their use. She crawled under the thin blanket of her surprisingly comfortable bed. The room was relatively soundless, which was both comforting and unnerving.

"Saba," she said, just above a whisper.

Saba responded immediately. "Yes, Skye."

Goosebumps trickled over her skin, raising her hair. "Can you play me music or sounds of the ocean?"

Soft noise filled the room. "How is this?"

It was an instrumental that Skye didn't recognize, and it played over the sound of crashing waves. Tears leaked from the crease in her eyes. Her lower lip trembled.

"That's perfect."

Saba listened but did not respond.

NINE

In the med bay, Skye found Char scrolling and reading a hologram article above the main workstation. Her attention was completely focused on the literature.

"Good morning, Char," Skye said.

Char brightened and said something Skye didn't understand. Her face dropped in frustration.

Skye tapped her arm. "Nanotech."

After a long debate and internal struggle, she decided to get it. It was a risk, but a calculated risk. She needed information and leverage. She'd be in a better position to gather information and possibly plan an escape if she could understand what was going on around her.

Char bounced on the balls of her feet and clapped her hands excitedly. She also continued to chatter. Even though Skye couldn't understand, she felt it was well-meaning.

Char ushered her to a nano-chair. It conformed to her figure, supporting her back and neck with ergonomic precision. In a rush of motion, Char swept through several cabinets, gathering equipment on the table. She gently wiped Skye's arm from shoulder to fingertips and laid it carefully on a cloth on the steel counter. She positioned a metal bar on her skin and brushed it the length of her arm in a downward motion. Char tapped the end of the metal bar on several points along Skye's arm that felt like little electric jolts.

Gradually, her head started to swim and ache. Char stopped and observed. She continued to talk to Skye, presumably trying to reassure her and tell her what was happening. Char patted her hand gently, then resumed with the little electric jolts. After setting the metal bar down, she wrapped the cloth around Skye's forearm. It created an inflating pressure, reminiscent of a blood pressure cuff. Skye sat quietly and still. She would have put her feet flat on the floor had they reached. Instead, they dangled and searched for a foot-bar.

"We're almost done, dear. You're doing so good. Much better than Joey, but that's understandable. The poor man had no idea what was happening to him. It must have been terrifying. I know it was terrifying. He told me about it. We actually joke about it now. I'm glad he's such a nice human. I was so anxious that the first of you to wake would be a nightmare and ruin everything. I can see that was a silly thought, now, after meeting you both," Char rambled.

"It's not," Skye said, her eyes closed to the subtle headache. "It's not a silly thought."

Both their eyes widened as they met. "You understand me," Char smiled.

"Yes. And you are also very kind. Not all humans are," Skye said.

"Well, then. I guess we got lucky," Char said, "and you're all done! How do you feel?"

"My head hurts. But overall, fine," Skye said.

Char unwrapped Skye's arm. A thin film covered her forearm and lit up a series of commands that Skye could now read. She understood Char, and presumably, all the other known languages in the Alliance territories.

Joey was right. It was freaking awesome. If Skye could have chosen a superpower on Earth, this would have been it.

"I can give you something for the headache so that you don't notice it. Headaches are funny things. It is the most common ailment in every galaxy system, and even the brightest minds have never truly found a preventative cure."

She tapped a little black stylus across Skye's armband. The headache dulled.

"Skye, do you agree with Joey? Do you think the other humans would want to choose the nanotech, rather than have it just given to them?" Char asked.

"Yes. Absolutely," Skye said. "Some people may not want it."

"But it seems so illogical not to get it. You would be so isolated," Char said.

"Fear is a big motivator. But I agree with you, which is why I chose to get it. But I would have serious reservations about it had it been forced upon me. I can't speak for everyone, so it's important to let them choose for themselves." Skye paused in thought. "It's not my place to make those decisions for other people. And if any human you meet tells you to conduct procedures on people without their consent, don't trust them. Those are not the good humans."

Char nodded. "I expect that goes for all people, not just humans."

"What if I don't like it? What if I want it removed? Can you do that?"

Char furrowed the mounds of skin above her eyes. "Yes. I have never done the procedure, but I believe there is a removal option. Some species do not take well to the tech. Do you think you will reject it?"

"I don't know yet." The pit of Skye's stomach dropped as a surprise panic attack overcame her senses. "What if something goes wrong? Could this kill me?"

The band blinked and chirped.

"It should aid you. That is its design. I have never heard nor read of anyone dying from nanotech bonding. When I say some species do not take well, I mean, some are not compatible, and the tech malfunctions or disables. It just stops working. For example, the Wella race from Munja need their tech replaced regularly, yearly if they're lucky. They short it out so easily, but it causes them no harm. We do study this sort of anomaly. The Alliance is built on information and transparency. Knowledge is our greatest power."

"What kind of control does it have over me?"

"Well, right now, it just helps you communicate. So, it takes the words you see and hear and translates them to the closest version in your native understanding. You can even amend the translation if it does not translate well. As you get used to it, you can use it to do and interact with many things. You can adjust it to monitor your vital statistics and give you reports on yourself, but that's something you have to set up yourself." Char brightened. "You can even set it up to regulate your preferred cleansing temperature! I personally love that feature."

Skye smiled. The panic retreated while she spoke with Char. Inherent paranoia lingered in the shadows of her mind, persistently, but also quietly.

"I look forward to figuring it out. I'll let you know if I have other questions."

"Of course! Anything I can do, honey, just ask."

Skye found Joey in the canteen. Her armband displayed a schedule for the day and a menu to order food. She had no idea what the items were, but at least she had options.

"Heeey, look who's got new tech!" Joey said.

Skye smiled. "I did. I totally caved. It's pretty amazing. You were holding out on me."

"You have no idea." He laughed. "And I told you it was amazing."

"What's good to eat? Now that I have options," she said.

He put his hand to his heart and looked offended. "You didn't like what I picked out for you yesterday? I'm hurt."

"It was fine, but obviously not what I'm used to."

"Did you ever travel on Earth? Did you visit other countries?" He asked.

"Once or twice. I didn't exactly grow up with money."

"Fair enough. Think of this as eating out in another country. The food is different, the customs are different, the people are different, but we're more alike than not. I think."

Skye narrowed her eyes and grinned. "Are you sure? Because I've noticed some pretty glaring differences, and I've only been awake a day."

"In all the ways that matter. I think."

They scanned through the menu and ordered food through the ship system.

"So, what is the plan for today?" Skye said.

"I think more of the same. The ship's mission is to observe the species here," Joey said.

"You don't like animal watching?"

"I'm more of a tech guy, to be honest."

"I could see that. I bet you were a total nerd on Earth."

"Absolutely!" He laughed. "What I wouldn't give for an old school video game system or some comic books."

"What do you do to stay entertained here?"

"It depends on who you ask," he said. "Most people here are working, and that's, like, all they do."

"With the exception of?"

"Zaima. Don't ask about entertainment with Zaima around. She's terrifying. And her idea of entertainment is very different from... well, anyone. I think." Joey looked a little pale.

"Yea, she came out of nowhere."

"I think she might be invisible sometimes, and she might be an assassin," he said.

Skye laughed. "Maybe you've read one too many comics already."

Joey protested and went on a rant about the value of graphic novels. Skye smiled and feigned attention, but her mind drifted to memories of her past. It was an odd, sad sensation, memories of things that no longer existed. Nostalgic ghosts. Problems that were so important yesterday no longer held any significance. So many things she would never see again. So many people. She humored the notion that it was real. She didn't like it.

TEN

They met Kas outside near the carrier. He wore a floppy canvas hat. Zaima laid across the front seats with her legs over the driver's side door.

"We will observe the enatomo again today," Kas said, tapping his fingers together. He brightened when he saw Skye's armband. "Skye! I'm so happy you decided to engage in the tech. I've been hoping to be able to converse freely with you."

Skye blushed. "Thanks. I'm glad I got it too. What exactly are we looking for?"

"We are here to observe and record details about the species," he said.

"So everything and nothing in particular," Zaima said.

"Oh," Skye nodded.

Joey and Skye climbed in the back of the carrier. Kas sat in the front. With little warning, Zaima blasted over the dunes. The enatomo moved location and were further from the encampment today. They parked under the shade of large leafy trees when they caught up to the herd.

Skye stretched under the shade. "Tell me more about them, Kas."

Kas looked pleased. "I'm glad you are taking an interest in the study, Skye. Unfortunately, there's not much to tell. At this point, they do not seem to be an intelligent species. They have short life cycles. They feed, mate, and produce offspring that immediately go into a dormant phase. The current generation will die. After a few months, the offspring emerge, and the cycle begins again. This is the newest generation."

"How long do they live?"

"About a year. Most of it is spent in dormancy, approximately twenty days are spent in conscious activity," Kas said. "Of course, I refer to a year of life on their planet. All planets have different orbital patterns and rotation velocity. Thus, a day, month, year on any planet is different from any other. I can express the conversions in a timeline you're familiar with if you like."

"That's so sad. Such a short life," Skye frowned. "And yeah, why not. I'd love a chart of different planets around here, and any information about the Alliance. Send it my way."

"Oh, I will," Kas said excitedly. "Also, about the enatomo, it appears that they have no memory, or they do not learn easily. There is very little useful data."

Zaima's head rested on the seat at an odd angle. "They're dumb livestock. I look forward to the end of the week when we can leave this boring planet."

Joey and Skye exchanged looks. Kas looked disappointed and annoyed by the comment.

"I think there is more to them, which is why we're here, to find out," Kas said.

"I told Jedre he should harvest one or two of them," Zaima said lazily.

"What?" Kas said, quietly alarmed.

"For science." She drew out the statement.

"No," Kas flapped his hands. "You must not. We do not know what the repercussions could be. We have not studied them enough yet."

"Relax, Kas," Zaima smiled predatorily. "They'll never notice."

"YOU DO NOT KNOW THAT, ZAIMA!" Kas yelled. His face turned a shade of bright white. He took a deep breath and returned to his usual coloring. "I will speak with Jedre. This is insubordinate and threatens the nature of the study."

He huffed and slumped in his seat. His fingers tapped against each other rapidly. Zaima smiled lazily at Skye and Joey before lying back and covering her eyes with her headscarf. The enatomo lounged near an oasis, either oblivious or unconcerned with the commotion on the ridge.

Skye pulled herself off the seat and angled out of the vehicle. "I'm going to go stretch my legs."

"Be cautious." Kas's eyes were trained on the enatomo as he scribbled on a tablet. The markings illuminated on a floating interactive screen.

Skye walked and stretched the muscles in her legs. She stretched her arms and back. Mostly, she wanted to explore the area.

The enatomo alternated between huddling in clustered masses and spreading out in uniform space. They didn't seem to have any interest in their surroundings, moving through the water and bouncing off trees without care. They rolled up and down the dunes.

Skye found the cliff edge near the carrier. She sat in the shade and dangled her feet. On the other side of the oasis, the enatomo rolled right off similar cliff edges and bounced when they hit the ground. It didn't faze them at all.

Skye followed their movement in a daze. It was hypnotizing, the swerving and rolling together and apart. It seemed random and nonsensical at first, but the longer she watched, Skye realized there was a pattern to the movements. It was a dance of sorts. Skye thought back to what Kas said and wondered if they were peacocking.

She decided she liked these elephant blobs. They were interesting and seemed relatively harmless. Sure, the tusks could do some damage, and they could undoubtedly squash her, but they appeared inherently docile. They snacked on plants. They nuzzled and cuddled each other. They were sweet.

They stayed in the field for hours each day, watching the enatomo and their behaviors. Joey opted to stay behind after the first few sessions. The tension between Zaima and Kas varied. Skye suspected Zaima did it just to get a rise out of Kas. She was entertaining herself. She certainly did not care about the enatomo or the study. Her job was different.

"We're nearing the end of this cycle, Skye," Kas said on the way back to the ship. "This generation will be expiring soon."

"How many days left?" Skye asked.

"Tomorrow, we will be leaving," Kas said.

Skye breathed deeply and sighed. "Where to next?"

"We will need to stop at a waystation to send a direct transmission to the Alliance. We'll probably head toward Jodra until we receive our next mission. We must be cautious. Not all Alliance members will be intrigued to see humans," he said delicately.

Skye raised an eyebrow. "Like the ones who blew up Earth?"

Zaima matched Skye's eyebrow raise with a half-smile. Her eyes brightened.

"Especially the ones who blew up Earth," Kas said, oblivious to the sharpness in her tone. "The Vanzkelga will likely try to eliminate any remaining humans. However, the rogues responsible for the attack have been detained. They await trial at the Jodra Core for crimes of interplanetary aggression."

Skye noticed a blob among the dunes. "Stop the carrier."

Zaima slowed. Skye hopped out before it stopped completely and stumbled. She regained her footing and approached the mass with caution, searching for life and movement. It was a tiny enatomo.

"It's breathing," Skye said.

"Is it sleeping?" Zaima said. "Dumb livestock."

She bent down and extended her hand. "I think it's hurt."

"Be cautious!" Kas said, tapping his fingers nervously.

Her fingers touched the creature. It flinched. She paused before putting her hand flat on its shoulder. She could feel it breathing. The muscles shuddered and it vibrated what felt like a whine.

"I'm not going to hurt you, little guy," She whispered.

She inspected it without trying to move it. She couldn't see any injuries. It vibrated again when she attempted to roll it to its side. Skye's heart ached for the creature. Gently she turned it and revealed a gash.

"It's hurt!" Skye said.

"Leave it," Zaima perched on the seat of the carrier. "It's going to die anyway."

Kas hesitated. "Unfortunately, Zaima is correct. It is due to perish soon."

"It's suffering," Skye said. "Can't we bring it back with us? Can't Char do anything?"

Kas hesitated and smiled with a sorrowful, pitying look. "Sure, we can try."

He helped her roll the enatomo gently into the carrier and secure it. To her credit, Zaima did not drive as recklessly on the way back. When they reached the ship, Kas told her to stay outside and went in to get Char. They would not take the enatomo on the Evander.

Skye caressed the skin of the creature. It vibrated under her touch, a weak purr. She sensed the change in vibration from earlier – fear and pain turned to gentler relief. When Kas returned with Char, they looked sympathetic. Skye slowly realized they already made up their minds about the enatomo. It was not a creature of significant importance. Enough to study, but not important enough to intervene.

Char examined it, cleaned it, and sealed the gash. The little creature was tense the entire time. Fortunately, Char worked quickly.

"All patched up," said Char. "You can let it go back now."

Skye stroked the side of the little enatomo's face gently. It had kind and intelligent eyes that looked up at Skye and studied her face. Its right trunk gently caressed Skye's arm, mirroring.

"Kas, can I monitor it overnight?" Skye said.

He hesitated. "I suppose. I don't see why not. I will get you a slate to record your observations."

"A slate?"

"Yes." He waived his tablet. "We use these to record observational data."

Skye nodded and wished she kept her mouth shut. She assumed that's what he meant. Now she knew the term for it. She mentally chided herself.

The enatomo remained strapped to the carrier while the crew ate dinner. When Skye returned, she found a tent and a hammock set up near the carrier. She examined the enatomo again and settled herself into the hammock, tinkering with the features on her new slate. A transmission from Kas blinked on her band and the slate. She brought up a holographic map of the Alliance and its territories - zooming in and out, looking at planets and clusters, stars and orbital patterns. The calculations and translated space and time conversions were embarrassingly above her comprehension.

The enatomo squirmed against its restraints and puffed frustration from its trunks. Skye approached it slowly. It stilled and quieted with her movement, then cooed.

"Tell me about yourself, little one," she whispered.

It slowly reached out and tenderly curled a trunk around her hand. They stared at each other for a long time before they were interrupted.

"What are you planning on doing with it?" The large man said as he walked near Skye's little tent. He maintained distance and eyed the curious pair.

Skye watched him carefully, taking a moment to recall his name. "Hello, Jedre. I don't think we've officially met."

His head cocked with the curl of his upper lip. "I asked you a question, human."

Skye scoffed and stood between the large man and the enatomo.

Skye's mind recalled dealing with her fair share of large, cruel humans on Earth. As terrifying as Jedre was, her most practiced defense was not showing fear.

She stared him down. He bared his teeth, his back-tentacle hackles rising. Movement behind the beast drew her attention and pulled her face to a confident smile.

"Hello, Kas, Zaima," Skye said.

"Hello, Skye," Kas said, tapping his fingers together nervously.

Zaima said nothing. She grinned and stood to the side between Jedre and Skye. Kas skittered next to her after checking on the enatomo. Jedre growled and crossed his arms.

"I would also like to know what you plan to do with the creature," Kas said.

Skye looked at the enatomo and gently laid her hand on its head. It purred and cooed. The enatomo still had its trunk curled around her arm.

"I don't have a plan. I just wanted him to feel better," Skye said. "I didn't want him to suffer needlessly, especially if he could be healed."

"It's going to die anyway," Jedre said.

Skye narrowed her eyes at Jedre. "So will you. That doesn't mean you shouldn't get medical treatment."

His eyes widened. His nostrils flared. Zaima barked a laugh and clasped her hands next to her chin, smiling enthusiastically. Kas was still. His eyes shifted between Jedre and Skye nervously.

Skye looked back at the enatomo. "Everything dies eventually."

Jedre shook his head and walked away. He grumbled something about wasting resources. Zaima sauntered back to the ship after him.

"It seems to have really taken to you," Kas said.

"He's a sweetheart," Skye stroked his head. His skin was velvety, silky soft. "And I think he feels a lot better."

Kas brightened. "How do you know its gender?"

Skye bit her lower lip. "I don't. He looks like a boy enatomo to me. I could be wrong."

Kas smiled nervously. "Okay. I'm going to go in for the night.

Please document your interactions in as much detail as possible," he paused and added, "try to be as scientific as you can."

Skye grimaced. "I will."

Kepseli was a warm planet, even at night. Heat seemed to permeate from the spongey ground. The sky at night on this planet was the same as the sky at home. The stars were different sizes, in different places, but the space between them was as dark as ever.

Skye watched as an asteroid burned across the darkness. The little enatomo squirmed and chirped. She examined the little creature and the straps that held him. Dark marks began to form where they rubbed his skin. She found the healing gash and brushed her fingers over it - causing the enatomo to shiver and whisper a cry.

"If I let you go, will you promise to be good?"

She looked at the eyes of the enatomo. They mimicked the starry sky's dark, dark blue, and black hues. Shining flicks of light in shades of green and purple glittered as they moved.

Her hands ran down the tightest strap and hovered on the latch. After a moment of unease, she snapped it open and loosened the straps. The enatomo trilled and wiggled. She wound the straps around themselves and tossed them in the carrier bed. The enatomo rolled off the edge onto the squishy ground. It shook, rippling its skin and tossing its trunks.

Skye waited to see what it would do. When it didn't run away immediately, she walked into her tent to get the slate. Careful not to turn her back on the animal, she watched it curiously following her. The enatomo sniffed and rolled around her tent before settling on the rug and fluffing down. Its trunks curled around its body, resting its head on its tusks.

"What should I call you?" Skye crouched down next to the enatomo. "You need a name, little guy."

It leaned against her and rested a trunk across her lap. She stroked its velvety skin idly. He was cool to the touch and nuzzled his face into her side. It took a moment of searching, but Skye recognized the faint familiar scent of the creature. It smelled of baby lotion.

"I'm going to call you Ollie," She said.

He purred while she recorded her thoughts and the name of the little creature in the slate. He became much heavier in sleep and barked little whines like a puppy. She crawled out from under its appendage and into her hammock. While she swung and drifted to sleep, she smelled the faint scent of mint and wished she could brush her teeth.

ELEVEN

Skye felt the hammock dip. The change in movement from a gentle sway woke her. Ollie propped his head on the edge of the hammock and laid its trunks along her side. The Kepseli sunrise was grey and blue and purple. The sun had not peeked over the horizon dunes. In her sleepy daze, she hadn't noticed Ollie chewing on her hammock.

"Stop that." She shooed him away. The fabric now had a small hole eaten into the side.

She laughed. "You must be hungry. Let's find you some food."

Realizing she didn't know exactly what kind of plants the enatomo ate, she tapped into the slate. *Vegetation.*

She scowled. "That's not very detailed."

She stretched and looked at the bright and alert little creature. "Let's go for a walk."

They wandered across a cluster of dunes to a miniature oasis. Ollie trilled and sniffed along the edge of the pool, taking a great interest in a patch of red cattails. Skye offered him a variety of plant snacks. She tapped on the slate, noting what plants Ollie liked and did not like. He chirped and trilled when something excited him. Huffs and grunts conveyed dislike.

Skye had trouble deciding if he was more like a cat or a dog. Maybe he was like a pet elephant. It depressed her to think she would never know. She made a concerted effort to keep her ball of feelings suppressed. Every once in a while, an emotion would bubble to the surface – mostly anger at the extremists who destroyed her home. She felt depressed and sometimes overcome with helplessness, insignificance, and homelessness. She felt anxiety at what was to come and the true intentions of her shipmates.

She was not naive enough to think the Alliance had her best interests in mind. There was no expectation that she would be treated like an equal, minorities never were. She was a species being studied, just like the enatomo.

A low whistling sound resonated in the air. Ollie perked up and listened intently. It oscillated between low and high tones before stopping. When it ended, Ollie let out a low moan that mimicked the sound. The tone resumed, and Ollie took off over the dunes. Skye ran after him, but by the time she reached the top, Ollie was already over the next crest.

She ran back to camp. Joey, Zaima, and Kas were talking outside the ship when she ran up. Her tent and hammock were packed away. The Evander hover-dollies carried boxes to the ship.

"Skye, where have you been?" Joey said. "We were worried."

"Something is happening. Ollie ran off," Skye said, out of breath.

"Who's Ollie?" Joey said.

"The little enatomo. He ran off after hearing some noise."

"We're packing up to leave. We don't have time to run after your little pet," Zaima said. "We should have just eaten it."

"What do you mean, it ran after a noise?" Kas said.

"Don't encourage it," Jedre said, coming from the ship. "Our time here is finished."

"Our time here is for an observational study. If there is a significant event occurring, we would be wise to record it," Kas said.

"Is it significant?" Jedre said.

Skye wasn't sure what was happening, but she wanted to follow Ollie. Her gut told her something was off, terrible even, but the fact that Jedre was asking the question felt like a trap.

"I don't know, Jedre. It feels significant, but I really don't know."

"Kas, you have time to take the carrier." Jedre frowned and turned back toward the ship. "If it's important to the research mission, it should be observed and recorded by an Alliance scientist."

"He wouldn't leave without us, right?" Joey said.

"You, yes," Zaima laughed. "Not without me. I will drive."

They loaded into the carrier. Skye gave directions as they rollercoastered over valleys and crests. The closer they got to the now audible noise, the more trails they began to see streaming toward a common destination.

They knew they arrived when they saw the swarm of enatomo around a giant sinking crater. One after another, the enatomo jumped into the void. Skye searched the masses for Ollie. He was the littlest one, trailing behind a creature twice his size.

"Ollie! Stop!" Skye yelled.

The little enatomo paused and looked back before resuming its trek to the crater.

Panic raised pressure in her chest. "We have to go get him."

Kas watched the scene intently, scribing on his slate. "We are here to observe, not intervene."

"Kas, he'll die," It came out more pitiful than she'd prefer. "I don't want him to die. We need to do something."

Zaima watched her with interest but emotional indifference. It was the pitying looks from Kas and Joey that sparked her anger and frustration.

Kas looked down, burying his attention in the slate. "We told you he was going to die. The enatomo do not live long. This is one of the few things we know. I wish you would not have formed such an attachment."

"I'm going to get him," Skye decided, jumping out of the carrier.

"Skye, please stop!" Kas called after her in panic and concern.

Skye ignored him and raced across the squishy ground. They did not follow. The carrier stayed on the top of the dune, observing from afar. The enatomo were faster than her, she knew, but she ran as fast as she could anyway.

"Ollie! Stop!"

The wailing sound continued. It grew louder and vibrated her body as she got closer to the crater. She realized it was the enatomo, singing in a group. They sang highs and lows, up and over, funneling down the planetary drain.

Ollie was almost to the edge. Her heart sank.

"Ollie! Please stop!"

He slowed and turned to look at her. The look of pity in the creature's features broke Skye's heart. For whatever reason, he was intentionally diving into a crater of death with his entire species. She didn't want him to go. She wanted him to go with her and be her friend. She knew – as much as she wished it – it wasn't going to end in her favor.

Ollie resumed the wailing song as he sailed off the crater edge. When the last of the enatomo were gone, so was the song. The quiet of the planet placed a heaviness on Skye's chest. Her tender-hearted friend was gone.

Her tears soaked the soft ground at her feet against her will. She would not walk to the edge and look into the void. Some images cannot be unseen. She pulled herself together and returned to the carrier. They regarded her in silence as she sulked in the back seat.

They returned to the Evander and boarded the ship. It was packed and ready to go. She avoided the crew and their eyes. She wanted to be left alone and was grateful for a solitary space to call her own. She retired to her chambers as the Evander prepared for departure. Warnings over the armband made her aware of the launch sequence activation.

Through the numbness she felt, her heart hurt. She lost a meaningful connection when there weren't many of those available.

She pleaded with her thoughts. Why couldn't she have just brought it on board?

The look Ollie gave her before jumping seared her mind. The enatomo were intelligent creatures. Whatever karmic cycle they underwent year after year was intentional. Ollie knew what he was doing. He knew the implications, and he knew it would hurt Skye, but he had to do it anyway.

Skye took a deep breath. Tomorrow was another day, one most of her people didn't have. She needed to push forward. She needed to do what was required to be done. Right now, her biggest job was to learn and survive.

TWELVE

The Evander dipped into the slipstream just outside Kepseli's atmosphere. It would be a day before they reached the trading station in Ziet. With the enatomo assignment concluded, they needed to refuel, restock, and report.

Kas worked feverishly to complete his reports. Trading stations sent official transmissions to the Alliance central command and maintained compatibilities across the territories for information sharing. He reviewed the data stored by Skye. The details she obtained were obscure, but impressive and not previously recorded.

However damaging the relationship between Skye and the enatomo, it garnered rare details and intricacies of the enatomo species. The council would take notice of this work. He had to credit Skye as a contributor. His mind drifted to the gossip streams of the Alliance community. He did not dare imagine the reaction of his mother. She did not approve of unorthodoxies.

He breathed deeply to calm his nerves and purposefully quiet the tapping of his fingers. With his assigned reports finished, he needed to review the data from his private research. Kas tapped into the locked slate records and watched the footage. Saba tracked the movements of all the crew, as necessary for safety and function. Kas arranged for the tracking footage of the humans to be sent to him in a secure file. He added to his collection of observations. Skye was by far his most interesting subject – and her bonding with non-human species. He found their differences to be most intriguing, and his best argument for preservation.

The biggest hurdle in his study was justifying his disobedience to the Alliance. The raw-footage of relatively free-living humans gave strong support to his cause. Kas requested that all Evander personnel, especially ship recruits, avoid unnecessary contact with the humans for the sake of the study. He had not yet developed a sufficient plan to prevent Alliance punishment to his crew. Though there were options, none of them were particularly good.

An idea struck him like a lightning storm. He must make Skye his apprentice. It would provide bureaucratic protection in the Alliance, something neither of them had on their own. Nervous, rebellious laughter bubbled from his throat. Fortunately, he confined himself to his room to work, and no one was around to watch him giggle in a crazed state. But he had to discuss this with Einar. The decision involved too many lives. He tapped a meeting request in his band, which was immediately accepted and scheduled over dinner.

He sent the same message to Skye. She needed to be a willing participant. If there was one thing Yar Tukk got right, it was the unpredictability of humans. Kas scoffed, taking a break from the reports. Instead, he created a list of reasons why Skye should become an Alliance apprentice scientist – should she need convincing, he would come prepared.

Skye fell asleep on her arm. A thousand needles pricked the numb limb while a little flashing, bouncing light beckoned to be touched. She stared at it for an uncomfortable amount of time, her sleepy eyes mesmerized. The nanotech on her arm blipped.

She reluctantly tapped the band, opening a message bloop. Kas requested a meeting over dinner and labeled it mildly important. There was no reason to starve herself, and she couldn't avoid them forever. Besides, there was so much she needed to learn. As depressed as she was, her survival took precedence. She replied affirmatively.

The little light was gone. Skye frowned and dumped her head onto the bed, only to be woken again by a melodic alarm twenty minutes before her dinner meeting. Skye bathed and changed. She found a compartment in the closet for cleaning her clothes and put in her laundry before leaving.

Walking alone in the ship made her feel vulnerable. She reflexively straightened her posture and raised her chin. Exuding confidence was her best defense, even when it was forced. She froze in the doorway of the empty canteen.

"Kas and Einar are in the Commander's private quarters. Your meeting will take place there," Saba said.

Dotted lines appeared and disoriented her vision. After a moment of acclimation, she realized the nanotech was mapping her directions. A chill ran over her arms. Skye ordered a meal to-go and took it to Einar's quarters. When she arrived at the large doors, she hesitated to knock. The door pinged in front of her hovering fist and opened. Saba announced her arrival.

Einar and Kas were seated at a small, round kitchen table. They stood when she entered. "Welcome, Skye," Einar said.

His chambers were larger than hers, as expected. A couch sat in front of a black window. There were adjacent single seats around a coffee table and a large workstation in a nook to the left. She assumed the closed doors to the left led to a bed-chamber and bathroom.

Einar and Kas watched her with amused interest. The plate settings on the table made her realize she didn't need to bring her own food. She blushed and set her meal on the small countertop.

Einar motioned for her to take a seat. "I prepared a meal for you,

Skye. I hope you find it palatable. It is a meal my family prepares for guests."

The meal reminded her of orzo in red sauce with chunks of meat. Her mouth salivated while he filled their cups with liquid.

"Thank you. It looks and smells delicious." She sipped from the cup. It smelled sweeter than it tasted and reminded her of white wine.

Kas and Einar discussed the Kepseli observation and the plans for arrival at the trading station in Ziet. Skye listened intently while eating her meal, her eyes shifting quietly between the two. Kas tapped his fingers nervously during a lull in the conversation.

"Skye," Kas said. "I would like to make you an apprentice scientist."

He waited expectantly for her response. Skye looked between Kas and Einar.

"I don't know what that means."

"Ah, yes, you would essentially be conducting observational study missions across the Alliance territories, much like the one we did on Kepseli. As an apprentice, you would be working under an Alliance scientist, such as myself," Kas said.

Einar sipped his glass of wine. "You would have a title and certain protections as a working member of the Alliance."

She blushed red heat with a rapidly beating heart. It felt like a gift. Her stomach fluttered. It felt like a trap.

"That sounds important," Skye said.

"It is an honorable title in the Alliance," Kas tapped his fingers.

"Is there anything special I would need to know or do?" Her eyebrow raised. "Would I get paid?"

"You will be required to abide by Alliance directives. It will be important to understand a bit more about the Alliance and its structure. It would be wise to do that regardless of your title," Einar said.

"You would have protections as my apprentice. You are a human, Skye. It would be prudent to set yourself up with some protections now. The Alliance's political climate is divided on the subject of humans, but people generally follow title directives," Kas said.

"It is a big deal to be named an apprentice scientist. It is a coveted position in our society, and one that eventually may lead to an honorable scientist position," Einar said.

"And you will be afforded a service stipend," Kas added.

"Why me?" Skye sat tall and wiped her mouth. "And you said an Alliance scientist – who would be my mentor?"

"I – I would be your mentor," Kas said, looking back and forth between Einar and Skye. "And I chose you because of your interest in learning, um, with the enatomo."

Skye absorbed the information. "And you think it would be good for me?"

"Yes. It is a gifted advantage to be chosen for an apprentice scientist," Einar said.

Kas hesitated. "It would be good for both of us."

She nodded. "I appreciate the honesty. I would like to know more about it. I'm open to it. I mean, it's not like I have anything better to do, and I'd like to be able to do something useful with my time."

Einar smiled, and Kas breathed a sigh of relief. "You are surprisingly pragmatic."

"I also have a favor to ask you," Einar said. "There will be more humans waking from their sleep pods soon. Would you join Joey in welcoming and acclimating them to life on the ship?"

Skye smiled warmly. "Absolutely. Just let me know when."

THE TRADING STATION in Ziet was a hub of activity. It reminded Skye of the big cities back home – cities that no longer existed. Her heart panged. To muffle their species presence, the humans were given poncho-like space suits. The material was fluid and oversized, designed to fit a variety of shapes and sizes.

Kas adjusted his suit. "Trading centers can be overwhelming at first, but you get used to them with more exposure."

Joey bounded down the crew deck and stopped short. "Oh, my God! It's Patrick Stewart! Look, look! It's Patrick Stewart! Sweet baby Jesus I've died and gone to Star Trek." Joey ran off to meet his idol. "This is the best day of my life!"

"He's going to be disappointed," Kas said.

"Why?" said Skye.

"His name is not Patrick Stewart. And he is – as you say – a dick."

Skye grimaced. "Oh."

Jedre loomed over Skye. His height was more apparent when he stood so close to her. "Humans should not be wandering unaccompanied, even on Ziet."

Kas tapped his fingertips together. "That is true. Jedre, will you take Joey with you –"

"No." Jedre stomped down the port and away from the commotion.

Zaima sauntered toward the fuss, turning to briefly flash a bright smile. "I will keep tabs on our Joey."

Kas tapped nervously. "Are you ready?"

A chill ran over Skye's arms. She wanted to see the trading station, but unease churning in her stomach caused hesitation.

"Yeah." She nodded through her marshmallow suit.

They headed to the city center through vendor lined walkways. People of all varieties shuffled through or zipped by on segue-like mounts. Drones whizzed and hovered overhead like hummingbirds. Skye kept pace with Kas and tried not to stare too much.

The cluster of people speaking in such a variety of languages and dialects overwhelmed Skye's ability to think. There was definitely a learning curve, one she hadn't yet hurdled. She resumed a purposeful and confident stride by the third block. Stares and whispers were abundant off the shelter of the Evander. Nervous energy followed her movements. She made a concerted effort to not react.

The tallest building at the center of the trading station reflected light from the city and glittered against the black sky. A spinning, blinking apparatus circled the top floors, like an amusement park thrill ride. Skye read the engraved name on the building as she followed Kas through the black revolving doors.

The Interstellar Alliance Trade Center atrium was open and rose several stories in all its glory. Skye watched as platforms transported people to different levels in graceful, unassisted arcs. She couldn't help but think of how many humans would have died without hand railings, and how many would have fallen off these borderless platforms.

The crash of an obese blob of a creature shocked her out of her thoughts. Skye smirked. Maybe they weren't so different after all.

Kas headed toward the platforms stiffly. A monster of a guard with the face of an angler fish stepped in front of them.

"State your business," the guard said.

"I am Interstellar Alliance Scientist 131NR085MT21, Kas Liska. I am here to transmit report. I am accompanied by my scientist apprentice."

The guard sniffed at them. His needled teeth sharpened against each other as his grin widened, his tiny black eyes focused on Skye.

"A human." A low groan rumbled from his throat. "How interesting. I will buy it off you, scientist."

"She is not for sale," Kas visibly recoiled.

He groaned again and whispered a chuckle. "I smell fear. Mmmmm. Name your price."

A ridge of fur rose along Kas's backbone. "This is my apprentice. No member of the Alliance may be bought or sold, especially not an apprentice scientist. I will have you reported. Now, move out of our way," he growled.

The guard grunted and stepped aside. Skye's skin tingled. She refused to look at the guard but noticed the air shift around her as they passed. He inhaled deeply and moaned again. She gagged and barely suppressed the urge to vomit.

Kas whispered and choked on his words. "I am so sorry, Skye." His eyes watered and scrunched with his face.

Skye surveyed their surroundings. Her walls were up, her poker face locked into its rightful place. "Don't worry about it. We'll talk later. Let's just do what we need to do and get back to the Evander." Her voice came out ragged.

As unnerving as it was, that creature recognized the scent of a human. How and when it came into contact with humans was both concerning and hope-lifting. Maybe other humans passed through Ziet – other humans who were still alive and floating around the Alliance somewhere. It also raised her attention to the fact they were undoubtedly being bought and sold.

He nodded and stepped in the center of an elevator disc. Skye followed close behind. They swiftly rose to another floor and crossed the landing to a bay of kiosks and enclosed offices. Kas entered a private office and closed the door. The glass to the outside immediately dimmed, and a workstation screen lit up the wall.

Kas submitted to a series of biometric scans and entered his identification code. He motioned for Skye to come near. The computer ran through the same sequence before awaiting her code.

Kas placed his hand on her shoulder. "Are you certain you are interested in becoming an apprentice?"

"Yes."

"I do not wish to force anything on you. I hope you find this position as much a calling as an opportunity."

"Kas, I think I have a lot to learn, but I also think this is an opportunity I shouldn't pass up. I don't think I'll regret it, and if I do, I'll learn to live with it."

Kas hesitated. "You are certain?"

"Yes."

He commanded the computer to issue an identification code. After a series of prompts and verifications, the machine scanned Skye once more and blinked her credentials: IAAS – 254KL01. Her armband blinked and chimed when her status recorded.

Kas smiled brightly. "You are now an official employed member of the Interstellar Alliance. This status offers you protections. However, as a human – the first human – it will draw attention. I will send you detailed reading on your protections and responsibilities. You must study them thoroughly."

"Maybe we should have done that to begin with," Skye smirked.

"The timing was necessary. If Kepseli is any indication of your talents, you will do well as a scientist. I will do my best to ensure you succeed, Skye."

Her heart swelled and choked up her words. "Thanks, Kas."

Kas took a moment to upload and transmit his reports. "Skye, you may use these hubs to transmit your reports as well. Would you like to send your report of the enatomo?"

Heat flushed across her skin. "I didn't know I'd be turning this in, but yea, I can send my findings."

She tapped in her new credentials. A link invitation immediately hovered in her vision. She sorted through the files from her band and dragged it to the link. *Transmission sent.* Her stomach squirmed in excitement and unease.

The trip back to the Evander was less eventful and less congested. Kas pointed out some interesting and useful vendors. They didn't stop for anything. Skye had the impression that crowds and people gave Kas anxiety. She could relate.

Jedre stood on the loading deck. "You finish your report, Kas."

"Yes, Jedre. We are finished. Has everyone returned?"

"We're waiting on Char," he grunted.

"Did Zaima and Joey return?"

Jedre chuckled. "The human is the reason we're waiting on Char. He was stabbed by the hevocian. If he survives, I imagine he will not attack one again."

"What! Where is he?" Skye said.

Jedre scowled with irritation. "In the med bay. Where else would he be?"

Skye ran through the ship, skidding to a stop on the textured metal floor. The open med bay doors offered a swollen, inflated Joey sitting on the examination table. His thin gown threatened to burst at the seams.

He murmured through bloated cheeks and lips. "Erm ehrlergic ter vees."

"What happened?"

"Ii wa na Atric Ewar."

Zaima smirked. "His excitement was not received well." She sat on a rounded nano-chair with crossed legs. Her arm lazily supported her head. "He keeps trying to talk, but I don't know what he says. He should just stay quiet until Char returns."

Skye removed her marshmallow suit. "What did this?"

"Ah, he met the pointy end of a hevocian vespula spine. They are not nice. They do not like excitement," Zaima said.

"It stung him?" Skye came closer but did not touch Joey.

Zaima made a violent jabbing motion with her wrist. "Stab. Char gave him something. He breathes, but the puffiness did not go away."

Joey struggled to reach an itch under his robe. His skin was already red and blotchy. His hair stood on end, emphasizing its frizziness.

"Do we have antihistamines or epinephrine?"

Zaima shrugged. Joey grunted and bobbed his head. Skye tapped her armband and sent a message to Char and Einar.

THIRTEEN

Char slipped through the streets easily, overcome with urgency and nostalgia. She grew up in its streets when her parents visited to report to the Alliance. It was practically her second home.

Mencuri, her home planet, was a mere parsec away. She kept contact with several medic peers who remained in the area. Char needed all the help she could get. While she found the assignment exciting and challenging, she also recognized when she was out of her depth. Humans were not her area of expertise. As it happened, one colleague was stationed in the trading station. Rumor had it, she was adept in the study of rare races, including humans.

The eerie feeling of surveillance crept up her neck. She scanned the street. The crowds began to disperse, and vendors closed their stalls. A pair of razvedka students studied displays at a bauble shop. An urtesi theorist droned on while a polite merchant slowly ushered him out. A lean traveler from Gafur scratched tokens at a gambling shaddy. Char smirked. The gafur were known for their intelligence, not their common sense. Everyone knew, no one ever won those instant games.

The stunning green tower of Ziet appeared in every cityscape view of the trading station. It was a well-known and well-kept secret among the Alliance. People knew of the rare species research that came from the facility, but rarely did they know how to enter. Occasionally, a curious and unlucky soul wandered through an entry port. For the tower security, it was a nuisance. For the scientist team on floor eighteen, studying curiosity traits among species, it was an exciting new test subject.

Char knew where to go, even without the instructions sent by her colleague. She slid open a heavy metal door and squeaked it closed behind her. The empty warehouse smelled of cleaning supplies. Her shoes pattered across the floor and clanked up a grated metal staircase. The only features on the second landing were a set of double doors and a small call box. She tapped in a numeric passcode into the lock on the door. They swished open and melded into the walls. The illusion of the empty, dank warehouse flitted away like pixels turning in a digital screen. A translucent green hallway loomed before her, ending in a disc and tunnel system.

Char's destination was a bit higher than floor eighteen. Her colleague, Mara, became a medic alongside Char, but their careers took drastically different paths. Much like Kas, Mara's interests lay firmly in studies and new discoveries. Char had her fair share of discoveries along the way, but her passion remained medicinal and altruistic in nature.

As she neared the top of the tower, the elevator disc slowed to a stop. Char walked off the platform to a view she would never get used to seeing. As high as they were, the people below were nothing more than specks, entirely indiscernible from one another.

A silky voice echoed through the hall, bouncing off the ceilings and glass. "Char!"

Char smiled at the sight of her colleague and old friend. Time treated her well. Mara was slightly taller than Char. Her curled blush-blonde hair naturally swayed to one side and clung to her shoulder. While Char preferred sensible and soft tunics, Mara prided herself on outlandish style. Her brilliant white eyes sparkled against the traditional mencurian pink of her skin.

"How have you been! It's been far too long since your last visit. I suppose that's to be expected when you're traversing the Alliance on a discovery vessel. I could never be cooped up in such a space for that long. I don't know how you do it."

Char smiled. "You look well, Mara."

"Thank you! I just had some work done by my pod-mate's cousin. She's excellent. If you ever want her number, just let me know. But I know you're not here for that. Tell me, what brings you to the green tower?"

"Your expertise on humans actually."

"Oh, Char! It's all business with you. Let's talk over drinks."

Mara led Char to her glistening living office. The room sparkled and moved to accommodate Mara. A set of lounge chairs formed next to a low table. Disc service delivered drinks and petite snacks. Mara flopped down in one of the chairs while Char sat gingerly and plucked a snack from the plate.

"So, what do you want to know about humans? I thought you were working on Kepseli?"

Char nibbled the cookie. Mara appeared casual and nonchalant, but it was as much an illusion as the building. Mara had always been competitive and kept her research guarded. Char knew to be careful in her inquiry. Had it not been necessary, she would not have come.

"I've been reading your reports, and I just found it so fascinating. I heard some questionable rumors about their medical practices, and I wondered if you had any insight."

Mara slid her a devious smirk over her glass. She sipped before answering. "There are some incredibly unbelievable stories, even for a Vanzkelgan. However, I came upon some humans, and authorization to conduct real studies."

Char gasped. "Where did you get real humans?"

"Several ships acquired samples before the big bang." Mara

fanned her hands, emphasizing the explosion. "Several hundred samples are floating around the Alliance. There's even a rebel group."

Char barely feigned surprise. "The Alliance sanctioned the studies?"

"Of course, Char. I don't work off the record. And after the whole controversy with the annihilation of Earth and the potential threat of humans to the Alliance, it was easy to have the research approved. I practically have an unlimited license."

Char's hand rested on her cheek. Her brow raised as she tightened a half-smile. "That's envious. So, tell me, what have you learned medically?"

"A bit. However, we've been focusing on their resiliency. These humans are both highly resilient and incredibly fragile, depending on what they're exposed to." Mara brightened. "I especially love the new ones! They have such a fighting spirit. Humans are so adorable when they're angry. And they're so tiny. This has to be one of my favorite projects yet."

Char's hand moved over her mouth. "Have you ever exposed one to a Vespula sting?"

Her face darkened into a knowing smile. "Yes, actually, but the results varied. All of them puffed up. Most went back to normal after some time, but some puffed up so much it cut off their respiration, and they died."

"They didn't all die?"

"No. Not at all. I think we lost one, but most were just fine after a session in the stasis pods."

"What have they told you of their medicine, how they treated illness on Earth?"

Mara tilted her head and sneered. "Char, they're a primitive species. I have no interest in *their* medicine. I can get my own answers much more quickly."

Char lowered her eyes and nodded. "I see. It's all very fascinating."

Mara leaned forward. "You know, if you come across any humans in your travels, I pay very well for sample acquisitions."

"I'll keep that in mind." Char sipped her glass and smiled brightly. "Enough about work. How have you been? Any new love interests?"

Mara laughed. "Oh, no. My mother wants me to settle down on Mencuri and bud off a few spawn to further the family tree. I told her it's not going to happen. Not now. I'm not about to give up my work just yet. What about you, Char? Are you bulking up to bear fruit?"

Char flushed. "No. I'm not having any children. At least not until my work is finished, and I find someone whom I find compatible."

"Good luck with that. I doubt you'll find any decent mencurian candidates while traversing the spacial planes."

"Well, you never know."

A sneer slit across Mara's face as she nodded. "Oh, Char. I do know."

Char left the green tower feeling ill. She swallowed hard, suppressing the acidic taste creeping up her throat. Her exhale chopped raggedly. She tried to recount how long it had been since she'd seen Mara. She tried to remember the woman she knew from her academy – warm memories shrouded in a dark cloud.

She composed herself and set a steady pace back to the Evander. Even if the council approved these studies, she was confident the study processes were not compliant with research standards. It needed to be brought to the attention of the scientific community. Humans required protection now more than ever. She tapped a message to Kas and Einar in her armband. They needed to hear her findings immediately.

On the ship, Skye stood alone in the storage chamber. One stasis pod was scheduled to open any minute. Obviously, Joey was not in any condition to greet newcomers. The swelling had gone down some, but he still resembled a fluffy pufferfish. Zaima was little help in the med bay. Eventually, Einar came to assist and helped him into a stasis recovery chamber. Joey apprehensively agreed to rest for a shift while they waited for Char to return.

A pressure release startled Skye out of her thoughts. The hair on her arms stood on end, and she shivered with a sudden chill. The newest human recruit pushed himself to a sitting position and looked around the room. He shrank back when seeing Skye.

"Hi there, I'm Skye. What's your name?"

The bearded man calmly surveyed the room with a scowl. "Vittu. Missä olen."

Skye grinned at her tech translation. "I'm going to assume Vittu is not your name."

"My name is Davin. Where am I?"

"Hi Davin, that's a long story. The short answer is that we're on a ship."

Davin climbed out of the stasis pod and stretched. His shirt rose, revealing swoon-worthy abs. He ran fingers through his stylish blonde hair while he examined the storage bay and the stasis pod. His silence goaded anxiety from the back of Skye's mind. She clasped her hands and rocked on the balls of her feet.

He planted his feet and crossed his arms. "Please explain how I came to be here."

"Well, I don't think there's any easy way to say this, so here it goes. We're on a space ship. We were plucked from Earth before it was destroyed. Earth is gone. And were members of something called the Interstellar Alliance, which is like a really big country in space that consists of many planets."

"I don't believe you."

"Okay," Skye forced a smile. They stared each other down in silence for several minutes before Skye broke eye contact. "Would you like a tour of the ship?"

"I would like you to show me the exit," Davin said.

Skye walked toward the doors and waited. Reluctantly, he followed. His stride was longer than Skye's, and she walked quickly to keep pace.

"This is the med bay," Skye pointed it out as they passed but did not stop.

Skye held out her arm to show him the band. "This is nanotech. It translates different languages and allows us to send messages to each other. It's incredibly helpful. It is available if you want it. They won't force it on you if you don't want it."

He forced a tight smile. Skye showed Davin his private rooms and introduced him to Saba. He didn't speak as she gave the tour. Instead, he looked around every corner, scanned the ceilings, floors, and walls, counting the doors and steps they took.

Skye perked up. "Hey, here's the kitchen! Why don't we get some food?"

Jedre walked out of the canteen and growled as they approached. "Not another one."

Skye stopped. A slight panic waved over her, and she looked to Davin. His back was straight. His face stunned, but only momentarily. He looked at Skye and stepped in front of her, squaring his shoulders to Jedre.

Skye peered around Davin. "Hello Jedre, this is our newest recruit –"

Jedre growled and walked the opposite way down the hall. Davin eyed Skye curiously. She walked around him and continued the tour to the now empty canteen.

"What do you like to eat, Davin?"

His nostrils flared. "What the hell was that?"

"That is Jedre. He's the ship's... he's part of the crew," Skye said.

"That's it. What kind of game is this? I want out," Davin said.

Skye grimaced. "I'm sorry. I'm not very good at this." Her stomach growled loudly, causing her to blush.

Davin sighed. "Let's get some food."

Skye grinned a tight smile. "Sounds good. What do you like to eat?"

"I like many foods. I usually have oatmeal for breakfast or soup and pancakes. I need coffee."

"Oh. Joey said coffee didn't survive."

His nostrils flared. "Who is Joey? And what do you mean coffee didn't survive?"

"Joey was the first one of us to wake up. He's, um, not feeling well right now. And yeah, he said there's no coffee," Skye shrugged.

Davin dragged his hands down his face. "I want out of this nightmare."

Skye's face crinkled. "I'm sorry."

She could feel the tears rimming her eyes. It didn't really feel real. Not until now. Not until she had to explain it to someone else. She missed home. She missed Earth. Davin sat at the table, quietly staring at his hands. He waited while she angrily subdued the unwelcome tears. It took her a moment, but she gathered her composure.

"I'm so sorry," she said.

Davin clasped his hands together. "I am sorry, too. I just don't believe you. I did not mean to make you cry."

"No, it's okay. I wasn't expecting it to hit me so hard. I guess I hadn't really mourned yet." She wiped her tears on her shirt. "I'll take you to meet Einar and Kas. That might help."

Davin nodded and followed her out. Saba greeted and announced their arrival, allowing them access to the bridge. Einar sat in a fabricated chair that dissipated when he stood. Kas shuffled through holographic reports. They stopped their discussion when Skye and Davin entered.

"Einar, Kas, this is Davin. Davin, this is Kas and Einar."

They greeted a stunned Davin, who nodded and strode forward with an outstretched hand. His chin jutted forward with a tight-lipped smile.

"On Earth, a common greeting was to shake hands," Skye quickly explained.

Einar curiously took Davin's hand and shook it. Kas followed with a dainty grip and cringed at Davin's firm shake. Zaima stepped out next to Einar and extended her hand. Davin took a startled step back, then gripped her hand while maintaining steady eye contact. Zaima grinned.

Skye smiled. She hadn't seen Zaima when they walked in. Today she was dressed in a navy-blue skin-tight suit. Her hair was black and wavy. Her skin was patched with black and white markings that seemed different every time Skye saw her.

When her hand slipped from his grip, she cooed an introduction. "Zaima."

"I received word from Char. She should be back shortly. Is Davin interested in the nanotech?" Einar said.

"I offered. I'll introduce him to Char when she gets back. I know Joey will need to be checked on first."

"How is Joey doing? I hear he inflated?" Kas said.

"Um, yea. He had an allergic reaction. On Earth, we had things to help treat it. I don't know how that works now."

"Our medicine is advanced, but lacking in knowledge of human illness and treatment. Perhaps you can catalog some of your knowledge on the subject. I know Char would be appreciative," Einar said.

"I will work on that. So, what's the plan?"

"The plan?" Kas said.

"Now that I'm an apprentice. What's our next assignment? What do we do in between studies?"

Einar looked to Kas as he spoke. "We already have our next assignment. There is a list of approved Alliance studies. Once one report is submitted, the next is assigned. You can access the information in your band. We have set a course to the planet Shehur in the Almas quadrant."

"Char has returned. You may find her in the med bay," Saba said. "All crew on board, Commander."

"Initiate departure checks, Saba." Einar tapped a sequence into his band.

Skye nodded and left the bridge. Davin trailed close behind, struggling to tear his gaze from the Evander crew. Zaima fluttered a finger wave as they departed.

FOURTEEN

Davin was quiet while they walked to the med bay. After Skye translated the conversation on the bridge, she glanced at him every few minutes and waited. Having been in the same position recently, she could relate to his skepticism.

"How did we get here?" he said.

Skye waited for him to meet her gaze before responding, ensuring he wasn't asking rhetorically. His eyes met hers. For a brief moment, his face flushed with sorrow before resuming its steely mask.

"From what I understand and what I've been told, that's a complicated question," she said gently and recounted the story of Earth's demise.

"You only know what you've been told. That does not inspire confidence. Hollywood has made it difficult to believe anything is real."

She looked at him knowingly. "I've seen enough to know it's not fake."

"How do you know that whatever they injected you with is not making you see what they want you to see?"

Skye slowed down briefly. "That's a valid point."

They continued to the med bay. An opaque screen was drawn across half the room through which shadows could be seen. Skye heard Char and Joey talk in muffled conversation.

"How's it going over there?" She called out.

The shadows stopped and turned toward her. The curtain retracted uncomfortably quickly, revealing Joey on the table. The swelling reduced but wasn't completely gone.

"Looks better than it did before," Skye said.

Joey whined. "I feel miserable. My skin hurts."

Char smiled less brightly than she did before. Her rosy skin seemed flushed.

"Are you feeling okay, Char?"

She perked up and abruptly gained some color. Her eyes, while still carrying sadness, showed some of her usual cheeriness. "Yes. Thank you, Skye. I wish I could do more."

"Einar suggested we catalog what we remember about medicine from Earth."

"That would be wonderful! And incredibly helpful. I've found pitiful reports on human medicine. It's just absurd. They mostly tell stories about attaching metal to bone and slicing people open and exchanging parts between humans. It's incredibly gruesome."

Skye and Joey exchanged a glance quietly. Char studied their expressions with an air of alarm.

Joey grimaced. "Well, there's some truth to it."

Char laughed nervously. "Seriously?"

Skye gently explained. "Some humans are – were very talented when it came to medicine. They spent many years of their lives learning how to heal people. Doctors, pharmacists, nurses, lots of different jobs - all these people worked together and shared knowledge to help people get better. I'm not exactly sure what you read, or how they reported it, but there is some truth to it."

Char gurgled an incomprehensible noise and clasped her hands. "I will attempt to comprehend it." After a few quiet nods, she looked at Skye and then Davin. "Oh! Hello. Who is this?"

Davin quietly watched the exchange.

Skye smiled. "This is Davin. Davin, this is Joey and Char."

"Hello," they exchanged greetings.

"Davin, did you want the nanotech?" Skye asked.

"No," he said quietly.

Char's shoulders drooped slightly. "You humans are suspicious creatures."

Skye smirked. "Yes, we are."

Her stomach rumbled. She realized they never actually ate. "Joey, are you hungry? We're going to get something to eat, and then I'm going to show Davin his room."

He clenched his fists and shook in excitement, before sending a thank you prayer to space. "I'm so hungry."

Joey squeaked off the table and joined them. Skye watched Char bring up some reports as they left. Her bright demeanor dimmed by her time on the Ziet waystation.

"I have food restrictions. What is there to eat?" Davin said.

Skye looked at Joey.

"I've been going by trial and error, but I'm not a picky eater. Saba?" Joey said.

"Yes, Joey."

Joey looked from Davin to the ceiling. "Can you give an explanation of the food options for Davin?"

"The meal options are organic and inorganic substances obtained from various planetary resources. Select plant-based ingredients are grown on the ship in the nursery. All animal-based ingredients are harvested dependent on the region and duration of time which the Evander is located."

Davin suspiciously gazed at the ceiling. "Are any ingredients toxic to humans, that you know of?"

"Yes. Although most ingredients have not been studied for their effects on humans. I've identified several substances that appear to negatively affect human biology and have been removed from the dieting options."

Joey and Skye silently listened. Skye's mouth was slightly open in a grimace.

Davin frowned at their reactions. "These are the questions you have not asked."

"I'm not going to pretend like I know everything. Not even a little bit," Skye said.

Joey chatted with Davin while they ate. Skye mostly listened. They were closer in age than Skye, both in their twenties and completed college, even though Joey acted like a teenager. Davin had been a musician from Finland who spent some time in the States. Joey was a self-proclaimed military brat who knew just enough about computers to get into trouble. Davin didn't say much. Joey could carry the conversation for all of them.

The Evander shook violently.

Saba's voice boomed throughout the ship. "Attention. Eminent storm presence. Assume appropriate safety measures."

"What are we supposed to do?" Davin said.

"Saba, what should we be doing?" Joey said.

Chairs equipped with safety harnesses unfolded from the wall. "You do not have assigned duties. Secure yourself to prevent damage."

They scrambled to the safety seating on shaking legs. Skye navigated the magnetic buckling. Once clicked into place, the harness adjusted to fit her body snugly. Joey mimicked Skye and snapped his into place. Davin followed.

Through gritted teeth, they endured a battering of spinning and shaking. The vibrations moved their skin to numbness. Skye's hair floated in front of her face. Her limbs hovered. With the gravity modulation shut off, unattached random canteen utensils floated freely.

"SABA!" Joey cried.

She did not answer.

The floating debris slammed into the ship surface with unexpected force. Their bodies compressed to the chair and the wall.

Skye's hair flattened as best it could. Even the gravitational force of a dozen planets could not tame her mane of thick waves. It was as if gravity had been applied to all surfaces of the Evander at once. Crushing, mind-numbing gravity.

Skye turned her head to see Davin's slack body pinned to the chair. With nausea-inducing effort, she turned her head to the opposite side. When her eyes regained focus, she saw Joey. He was red with exertion, resisting the forces trying to flatten him. Breathing was difficult. Seeing was difficult. Black shadows crowded her peripheral vision. She closed her eyes and focused on each breath. With the swiftness of a snap of the fingers, she was out.

Something tapped her face. "Human. Wake up."

Her heavy body suspended against the straps of her harness. The skin on her face hung with unnatural weight. A clear string of drool slipped from her mouth and clung to her arm and leg.

Tap. Tap. Tap. "Skye."

A thick finger poked the side of her head.

"Wake up!" He yelled in frustration.

Her eyes focused on her knees, but she could not bring herself to move. Her mouth swallowed the excess spit. Her head rolled, and she released a groan. Her limbs were leaden and uncooperative.

A blue face hovered inches from her own. Subconsciously, it was not a face she wanted to see. His face caused angry emotions to bubble to her brain, releasing the urges of a toddler tantrum.

"Get away from me," she said.

Her voice came out slow and slurred. The shock on his face delivered unexpected happy feelings that immediately made her feel bad about herself.

"This is not the time."

"What could you possibly want from me?" she whined.

Her vision doubled and made her nauseous and dizzy. Her head fell to one side. A large hand cradled her head, tilting it upright with alarming tenderness. He searched her eyes.

"Your shipmates need your help, Skye."

Her breath caught. She took a deep breath and searched his face for insincerity. She noticed the deep bleeding gash on his forehead.

Her hand floated to his face, and clumsily brushed the wound. "You need Char."

He winced and grabbed her hand. "No. Right now, Char needs you."

Her heart pounded as her head continued to sharpen. She looked down uncomfortably and tugged on the buckles of her harness. He gave her a moment and then assisted, releasing the latches with ease. She wriggled against the straps and stepped out of the chair. Immediately, she crumbled to the ground. Her face rested on the cold floor. She groaned and pushed her upper body up with her arms.

"My legs are asleep."

He looked startled and deeply concerned. She moved them gently in a circular motion, encouraging circulation to return.

"Are you hurt?"

"I don't think so. The feeling should return in a minute."

He scooped her up off the floor and walked out of the canteen. Her arm naturally wrapped around his shoulder and brushed the extensions on his back. His skin was almost indescribably rough and soft, like a cross between chinchilla fur and sharkskin.

Her head bobbled involuntarily. "What happened?"

"We ran into interference during a slipstream transfer. Someone tried to disable our ship."

"Where are we now?"

"We made it to Almas and are en route to land on Shehur."

"Where are you taking me?"

"Storage bay."

Skye had been watching the path ahead while he answered her questions. She moved to study his face. The wound crusted over, and the active bleeding congealed. The angles of his face seemed ashen. This close to his face, she could see his eyes were a deep teal blue with a dark outer ring. They shifted to her face. He recoiled and stiffened when he realized she was staring at him.

She could feel the growl reverberate through his body. "What is it?"

She shook her head and resumed looking at the path ahead. There was an audible commotion as they neared the storage bay.

"I think I can walk. What's going on?"

He set her on her feet and ensured her steadiness before stepping back.

"Two stasis pods decompressed. The humans have responded violently. Char came here to check on them when she realized they might be affected by the slipstream interference. They have acquired a weapon and are holding her hostage. They have not responded favorably to our efforts to calm the situation. If you cannot resolve the situation, it will be resolved, and it will not end well."

She wanted to ask more questions, but she understood the reasoning. Her initial reaction was one of hesitance. She was not a hostage negotiator. However, she was one of the best chances of calming two angry, confused, and scared humans. Joey was the better option, in her opinion, but he was still unconscious.

The voice of Eleanor rang in her head. *You got this, Skye. Work the problem.* She straightened her shoulders and approached the door. It did not automatically open.

"Saba, slowly open the door on the left, please."

It silently drifted open to reveal a dimly lit storage bay. She half stepped in the door and announced her presence. "My name is Skye, and I'm coming in!"

Immediately, a shrill voice protested. "Stay away!"

"I'll kill her! I swear, I will." A dense and deep male voice threatened. "We will not stand for any tricks from you monsters!"

Aside from a throbbing headache, Skye's mental acuity returned to normal. On a normal day, she may have approached the situation delicately. However, she was in a foul mood, and she was doubly upset that they harmed Char. She hadn't realized until this moment how attached she'd become. She genuinely liked the woman. Her being mistreated made her angry.

Skye spoke loudly and confidently. "If you hurt her, you're not making it out of here alive."

She waited for a response. She heard an audible gasp. Jedre was close behind her with a weapon raised to his shoulder. Skye gestured for him to wait and stand back. The two humans were quiet.

When they didn't respond, she continued. "If you kill her, I'll make you wish I had killed you, after I drag you out of there."

"Who are you?" the woman said.

"My name is Skye. Who are you?"

After a pause, the woman answered. "Listen, I don't know how I got here. There's been a mistake. This is a big misunderstanding!"

"Do you have a weapon?"

"Yes!" the man said.

"No!" the woman said. "No, I don't want any trouble!"

Skye took another step, clearing a path to the door. "Come out slowly."

"Stay where you are! Don't go out there! You are insane!" the man yelled frantically.

A woman of average athletic build with pin-straight blonde hair peeked out behind the storage pod just enough to see Skye in the doorway. She slowly approached while the man continued to yell.

Skye heard Char whimper, sparking a rage-filled warning. "If you hurt her, I will kill you!"

The woman hesitated; her face plastered with fear.

"Listen, I know you're terrified. I know you're confused. I'm here to help you, and I'm not going to hurt you. No one here is going to hurt you." Skye took a step outside the storage bay, straddling the doorway. She locked eyes with Jedre. "Clear the hall. Out of sight."

She waited while he reluctantly complied, then returned her focus on the woman. "I want you to come here and stand just outside this room."

"Okay, okay," she raised her hands and shuffled out of the room.

Skye made room for her to pass. The woman followed Skye's instruction and stood with her back flat against the hallway wall.

"Do not move from this spot."

The woman nodded. She crouched to her knees and cried hysterically. After a moment, Skye walked further into the storage bay, holding her palms up.

"Stay back!" the man screamed.

She saw a pipe wave over the stasis pod, followed by a hollow clank. Char cried out and whimpered.

"Shut up! Shut up!"

"Let. Her. Go." Skye said evenly. "You have nowhere to go. She has done nothing to you. Let her go and put the pipe down."

"Get away! I'm not going down without a fight! You monsters can't fool me."

"I'm human, and I'm the only chance you got, asshole."

A thin man with a pronounced round head stepped out from behind the pod. He held the pipe like a cricket bat and shook it menacingly.

"Char, are you okay?"

A strangled sob whimpered from the dark, "Skye."

"Shut up! How can you understand this monster!"

"Listen, idiot. You either come peacefully with me, or I invite the real monsters to come in here and tear you apart."

She watched him fluster and issued her commands with unwavering confidence. "Char, move toward the door and exit left."

Skye put her hands on her hips and faced the man. She stared him down as Char started to crawl toward the door. Once in the clear, Char stumbled to her feet. As she passed Skye, tears rimmed her eyes, and her hands clasped at her heart. Skye curtly nodded with a tight smile.

She returned a menacing gaze at the man. "Drop the pipe and put your hands behind your head."

When Char neared the door, the man lost his mind. He charged Skye. Startled out of her tough facade, Skye brought her hands up to shield her head. The pipe clanked noisily on the floor and rolled to an abrupt stop. The man dropped to the ground like a bag of sand.

Zaima appeared in a tight black suit with white striped print. Her face markings vibrant, and her straight black hair pulled back into a long tight ponytail. Her arm poised over the man in victory after delivering a severe blow. The man was out cold.

Skye relaxed. "Thank you, Zaima."

She cocked her head and grinned. "My pleasure."

"What are you going to do with them?" Skye said.

"We will go have a chat, and meet with Einar," Zaima said.

"Do you have rope or anything to tie his hands?"

"Rope?"

"Yes. Something to bind his hands," Skye said.

"Ah," Zaima nodded.

She produced a long, thin sliver of metal and proceeded to wire it around his wrists and arms behind his back. She picked up his collar and dragged him across the floor. Skye cringed at the handling of the man but did not protest. In the hallway, the woman crouched on her heels and covered her face.

Skye touched her shoulder. "Come with me."

She looked up, terrified, and complied. Her muffled sobs accompanied the sounds of their shoes on the metal floor. They were not going to the bridge.

Zaima dragged the man into a plain square room with two chairs and a table. She dropped the man on the floor and gestured for the woman to sit.

From the wall next to the door, Zaima produced another chair. She set it down across the table from the woman. The woman gripped the seat under her and stared wildly at Skye and Zaima.

Zaima rested her chin on her fist. "What do you want me to do with the man?"

Skye checked his pulse. He was alive, just unconscious. Drool pooled under his mouth. His arms developed a purple tint and red marks under the binding.

"Let's put him in a chair with a safety harness and keep his hands secure, but not cut off circulation."

Zaima removed the wire binding and propped him in the chair. The harness slipped out of the chair like a chainmail snake and buckled securely. She set his hands on the table, which were immediately secured by similar straps. Skye made a concerted effort to remove any surprise from her reaction. Zaima nodded and exited the room. The silence lingered as the door pressured close.

Skye sat across from the woman and studied the pair. The woman's hands trembled as she crossed and rubbed her arms. She looked around the room, avoiding eye contact with Skye. Her gaze landed on the man, drawing a sob from her throat.

"What is your name?" Skye said.

Her large, doe-eyes widened when they met Skye's. "Farren."

"Hi, Farren. I'm sorry for what you had to go through today."

Farren's face crumpled, tears spilled from the corners of her eyes. She wiped them and took a deep breath, straightening her back and her composure. "I don't understand what's going on. Where am I? How did I get here?" She began to cry again. "I woke up in a coffin."

Skye waited while she sobbed. She smiled empathetically and leaned her arms on the table. Farren took several more breaths, flaring her nostrils and stiffening her chin. She held her arms tightly crossed.

"They're stasis pods, to keep people safe during transit. I also woke up in one, but my introduction to this place was far gentler and more planned."

Farren's lip quivered. "This place?"

"We are on a space ship," Skye said.

"A space ship?" Farren's eyebrow raised. Her face shifted between confusion, fear, and skepticism.

"There's no easy way to explain this." Skye tried to keep the story neutral and factual. While she was becoming tired of telling the story, she would not deny anyone the history.

"Aliens? They're aliens," Farren recoiled in disgust and horror. "Have I been probed?"

"I don't really like using that word and no, not to my knowledge. They don't do that," Skye said.

"Are you sure?" Farren relaxed the tension in her shoulders slightly.

"Pretty sure," Skye forced a tight, matter-of-fact smile.

"So, now what? We're going back to their planet? Are we slaves?"

Skye recoiled with concern and confusion. "No. No. We're guests. Most of the crew come from different planets, so I'm sure we'll eventually visit someone's home, but not yet. The Evander is a scientific discovery ship. It studies planets in the Alliance. Earth was one of those planets before it was destroyed."

"I don't believe you. Why would Earth have been destroyed?"

"I know. It's unbelievable. I didn't believe it either at first. But I can think of many reasons and ways Earth could have been destroyed by humans. It just so happens that it was destroyed because a human killed a particular Alliance scientist. It sure is complicated."

"So, what do you want from me?" Farren eyed Skye.

"Nothing," Skye shrugged.

"So why am I here?"

Skye felt the anger and frustration radiate off Farren. She could relate and tried not to let her emotions be influenced. A light blinked on Skye's armband.

Farren jumped. "What is that?"

"I don't have answers for all of your questions right now, and I know you have a lot of questions. I need to report to the ship's Commander, but I'll be back when I have more information for you."

"You're leaving me here? What about him!" Farren gestured to the sleeping, angry man.

"He'll be fine until I get back," Skye said and looked at the ceiling. "I'll be notified if he wakes up. Right, Saba?"

"That is correct, Skye," Saba said.

Farren looked around for the speakers. Skye returned her chair to the wall as smoothly as she could, considering she didn't know what she was doing. Saba assisted.

"Obviously, you're being watched. Don't do anything stupid," Skye said as she left.

FIFTEEN

Adrenaline flowed freely through her system. The consequences of the newcomers' actions weighed on her mind. Skye paced in the hall while she thought. Her leg bounced when she stopped, a nervous habit from her childhood. She resisted the urge to kick the wall. Letting her temper control her actions would help no one, and Saba didn't do anything wrong.

Focus. She clapped her hands loudly and walked steadily to the bridge. The doors opened with her approach. She slowed and caught her breath before entering.

She quietly studied the Evander's crew. Einar and Kas spoke in serious conversation near Einar's workstation. Zaima perched on a seat near Jedre. Char stood and looked visibly shaken. They stopped their conversations when Skye arrived and focused their attention on her.

Einar brightened slightly but maintained a dark, midnight hue. "Thank you, Skye, for coming so quickly. We need some insight and clarification on the recent events." He calmly walked toward Skye.

She smiled nervously. "You're welcome, Einar. Absolutely."

While she remained aware of the others in the room, Einar had her full attention. She noted the shift in his color once again, mimicking and mingling the appearance of others and herself. His eyes were dark and held great intelligence. He was the epitome of the strong silent type, and Skye chided herself for not giving him more notice before. He came off as such a docile individual, until that moment. This man was a well-hidden force.

He smiled – something Skye once brushed off as comforting – now sent tingles across her skin. "The two humans who emerged unplanned have not responded well."

Skye looked at her shoes. "No."

"In your estimation, do these humans pose a threat to the crew?" he asked.

Skye weighed the question. She could feel the importance of her answer. Diplomacy was not something she would have listed as a strength on Earth. It occurred to her that giving biased opinions haphazardly could result in severe consequences, for whatever was left of the human race. The way he looked at her, she felt he'd be able to see through any lie.

"Honestly, I don't know. Humans are –" she tried to find the proper wording. "Humans are a diverse species. We are very different from one another. Our thoughts, actions, beliefs, appearance, natural tendencies -" she heard herself rambling and cringed. "All these things vary from person to person. I think they experienced a traumatic event, and that is what caused their behavior. Do I think it will impact their thoughts and feelings and actions in the future? Yes, probably. Do I think they're dangerous? No, not really. Definitely not the woman. The guy, maybe. He's still unconscious."

Einar nodded and assessed her response. "There have been reports of human violence on Earth. How true would you say they are?"

Skye took a deep breath and clasped her hands behind her straightened back. "Without reading the report, I cannot give an accurate response. However, my personal experiences lead me to believe that those reports hold some truth."

Einar grinned. "That is a fair answer."

Kas tapping his fingers. His nervousness made her more nervous. Zaima crossed her legs and rested her chin on her fist. A predatory grin pulling on the corners of her mouth. Skye swallowed hard. Jedre stood with his arms crossed. To her surprise, he looked less angry than usual.

Einar tilted his head and walked a few paces. "You threatened the human man, a member of your own species. You threatened him with death."

Skye met his eyes. "Yes."

He waited a moment, then gestured with his hand for more. "It seems unlikely that you would choose to murder a member of your own species for harming Char, whom you barely know and who is not your kin."

Skye cocked her head to the side. Her eyebrow raised, and jaw jutted—every fiber of her being reigned in her attitude while she waited for an actual question.

Einar's face softened. "Why would you threaten him in such a way?"

"I don't know him at all, and he was threatening Char." Skye gestured with her hands, forcibly keeping the volume of her voice respectful. "Even if she's not my *kin*, I think of her as my friend. I'd have been very upset if he hurt her." She turned her attention to Char. "Are you okay, Char?"

Char's eyes and her face blushed and swelled. "I'm okay. Thank you, Skye."

Skye nodded and took a deep breath. "I know they were scared. People can sometimes react violently when they're scared."

"Would you have killed him, like you said?" Zaima said.

Skye hesitated. "I think probably not."

Zaima smiled and slapped her knees. "You are good at pretending. I believed you."

"Luckily, he did too." Skye grinned lopsidedly at Zaima before turning her attention back to Einar. "What are you going to do with them?"

Einar raised his thin eyebrows. "It depends on their actions. If they are able to acclimate, we will allow them to function on the ship. If they are not, we will need to examine alternative options."

Skye nodded. She did not ask what the alternative options would be. "How are Joey and Davin doing?"

Saba answered. "Joey and Davin have retired to their rooms. We will be arriving in Shehur within two hours and eight rounded minutes."

"Perhaps it is prudent to put the new humans in their own rooms until they can get acclimated," Einar said. "Are you able to manage, Skye?"

"I should be able to, but I wouldn't mind having some assistance, just in case."

"Jedre can accompany you."

Skye cringed. "Jedre wouldn't be my first choice, no offense. His appearance may be alarming to some humans, especially those who are already untrusting. Is Zaima available?"

Skye watched as the crew responded to her request with curious grins and astonishment. Zaima's was the largest of all.

"You think that Zaima is less alarming than Jedre?" Einar said.

Skye felt like an outsider to an inside joke. "No offense, but yea."

"Then, Zaima it is," Einar smiled.

FARREN FOLDED her arms on the table and rested her head. She had so many unanswered questions, but only a few that truly mattered to her. If she was honest with herself, she already knew the answers. If Earth was gone, her family was gone. The chances of them being rescued and not on this ship couldn't be very good. One in a billion.

One in three-billion. She didn't know the odds, but she knew they weren't good.

Her heart broke. Her thoughts replayed moments of her life, memories she never knew the importance of until now. The last conversation she had with her daughter was when she was putting her to bed. Her daughter wanted to stay up, then she wanted to cuddle. She negotiated 2 minutes of cuddling, but told her mom that "I not like you!" Farren responded that she loved her very much, and it hurt her feelings when she said she didn't like her. She cuddled with the little girl until she fell asleep.

Her newborn boy was sleeping in the room next door. She checked on the little boy, resting her hand on his chest. She always had a deep fear that he would stop breathing. She remembered having the same fear when her daughter was an infant.

She remembered her husband rubbing her shoulders as she studied. She was exhausted. There were only a few more weeks before she took the nursing boards. She finally graduated from nursing school, and her little family was finally going to get some sort of normalcy.

She wished she had spent more time cuddling and holding her babies. She missed her husband's warmth. Her heart hurt. The sobs renewed in her chest, and the tears flowed.

The man was still unconscious when Skye returned. The doors slid open to let her in, then quickly sealed behind her. Farren noticed the woman in disguise waited in the hall.

"We're moving you to your own room while we survey a new planet," Skye said.

"I really just want to go home."

Skye said quietly. "I know."

"Just put me back," Farren said.

"Put you back?"

"In the sleep coffin."

Skye thought for a moment. "Saba, could we do that? Put someone back in stasis?"

"Yes, Skye."

Farren perked up. "I would like to do that. If what you're saying is true, I need time to mourn."

Saba chimed. "You will wake up as if no time has passed at all."

"I don't care."

Skye turned back to the door. "It's something I can look into for you, but what good will it do?"

Her throat tightened as she composed her thoughts. Tears threatened to flood past the rims of her eyes. "I have lost my life. I have lost my children. I need something I can control. This is something I can control. Just put me back to sleep."

Skye nodded. "If you think it will help. But right now, we need to move you to another room. Come with me."

When they exited, Zaima wasn't visible. Skye assumed she was still around. She led Farren to the area housing the human recruits. With Saba's help, she located Farren's room and showed her some of its features.

"Are you hungry?"

"No, not really. Let me know when I can go back."

Skye left Farren to herself and started back to the room for the unconscious man. Halfway there, Zaima walked beside her.

"Do you think the next one will be more fightful?"

Skye hesitated and considered Zaima's word choice. "Probably."

Zaima stopped outside the door. She grinned. "He is awake."

The door opened to Skye. She watched the struggling man grunt and roar as he tugged against the bindings. She took her time, casually retrieving a chair and setting it across from him. He spewed profanities and derogatory remarks. She stared at him with contempt and waited for him to exhaust himself.

It took some time, but eventually, the huffing and yelling waned. Skye relaxed in her seat and crossed her legs. She leaned forward, about to speak when his eyes went wide, and he shrieked in horror. Zaima materialized over Skye's shoulder with a toothy grin.

"Demon! Let me go!"

"The more you struggle, the worse it will be," Zaima said.

"You cannot keep me here! Do you know who I am? You are dead when my family finds you!"

Skye did not relent, her face remained emotionless. "Earth is gone. You are on a space ship. And if you continue acting this way, you're going to get yourself killed or worse."

"I don't believe you. You stupid girl and your lies."

Zaima snarled. "This human is unpleasant."

"Yes. He is." Skye got up from the table. "Let's go."

"You can't leave me here! You stupid – " The man continued to scream after they left.

"What do you want to do with him?" Zaima asked.

"Leave him here. Maybe we can return him to stasis too."

Saba chimed from overhead. "Landing protocol complete. We have successfully arrived on planet Shehur. Please report to stations for initiation of observational support."

"What does that mean?" Skye said.

"You need to see Kas. The next study mission has started," Zaima said.

A little blinking light pinged on Skye's armband. Kas summoned her to meet on the crew deck.

SIXTEEN

Kas unpacked a crate of equipment on the crew deck. "The evasive species is rumored to live in these canyons."

"Do you mean invasive?" Skye asked.

"No, evasive," Kas said. "No one has been able to identify or observe it properly."

"Then how do you know it's even here?"

"It has been reported that one, possibly more, unknown species inhabit the planet and have aided stranded travelers."

"So, this is the first time an observational crew has been here to check it out?"

"No. This is the seven-hundredth and fifty-first attempt to make contact," Kas said.

"Oh."

"The Alliance is very interested in discovering how this species eluded previous inquiries," Kas said.

"You seem excited about this one, Kas, and serious."

"Yes, I suppose I am. This mission is a rite of passage among Alliance scientists. Everyone wants to be the one who finally reveals the species on Shehur. It's nicknamed the quiet planet for a reason," he chuckled.

Kas set a thin navy space suit, a set of boots, and a vest on the table in front of Skye. "You will need to dress for this study. You will not be able to breathe or survive on the planet without protective equipment. Because we do not know the nature of the species, you will also need to be armed with a weapon. We will get to that in a moment."

Skye slipped the suit on over her clothes. It compressed and melded to her body, covering her head to toes. Only her face remained exposed, though she assumed that would be remedied before they exited the Evander. She slipped on the durable black boots, which also compressed to fit her feet snugly and comfortably. The vest banded into place over her shoulders.

She questioned the use of her band under the suit and looked at her forearm. To her delight and surprise, the band was visible. Upon thorough examination, the band either melded with the suit or the nanotech showed her the band command functions in an overlay.

"What are you doing?" Kas asked.

Skye lowered her arm. "I was examining my armband through the suit."

"Ah, okay." Kas was dressed the same, with only his face showing. "When we release the exterior door, we must have our facial covers active."

He pressed his right temple, and a transparent mask bubbled out of the suit, sealing his face. He tapped it again, and it retracted. "For now, we can leave it off. We must go to the ship weapon storage."

He wasted no time. Before Skye could comment, he exited, and she was running to catch up. The weapon storage was in the heart of the Evander. Kas led Skye through a series of hallways and turns, further than she had ever explored. They stopped at a set of blue striped metal doors that did not open automatically. Kas entered a code and scanned his hand and ear. Skye watched in fascination.

The storage room was anti-climactic. There were rows of storage bins and cabinets. Several cases with drawers inside lay open on a workstation like ugly matryoshka dolls. Kas opened a cabinet on the left, retrieved a case, and snapped it open. It revealed two plain-looking metal rods and two coin-sized metal disks.

Skye watched. "How does it work?"

Kas delicately attached a metal disc to his vest, and then one to Skye's. "It is a personal positron defense. You aim the director." He held up the metal rods and handed one to Skye. "and it... causes damage. It is particularly useful if you find yourself being threatened. It is connected to the nanotech and will form a protective shield when you sense danger. It may take some wearing to calibrate. I assume you are the first human to use it." He activated the shield with a slight tap of his thumb then deactivated it with the same movement. "You can also use it manually."

She followed Kas's lead and tucked the director into an inner pocket of her vest. He returned the open case to the cabinet and retrieved a set of stylus sticks.

"Medkits," He said, giving one to Skye.

Without further warning, Kas shuffled Skye out of the weapon bay. The doors sealed behind as they hustled back to the crew deck. In the bay, he activated his face shield and motioned for Skye to do the same. It sealed over her face.

After a moment of suffocation panic, Skye took a deep breath. There was a sweet smell to the air supply that was familiar, but she couldn't identify. Irritating nostalgia tugged at her mind while she followed Kas to the exit lock.

They sealed themselves in a small foyer room and waited for the pressure to normalize between the outer atmosphere and the Evander. When the exterior door hissed open, Skye was overcome by the barren desolation of the planet. Shehur was flat and blue.

His voice transmitted in her ear. "We must hurry and set up a site before the air changes."

Kas scampered over to a vehicle packed with crates. Skye followed behind and got in the passenger seat. He was a much more cautious driver than Zaima. About a kilometer from the Evander, Kas stopped and grabbed a white box crate from the carrier. He unfolded several snaps and fasteners, allowing the structure to unfurl. He stepped away while it inflated and popped up.

Skye watched as he tapped commands in his band. The self-loading crates transferred to a hover dolly and shuttled into the new tent. Skye held her arms, patiently waited for instruction. Kas snapped up a dual workstation and seating area. He loaded the other crates into the tent and pulled a cover over the vehicle interior. Skye took mental notes.

"We only have a few minutes left before the air changes, hurry in the tent. We can set up the basics in there," Kas said.

Skye sealed the tent behind them. "What happens when the air changes?"

"The atmosphere on Shehur is a unique gas combination, mainly hydrogen and helium. What makes it special is that it is not truly a gas planet, as you can see." He stomped his foot soundlessly. "The composition of the planet itself is heavy in minerals, and the air is heavily laden with fog storms. We must do most of our work in the patches of open air."

"Is the fog harmful?"

"Not especially, but it is difficult to function in an environment you have never explored, especially if you cannot see where you are going." He froze, reconsidered his words, and then shook his head. "Not confidently see where you're going."

"Fair enough."

"I have sent you several reports on Shehur. You should study them while we wait for the fog to pass."

Skye took a seat at the workstation and found the information. A file with forty-two reports blinked on her screen. They were separated based on a system that assigned quality rating, then chronologically. It told a story of the most pertinent information. She found she could also rearrange the files to read in true chronological order, or randomly. The system in place was superior for delivering information.

Kas tapped away on his workstation and shuffled through crates of equipment. He assembled a metal table, then started whirling together a metal instrument.

"Saba, are the readings calibrating?"

"Calibration in process. We will have atmospheric patterning in place momentarily."

"Sometimes, we are not able to get the best readings from the ship. We must set up instrumentation that functions best on the planet's atmosphere," Kas said.

Skye swiped at a holographic report. "Why can't it be done on the ship, like an antenna or something?"

"If the ship itself interferes with the accuracy of the readings, we must separate the instrument from the ship. Most of the time, we do not have this issue. However, on Shehur, there are complications," he huffed, "and unknown causes of complications. Keep reading, and you will understand better. The next open-air patch will begin in forty-seven minutes. It will remain for seventy-two minutes."

"That doesn't seem like a lot of time to explore," Skye said.

"It is not," Kas frowned while he tinkered with the instruments.

"Patterning complete. It is accessible through your armband," Saba said.

Skye continued to sift through the reports. It took longer than if she were reading in her own language. The translation of the nanotech was fascinating. Some reports were far better written than others but contained little useful content. Others were packed with interesting tidbits, but the explanations were contrived. Eventually, she came upon an incredibly detailed, incredibly well-written piece. It read like a book and consumed her attention so completely that she hadn't noticed Kas speaking to her.

Kas tapped her shoulder. "Skye, did you hear me?"

"No, what?" She startled.

"We have seventeen minutes until the fog breaks. Bring up the planetary map on your armband."

Skye hesitated.

Kas gently held her forearm and tapped her banding. "This is how you bring up a specific planetary map." He looked to her for understanding. When she nodded, he continued. "This is how you set points of interest, waypoints, track your location, my location, and set a path. The programming will alert you to the best-suggested pathing and highlight any foreseen obstacles." He removed his hands and then clasped her hand in his. "It is imperative that you utilize these tools."

The seriousness in his concern heightened her attention. Her nerves blazed as it were. The narrow window of workable time only made the pressures that much more intense.

"I understand," she said confidently.

"I am admittedly not fluent in human nuances. I want to make sure you are ready to take on this advanced mission. You have not had adequate training. I acknowledge that it is both my fault and responsibility to correct. It is my obligation as your scientist mentor to lead your training properly. I am suddenly concerned that you appear more competent than you truly are, and I have misinterpreted the impression I have of you."

After a moment of comprehension, a nervous grin spread across Skye's face. "Thank you, Kas. I believe there was a compliment in there. I'm as prepared as I'm going to be, and I'm handling this the best I can. We can have a more detailed discussion about human nuances after the mission. I'm all in."

"All in," Kas hesitated. "I very much look forward to that conversation best suited for a later time."

Skye set alerts on her armband for the movement of fog and windows of opportunity for exploration. Kas mapped their next location. They would consistently need to move swiftly and efficiently. The plan for the first day was to set up a tent trail. The mission was allocated two planetary weeks, with the opportunity for an extension, if warranted. Kas had the authority to make the extension, but it would require detailed justification in his report.

They exited the tent into a wall of fog. It was solid, no seeing through it, and the moment they stepped out, Skye felt entirely alone. Her heart and breath quickened in temporary panic. Her shield activated.

As the alarm buzzed on her arm, signaling the atmosphere shift, the fog dissipated. It did not simply pass as moving storm clouds. Though, admittedly, she was not an expert on weather patterns. The way it evaporated electrified her nerves. Its abrupt transition mesmerized and terrified Skye. The sudden vivid color gave her a surreal appreciation for the unusual beauty of the planet.

The rocky terrain of grey-blue ground speckled in glistening silver. The star around which Shehur revolved sat high above their heads. Her suit kept her temperature comfortably chilled. She had no clue what the planet's actual temperature was, but the star seemed to warm her face.

Kas uncovered the carrier. As soon as they were seated, they were moving. The urgent demands of the mission encouraged Kas to travel at higher speeds. Even so, he was rightfully cautious. They flew across the terrain for a complete hour and took the last minutes to set up another tent station. They had to complete the set-up prior to the fog arrival; otherwise, the tent wouldn't keep it out. The thought of sitting in the isolation of the fog for extended periods triggered panic in Skye.

They moved from site to site, waiting and running. Skye spent her downtime reading reports and sleeping. They scheduled meal breaks in each tent with the rations packed in the carrier. She tried to conceal her embarrassment when the issue arose and learned the suits were equipped to eliminate species waste. She understood why Kas might have difficulty reading human nuances. They were complicated.

They finally unpacked the fifth and last tent in the carrier. The set up was done more quickly with each station. Skye hadn't seen any living creatures apart from Kas the entire day. She'd fallen into a comfortable routine over the hours. She examined the fractured rock beneath her feet and stared out over the barren terrain.

The further out they went, the rockier and more mountainous the landscape became. They were currently at the base of a large mountain chain. She could see crevices and alcoves along the valley, but nothing that moved. There was no vegetation to feed on.

After eight hours of travel, they awaited the last fog passing to start their trip back to the Evander. The empty carrier moved more swiftly than before, but Kas remained a cautious driver. The alarm beeped on Skye's armband.

"Kas, the fog is about to drop. Should we shelter at the next camp?"

"I have set the carrier on autopilot with a mapping of our route to the Evander. Since we have already traversed the path once, it should provide enough detail to navigate through the fog unencumbered."

Kas raised the cover on the carrier to seal the fog out. Skye's heart raced. She was slightly less fearful since it was not surrounding her body, but the view in the isolated carrier was claustrophobic. They traveled silently and hyper-aware, watching the navigation beacon through the map.

The journey back to the Evander was much quicker than the trip out. Half the travel was spent in terror-stricken blindness, the other in clear open air. Skye tapped her observations into the slate. The fog was unlike anything she'd ever seen. On Earth, she watched videos of tornadoes forming from storms and cloud cover descending on mountain hikers, but she never experienced it herself.

They pulled under the Evander hatch just as the next fog cycle was about to descend. After sealing themselves in the containment chamber, they could finally remove their suits. Skye peeled it from her body like a second skin and hung it in the wash capsule.

"That was a very productive first day, Skye. I am going to record my thoughts. I suggest you do the same, and I look forward to reviewing them," Kas said.

"Of course. Kas, am I able to read your reports?"

"Yes. You have access to all my accounts as my apprentice. Please review them regularly."

"Oh, okay. I will."

KAS WAITED for the door to seal entirely before collapsing onto his couch. The anxiety from this mission quickly exhausted his body. There were many reasons why he'd never taken an apprentice before, but the main one was that it terrified him. To be responsible for another individual's education and care was something he could have gone his whole career without, had the circumstances been different. He rested, perfectly still, while his mind ran through the choices he'd made and the things he still had to do.

He smiled, recalling when he was assigned to the Evander. He'd been fortunate to be paired to Einar's command. Every discovery ship needed a scientist to direct their studies, and every scientist needed a ship. Some crews treated their scientists as separate entities, never fully integrating, and Kas would have adapted to that approach just fine. Einar's system was always one of strategic inclusion. Kas recognized and appreciated the loyalty it created among the crew.

His mind drifted back to Skye. He breathed deeply, in and out, to calm his growing anxiety. His primary fear was one of inadequacy. She was untrained, and he was unprepared. He had no training plan, and he chided himself for the oversight. His education had been rigorously structured - the best the Alliance had to offer, his mother made sure. However, in its isolation, it failed to teach him the social requirements and organization of a teacher. Perhaps, he'd been focusing too much on the content and not enough on the process. With a great stretch of his muscles, and an infusion of inspiration and energy, he began to work on his teaching plan.

SEVENTEEN

Skye decided to get something more substantial to eat before heading to her room for a shower and sleep. She found Davin, Joey, and a very hostile man with a round head.

He threw his chair aside. "You!"

Initially taken aback, Skye flinched and then strengthened her stance. She looked him up and down. Her eyebrow raised, and lips pursed. "You."

Davin and Joey got out of their chairs too.

Joey moved between the man and Skye. "Woah! Calm down."

"Do not tell me to calm down! This is the bitch who left me in that room strapped to a table."

"Wait, what? Skye, you didn't?" Joey cringed.

Skye cocked her head. "I wasn't the one taking hostages and threatening people with pipes. You guys let this idiot out?"

"I was in there for hours!" The angry man raged.

Davin stood to the side between Skye and the others. "Einar told us where he was and asked us to get him some food and show him to his room."

Skye's lip curled as she nodded her head. "Have fun with that. I'm going to check on his victims and make sure they're okay."

Skye left the man screaming while Joey tried to calm him.

Skye knocked on the door to Farren's room. "Hello, Farren?" She waited but didn't hear anything. "Farren?"

"Skye, is that you?" Farren whispered.

"Yea, can I come in?" Skye said.

"Yes. I don't know how to open the door," Farren said.

Saba unlocked and opened the door. Farren curled on the bed, hugging her knees to her chest. She wore the same clothes as before. Her eyes were rimmed and exhausted from crying.

Skye didn't see any plates around the room. "Have you eaten? Has anyone come to check on you?"

"Yes, the scary woman from before brought me food. I didn't eat much of it. I'm a vegetarian, and I didn't know what it was."

Skye looked to the ceiling. "Saba, do we have any plant-based meals I can get for Farren?"

"I will have a food pack prepared for you, Farren," Saba said.

Farren's cheeks raised in a pseudo-smile. "Th-thank you."

Skye sat at the table. "Sorry I've been gone so long. I had a mission to attend to."

"You have a job?" Farren relaxed to a cross-legged position.

"Yes." It dawned on Skye for the first time. She did have a job.

"Would you like me to show you around? Would you like to meet the crew?" Skye said.

Farren grimaced. "No, not really. I would like to go back to sleep."

She jumped when the door opened unexpectedly. Recruit Stabby entered with a box of food.

Farren crouched on the bed. "What the hell is that?"

Skye sat relaxed in the chair. "That's recruit Stabby. It's Joey's creation." Skye lifted her ankles clear of the knives attached to Stabby.

"Recruit Stabby has brought your meal," Saba said.

The little robot bounced off the bedside. After a moment of hesitation, Farren grabbed the box of food. Recruit Stabby beeped cheerfully and exited. The box contained a variety of what looked like steamed and boiled vegetables.

Farren poked at a floppy purple radish, for lack of better term. "What is it?"

Saba chimed. "The meal consists of vegetation from the farms of the Ahila planet. They provide the majority of root and plant vegetation farms in the Alliance. Many of the species of vegetation can be found growing in the nursery on this ship in limited quantities."

Farren released a gentle sigh. "Thank you."

Skye left while Farren thoroughly examined the meal. She tapped a message into her band, requesting a meeting with Einar. The med bay was dark. Skye walked into the empty space and looked around.

"She's not here." A deep voice growled behind her.

Skye spun around to find Jedre leaning against the door. Her skin flushed, suddenly overcome with irrational guilt. "I wanted to check on her."

It dawned on her that she didn't know where Char's chambers were, or any of the other crew. She knew they were separate from the human quarters.

"Your humans are depleting my nursery," his eyebrow raised.

She matched his expression with a hand on her hip. "*My* humans?"

"There's a limited supply of vegetation from Ahila. It takes time to process and regrow it on board. If your humans continue to eat it by the boxful, it won't last to the end of the mission, let alone to the next waystation."

Skye crossed her arms. "Farren is vegetarian. She doesn't eat meat."

"There is very little *meat* on board this ship. She has a multitude of options," Jedre shook his head.

Skye adjusted her stance and her attitude. She could recognize a learning opportunity when she saw one. "Show me what you mean. If you have time, that is."

His face darkened as if he just realized he'd been talking to a human. Without a word, he turned and walked down the hall. Skye hesitated, then chased after him, caught up to his long stride, and kept pace. They walked in silence. She followed him to a section of the ship she'd never been. He paused in front of a grey and green colored door. It opened with his presence.

Tube and capsule terrariums lined the nursery. Silver storage cabinets lined the back wall. Tables of plants were arranged in rows under grow lights that dangled crystals and reflected in all directions. Skye entered slowly, in awe by the beauty and warmth of the room. It reminded her of home and all the parks and gardens she'd ever been to. She breathed deeply.

Jedre held tension in his shoulders as he watched. "Most people don't like the heat of the nursery. If you don't like it, leave."

She quietly joined him at a table of growing plants. "Not at all. It reminds me of home."

He huffed. "These are all non-meat food options. They come from all over the Alliance and are separated by region."

Jedre went over in detail the different regions, plants, edible and non-edible parts, rarity, and growth restrictions. Skye made notes in her slate. She would never have remembered the detail of the information. She would need to study it.

"This is what is left of the Ahila region," he growled.

The table was half-bare. Tiny sprouts pushed out of the soil in most pods, but only a handful of large, full leaved plants remained.

"I'm surprised you can't just replicate them with some sort of machine," Skye said.

His eyes rolled. "We can."

She gently touched one of the baby sprouts, half expecting Jedre to slap her hand away. "So why bother doing all this work growing them."

Jedre sneered. "You sound like a Vanzkelgan."

Skye raised an eyebrow and scoffed. "I take offense to that."

"It's not the same. We can produce mass quantities of replicate vegetation, but it's not the same as the real thing. The Vanzkelgans created the tech, and it is incredibly common across the Alliance. But it doesn't provide the same nutrition."

"It's fake," Skye shrugged.

Jedre winced. "For any true botanist, sourcing and growth is the first choice. We have the means for replicating vegetation, but I would only use it in desperation," he rubbed his chin and grinned, "or perhaps I will use it to feed your humans."

"Have you ever had to use it before?" Skye said, looking around.

He watched her from the corner of his eye. "Yes."

Skye felt her line of questioning made him uncomfortable and defensive. She also reasoned it could just be Jedre being Jedre. She still wanted to check in with Char, and a little blip on her armband suggested Einar accepted her request for a meeting. She noticed Jedre watching her.

"Thanks for the lesson. I got to go," she smirked and closed her slate, "and thanks for not being a jerk. I appreciate it."

Jedre reeled in confusion and disgust. "I do not think that translated properly."

Skye laughed and left, quickly realizing she didn't know the way back. She tapped her band and queried Char's location. A blinking path lit up her vision, triggering a wave of light-headedness and nausea that soon passed.

She followed the dots like Pac-man through a maze of halls and ladder shafts. It ended in a hallway with several non-descript doors, one of which marked her destination. She questioned whether knocking was culturally appropriate, or just something they did on Earth. While she stood there, the door opened. The room revealed a calm Char reading at her workstation.

Char brightened. "Skye! I was not expecting you."

Insecurity washed over Skye. "I just wanted to check on you and make sure you were okay."

"Yes, thank you. It was frightful, but I am unscathed," she nodded triumphantly.

As the words left her mouth, they felt wrong. "Not all humans are like that."

"Oh, I know. After all, we have you and Joey. Davin is coming around too. I'm sure the new recruits will eventually adjust."

"Actually, is it possible to return a person to stasis? Saba said yes. How would I go about doing that?"

Char frowned. "Skye. You can't just return all the humans you don't like," she tilted her head thoughtfully. "Actually, I suppose you can, but it's not exactly ethical."

Skye laughed weakly. "No, Char. As much as I'd like to, not for him. Farren, the woman, would like to be put back in stasis."

Char saddened. "Oh. Yes, it is possible. I can make arrangements if that's what she really wants. Poor thing. Her awakening was quite traumatic."

"How long will it take?"

"Give me a day or two. By the time you get back from your next excursion, I will have an update." Char tapped some notes on a slate.

The band on Skye's arm pinged. Einar inquired if she still needed to meet. She confirmed and departed. She had the mapping system direct her to Einar, as it appeared, he was not on the bridge. He was in a lower level of the ship. Skye hurried along and stopped when the dots ran out.

She was in the bowel of the Evander with the inner workings of the ship. The dimly lit halls flared her paranoia. A sudden fear of monsters renewed from her childhood. Up ahead, she saw Einar talking to someone. The creature was grey and salamander-like. Skye tried to politely maintain her distance until they were finished. When the creature caught sight of her, it sprung forth and skittered along the wall and ceiling. Skye let out a startled scream as it came near, far too quickly for her comfort.

Einar strolled toward them. "Kuza. Ease down. This is Skye."

Kuza dropped from the ceiling. His smile widened with his already large eyes. Panic coursed through Skye's system, clouding her thought and better judgment. She stood, not recalling when she dove to the ground for cover.

She trembled. "H-hello"

"H-hello," he mimicked.

She took a deep breath and forced herself to relax. "Hello, Kuza. I'm - I'm here to meet with Einar. I didn't mean to disturb you." Her hands visibly shook.

"Not at all, human Skye. It is an absolute pleasure to meet you." Kuza trilled.

"Kuza is the ship engineer. If there ever is a structural or mechanical issue that you cannot resolve, Kuza is available to assist. Skye is an apprentice scientist, Kuza."

Kuza trilled. "That is a rare honor. Congratulations to you, Skye. Kas has never taken an apprentice before."

Skye spoke quietly. Guilt settled in her stomach. "Thank you."

"Thank you for your assistance, Kuza." Einar touched Skye's shoulder and ushered her back the way they came.

"Visit again, human Skye." Kuza called before disappearing down the hall in a flutter of sparks.

Skye smiled but said nothing. When they reached the ladder platform, Einar tapped the wall and opened a disc elevator system.

"Wish I'd known that was there," Skye thought out loud.

Einar chuckled. "What did you need to speak to me about?"

"Farren wishes to be returned to stasis. Saba and Char said it's possible. I guess I just needed to make sure it's okay to put her back."

He tilted his head slightly. "You're seeking permission."

"Should I not bother you with these kinds of things?" Skye shrank slightly.

He smiled. "Do you think it is what she really wants?"

Skye grimaced and thought for a brief second. "Yeah."

"Do you think it is for the benefit of the ship to return her to stasis?"

Skye nodded. "Yes. I don't think she's a danger, but I don't see any reason to keep her awake if she doesn't want to be."

Einar smiled gently. "Perhaps not."

The elevation system opened to the bridge. Einar walked regally and with leisurely purpose to his seat. Skye followed and waited for him to continue. She didn't feel like she had a conclusive answer.

He met her eyes and smiled. "You do not need my permission to return Farren to stasis, or any other human for that matter. Thank you for keeping me apprised of the situation. I trust you will continue to do so in the future."

Skye nodded. "Thank you. I will."

When she turned to leave, Einar cleared his throat. "Skye."

She blushed, unsure of what she did wrong. "Yes?"

He met her eyes once again, but in a more serious gaze. "If you ever find yourself unsure of a situation, you may come to me or Kas, or any appropriate member of the Evander for counsel."

She nodded. "Thank you."

His tone deepened. "If you ever find yourself faced with a threat to yourself, the Evander, or the Alliance, you will report to me immediately."

Her body stiffened and flushed with heat. "Yes."

He held her gaze. "You are dismissed."

She nodded and spun on her heel. When she found herself halfway back to her room, her heart was still racing, and the hairs on her arms stood tall. Her armband beeped. She set an alarm to ensure she slept enough before the next excursion. She would need to update Farren later. She'd be happy with the news.

EIGHTEEN

The morning was cold and empty on the crew deck. Kas sent a message saying he'd be later than expected. Skye examined the equipment while she waited. Machines and instruments covered the shelves and tables, unmarked gray metal crates lined the far wall. Skye retrieved her suit and gathered the supplies they used the day before. She received an agenda for the day and thoroughly read the reports Kas suggested.

Kas flustered into the room. "Skye, we must be on our way."

He dressed in his suit and added several crates to her pile. They hover-dollied the equipment to the exit chamber and sealed their suits. The fog was about to drop, so they quickly packed the carrier and sealed the hatch.

Kas programmed the last tent destination into the carrier and set the autopilot. Skye noted her thoughts in the slate during the trip. She wished for music and played snippets of songs of the past in her mind. They passed the last encampment as the fog lifted, and Kas took over the navigation.

He adjusted the direction to run parallel to the mountain range. "Cave systems have been detected in the mountains by our initial scans. It confirms the data received from previous endeavors. We will establish monitoring scout systems to trace the caves and record any movement."

"Sounds like a plan," Skye said.

Kas scrunched his brow. They allotted enough time to set up the tent and unpack the carrier before the next fog dropping. While they waited for it to pass, Kas showed Skye the monitoring scout systems.

She looked over his shoulder. "They're hover drones?"

Kas tapped the schematics in the sleek little metal ovoid. "I suppose that's an accurate description."

It floated like a drop of mercury in zero gravity and appeared to have no front or back. Kas tapped on the workstation, and a panoramic view of the tent sprung to the screen.

"It will gather data and transmit directly to the Evander and the tent stations."

Skye cradled the drone, her hands appearing massive on the screen. It felt like a slippery water balloon and plopped out of her grip.

Kas set it back in its crate and turned off the projection. "It employs gentle elusion tactics to avoid capture."

Skye checked her armband. "How many are we sending out?"

Kas picked up the lightweight box. "There are four."

Skye raised her head in concern. "Will we have time to set them all at once?"

"We can set two now, and after the next fog, set two more. There are two cave systems near the tent station and two further off about thirty minutes. Once we set the droids, we will head back to the Evander and monitor from there."

"Then why don't we split up? You take two, I take two. Take the carrier to the further sites, and I'll take the closer sites."

Kas thought about the proposal uneasily. "It seems unnecessarily reckless. Why not just wait?"

"Either way, it's up to you, Kas. I just thought with everything that's been happening on the Evander, it would be prudent to get back quickly after completing our work."

Kas nodded a contemplative scowl. "I suppose that makes sense. You should be able to set the droids in the near cave systems and get back to the tent within forty minutes. You should have excess time. I will take the carrier to the other sites and set up there. I should make it back in time, but if I do not, I will wait through the next fog in the carrier. When it lifts, we will return to the Evander."

Kas programed the droids and gave Skye two crates on a hover dolly. He showed her the activation protocol in her armband that would track the movement of all four droids.

"If you run into any trouble, you will alarm the Evander and me to your distress. We will come immediately." He showed her the safety system on her armband.

"What about you? What if you run into trouble?"

Kas shook his head gently. "I will send an alarm. It will notify you and the Evander. You will find safety. The ship will come for us."

"Have you ever needed to use it before?"

"Yes," he said solemnly.

Skye left it alone. The blip on her arm said it was time to go. Kas drove away on the carrier while Skye headed toward the closer cave system on foot. The terrain didn't hide much, and it took her less than 10 minutes to find the entrance.

She approached with caution. Caves always gave her the willies on Earth. On a desolate planet with potentially lethal monsters hiding in the dark, her imagination ran wild. She reminded herself that the species that lived here preferred to be left alone and undisturbed.

Good for them, Skye thought. *Less likely to have their planet blown up.*

The opening of the first cave was quiet and dark, like every other cave she'd ever seen. She opened the first case, programed, and released the droid. It hovered in place while it acclimated to the new location, then set off into the cave. Skye watched it until it was out of sight.

The next cave entrance was further away. She jogged to keep good time. The hover dolly trailed after her, tethered to her armband location. Initially, she passed the second cave entrance. She had to backtrack along the tall cliffs.

A pathway snaked through a fissure in the rock and lead to the entrance. Enormous boulders jutted into the path, making the trail vary between narrow and wide spaces.

The small second entrance hid in the wall, barely big enough for Skye to slip through. It opened to an ample cavernous space that branched off in multiple directions. The lack of stalagmites caught her attention. They were something she expected to see in caves. The smooth interior felt odd without their presence.

A winding rumble sounded overhead like a landing plane. Skye checked her armband. It showed no alarm, no presence of the ship, and no discernable activity around her. Her skin tingled. She quickly released the second droid and ran after the sound. When she peered beyond the rocks, she saw a ship landing near the tent station. It was not the Evander.

She tapped the alarm feature on her armband. A red blip radiated her location to Kas and the Evander. She saw the unknown ship crew check a slate and slowly turn their heads to her direction. Her skin crawled. She tapped it again to shut it off and ran for the cave entrance.

When she turned, her head smacked into the droid. It was hovering just behind her back. She chided herself for not activating it properly. It and the hover dolly trailed after her. When she dropped into the cave, she untethered the dolly from her location and hid it in a crevice. She tapped the droid to acclimate it and send it on its way. It hovered momentarily, then floated down a corridor to the left.

Voices outside the cave entrance sent fire through her blood. She fled down a corridor on her right and didn't stop running until the third branch. Though the opening was snug, she tucked herself into a deep vertical fold of rock that wound around a corner, out of sight. There was enough space to crouch down and listen. The fear and excitement triggered her nervous bladder. She was grateful for the suit and wished she had a better plan, aside from hiding behind large rocks. They did nothing to hide their presence. Skye wondered if it was due to confidence or stupidity. She hoped the latter.

A voice echoed off the cave walls. "We can't search the caves. We don't have time. You saw that alarm beacon as well as I did. Their ship is going to be here soon."

A deeper voice spoke quietly. "They have humans. Let them come."

"This isn't the way to do it."

"Clearly, it's more afraid of us." The deep voice continued.

Adrenaline spiked Skye's blood. Her heart raced, making it harder to hear them properly. She peered around the rock, straining to see in the dark. Torches cast dim shadows on the wall. She quietly resumed her hiding place.

Clearly, there were things that Kas and Einar didn't tell her. She didn't expect them to tell her everything. They had no reason. In fact, they'd been more than generous with her and the remaining members of her species. But they never mentioned anyone specifically hunting humans. Perhaps they didn't want to alarm her. Unfortunately, she hadn't prepared to defend herself.

Defend herself. Kas had given her a weapon. She slipped the cold metal from her vest and held it to her chest. She imagined herself making a break for it, fighting her way out. But the logical half of her brain poked holes in the daydream. The likelihood of her fighting her way out of a cave with little to no cover and the enemy blocking the exit were slim.

She would wait. They would either leave on their own or find her, and she would defend herself. The Evander would come. Kas would come. She just didn't know how long it would take, and how long the shield would last.

The deep voice echoed through the cave. "If you're human, come out! We're not going to harm you."

Skye recoiled and shifted further away. *Yeah right.*

"We are human, and we are looking for other humans."

Her body froze while her heart beat loudly in her chest. So loud, she feared they could hear it. Her mind fluttered with possibilities. It had to be a trap. She wondered if this tactic worked for them in the past. Even if it were true, Skye hadn't met too many humans she trusted or liked.

Another voice echoed. "Rhys, we have to go. Their ship is coming. Victoria said it's urgent, we must leave now."

A feeling of panic and nostalgia washed over Skye. The third voice had a familiar accent. They all did, but the third one reminded her of home. They might be telling the truth. Her mind was blank. She crouched and grasped her head. The urge to ambush them was overwhelming. She wanted to see them.

Self-control. She reigned in her emotions. Rushing would do her no good. Maybe they were human, maybe not, but she knew nothing else about them. If the newest Evander recruit was any indication, not all remaining humans were all that great.

No. She would watch them. She would bide her time. And if they were honest and trust-worthy, maybe she would trade one ship for another. Her position on the Evander was cushy compared to most. It's certainly a hell of a lot better than anything she had on Earth.

The deep voice roared. "Come out!"

Skye retreated behind her rock and curled into her knees.

"What the hell is that?" The voice seemed startled.

Skye heard a blast and falling debris.

The deep voice resigned. "Let's get out of here. Everyone back to the ship." He shouted. "Your last chance!"

Skye stayed her ground and did not move. The sound of shuffling feet, followed by deafening quiet, rang in her ears. She would not move until the Evander came to her. In the dark of the cavern, Skye opened the tracking on her armband. Kas sped along the cliffs, still far away. The Evander moved more quickly. Within minutes, it arrived at the tent, circled the area briefly, and landed. Skye watched the tracker the entire time.

Kas shifted toward the ship, and her heart warmed. She stood on wobbly legs and stretched them out. She cautiously made her way toward the entrance. The floor crunched under her feet. She looked under her boot to find shards of silver eggshells. It looked like an egg full of glitter exploded on the floor. She worried it might have been one of the elusive creatures Kas was looking for. She solemnly realized it was probably the little droid.

Skye retrieved the hover dolly, tethered it to her band, and climbed out of the cave opening. She was immediately consumed in fog. Surprise cemented her feet to the ground. She could see the glow of her armband, but nothing else. The hover dolly bumped into her calf.

"Skye!" The blast of noise made her recoil.

"Holy hell. I'm here. You don't have to yell." She stretched her face and blinked.

Kas sobbed. "Oh, Skye! I thought something happened to you! – hic – when the alarm went off, I thought the worst, then it shut off, and I thought maybe you did it by accident, but then YOU WOULD NOT RESPOND!"

"I didn't hear you at all. I was hiding in the caves."

Skye checked her band. She could just make out the numbers when she held it against her faceplate. Eighteen minutes before the fog lifted. She stood uncomfortably, unsure whether she wanted to try to walk to the ship or go back to the cave. Neither felt like a particularly great idea. The hover dolly brushed her calf again.

"Stay there – hic – until the fog lifts," Kas said, regaining composure.

Skye reached down and grabbed the dolly. "Actually, I have an idea. I'm heading to the ship."

"– hic – Be careful!"

She slowly tapped commands into the armband and sat on the hover dolly. After crossing her legs and balancing her weight, she slid the metal weapon out of her vest and tapped on the shield. The fog dissipated in her little bubble. It was a pleasant benefit that she secretly hoped for but wasn't expecting.

She tapped her band freely and tethered the dolly to the Evander. It began slowly, gradually picking up speed. It was terrifying flying blind, but the dolly maintained her balance and boosted her confidence. She held on to the edge with both hands and zoomed over the terrain. Swirls of fog danced in her wake.

When she neared the ship, the dolly slowed to a gentle hover. In the final approach, the fog lifted. She saw the crew watching from the bridge. The overjoyed look on Joey's face made her smile. Skye hopped off and directed the dolly into the pressure chamber as the hatch to the crew deck unsealed. When it was safe, she removed her suit and stored it in its cleaning chamber.

The quiet deck blasted with noise when the main doors opened. Joey bounded in excited laughter. He gathered her in a tight hug, lifting her off her feet and swinging her around. While not something she'd typically welcome, she couldn't help but laugh while the excitement ran high in her system.

He set her down and shook her gently by her shoulders. "First of all, that was AWESOME! You looked like Goku riding a cloud straight out of Dragon Ball Z."

Davin hugged her. "Glad you are safe. We were worried when your alarm sounded."

Kas hesitated. Skye read he wanted a hug too, so she opened her arms to him. He sobbed and hugged her tightly. "I'm so sorry! – hic – I thought you had been killed."

Tremors rumbled through her muscles. "Nope, still alive."

The crew made room as Einar stepped forward. "What caused you to sound your alarm?"

"There was another ship. People got off and were looking around our tent station. When I sounded my alarm, they heard it too, and then they came to find me. I hid in the cave."

"You were lucky they did not find you," Einar said with barely a slip of emotion.

Skye studied his poker face. "Were they hunters?"

"Hunters?" He flashed confusion.

Skye nodded, maintaining the seriousness of the exchange. "They were looking for humans. They tried to get me to come out, saying they were looking to help humans."

He gave a curt nod. "Be sure to make a detailed report. We are all glad you are safe, Skye."

Einar left. Most of the crew followed and returned to their posts. The unanswered questions that went with him weighed heavily on her stomach.

NINETEEN

THE FOLLOWING DAYS PASSED UNEVENTFULLY. THE FOG CAME and went. In two days, the mission would end. The Evander would receive a new order. Skye took notes on any little details she encountered or noticed. She worried that there wouldn't be enough to create a sufficient report. She'd also been working on a report for Char. The newest revelation was how tired this planet made her.

Skye watched the fog swirl around the droid like it was playing with the little robot. Skye rolled her tight shoulders to shake off some exhaustion. While she watched, she wondered if her eyes were playing tricks on her. She started recognizing shapes and patterns where there was nothing.

She tapped her com device. "Kas, I'm heading back."

"Are you okay?" He responded immediately.

"I think I need to lie down," Skye stretched and looked across the barren planet.

"Please visit Char if you are ill. I will meet you at the ship."

Skye trudged to the ship, following the map through the fog. It lifted as she reached the Evander. Her natural reaction was to look around once she could see clearly again. The cave entrances were easy to see, now that she knew where they were. She stopped at the door with her hand poised on the latch. Her eyes blinked and squinted to clear her vision.

In the distance, in contrast to a cave opening, appeared to be lingering fog. Skye watched it while moving her head side to side. She wanted to make sure it wasn't just a smudge on her faceplate. She stilled as the fog figure moved. It shifted into the shape of a human and turned into the cave.

Tingles ran up her arms and legs, through her spine and across her scalp. Her mind raced. It told her to run after the figure. It told her she just imagined it. It told her to contact Kas.

She tapped her com. "Kas, I saw movement near a cave entrance. I'm going to check it out."

She sent the location to Kas through her band. With her energy renewed by adrenaline, she quickly set off toward the hills. By the time she reached the caves, there was no sign of life, no smudge of fog, no movement. Skye quietly treaded inside, assessing her surroundings with every step. There was nothing out of the ordinary. It looked like every other time she visited the opening in person or watched it on a screen. She checked her band, no response from Kas. The fog was scheduled to drop in six minutes.

A figure apparated like a ghost seeping from the walls and descended to the ground. It molded and mimicked her form until Skye stood face-to-face with a mirror image cloud replica of herself.

Her heart pounded in her chest. "Hello. My name is Skye."

It tapped its cloud facemask, prompting Skye to touch her own. The figure removed its faceplate. While Skye had the sudden urge to remove her own, she stopped and shook her head.

"I can't." Skye breathed heavily.

The droid hovered a short distance behind her. The fog form turned its head toward the droid and dissipated, swirling around Skye as it left. Skye did not move. She waited for the form to return. When it did not return, she slowly searched the cavern. After an hour of waiting and searching, she activated the droid's explore function and returned to the Evander. She notified Kas.

On the ship, she stuffed her suit in the cleaning bin and got a box meal to eat in her room. Her band pinged as she sat down.

"Skye. I received your messages. I will meet you at the ship."

It didn't feel urgent, so she finished her meal. She sat at the table, staring at the wall of her tiny room. The energy drained out of her. Another ping on her band marked the arrival of Kas at the ship. She sighed and pushed herself from the table. Every step weighed heavily on her joints. When she reached the crew deck, Kas was stuffing his suit into its cleaning chamber.

He bounded over to her with the energy of a toddler. He was absolutely beaming. "Skye! I have great news." He got uncomfortably close to her face and whispered. "I made contact."

She felt dizzy. Her eyes widened and glossed. Her brows raised. Her mouth gaped with a sudden lack of oxygen. Skye noticed the pointiness of his teeth as he grinned. She noticed the fine hair that covered his face. The color patterns were more intricate than she realized. She smelled his breath on her face. She could see him inhale and exhale deeply, as smoke, *or fog*, swirled from his nostrils. A chill spread through her body.

She only realized she'd fallen when she hit the floor. The precious little breath that remained was knocked from her lungs. Blackness clouded her periphery. Her vision blurred, and like a flick of a switch, her consciousness ceased.

Joey sat on his bed with the door to his room open. He played with the different features and settings on his slate. He could not just sit, and the device served as a welcome distraction. His mind needed something to ponder and tinker and entertain. Joey watched Davin bob up and down on the floor.

"You should get the nanotech," Joey said.

Davin paused mid- push-up. "You should join me. I could use a workout partner."

"Eh. I'll think about it," Joey said.

Davin moved on to his abdominal routine. "Suit yourself."

"I'm going to go explore the ship," Joey said. "Or see if anyone needs help with anything, or see if there's anything I can do."

Davin grunted. Joey wandered freely down the corridors. He was able to pull up limited schematics of the Evander, and while he didn't understand much of it, he found it fascinating. On Earth, Joey worked as a robotics engineer. He dreamed of building his own mobile suit Gundam Wing, C-3PO, or iron giant. In reality, he finished school and found a job designing commercial products. His last completed design was an automated cat litter box.

"Saba, what is this room?" Joey asked.

"You are in front of a mechanical and maintenance storage compartment," Saba said.

"Thank you," Joey said, moving on to the next area. "Saba, how do I work the disc and tube system?"

"Once you activate the disc system, you may choose a destination via the nanotech. Please operate safely and refer to the operational guideline report available in the inStar library."

A notification blipped on Joey's band. He brought it up on the slate and read through the user manual. "Thank you, Saba."

An urgent notification followed. "Quarantine in a secure location. Possible contamination."

Joey froze. "Saba, what's happening?"

"Quarantine in your quarters, Joey. I have mapped the quickest route. Do so now," Saba directed.

Joey followed the dotted path in his vision. Commotion by the med bay drew his curiosity. The urgent notification blinked on his band again, redirecting his attention. Reluctantly, he followed the insistent dots to his room. The door whooshed behind him, sending a chill over his skin. Although he was growing accustomed to it, the loneliness of his room was not a welcome feeling.

TWENTY

It was an odd sensation. Skye registered the movement, but she couldn't actually feel the hands shuffling her body. Each inhalation of her shallow breath swelled her tight chest. Her skin was numb. Her muscles did not respond when she wanted them to move. Her eyes were open, but she could not see. Shifts of light passed over the gray haze clouding her vision.

Panic. More pressure built in her chest. She couldn't even cry. She screamed internally – the savage wail of a trapped banshee.

She focused on the steps of the person carrying her. She felt high, both in proximity to the ground and mental state. She didn't think it was Kas. It didn't feel like Joey either. Possibly Davin. They set her on a table, presumably in the med bay. Muffled and alarmed discussion did not translate. Someone rearranged and prodded her body.

They moved her to another table. The air pressurized and smelled sterile with a hint of fresh-cut grass. The dizziness returned, and she questioned whether or not the chamber was truly spinning. The weightless, floating sensation calmed her momentarily before the cold of the table seeped into her skin. The cloudiness receded from her vision, allowing it to become sharp and clear. She was in a tube in the med bay. With a deep breath, she blinked the tears from the corners of her eyes.

Something heavy flopped on her face. A renewed sense of panic rose in her chest as she strained her body to move it. It moved. It was her arm. She stared at it as if it belonged to someone else. She could not feel it, but it responded lazily to her commands. It flopped on her stomach and slid to the table.

Pins and needles flared the nerves in her skin. She focused on her breathing and slowly worked her muscles. After an eternity, the feeling slowly returned to her body.

She lay there with open eyes, afraid to move. Panic bubbled in her chest repeatedly, and she repeatedly squashed it down.

"Skye. Can you hear me?" Char said.

Relief warmed her insides as the nanotech properly translated the words. Her eyes searched for the owner of the voice, prompting her head to roll sluggishly. Her voice failed, and her inner monologue cursed.

"I'll take that as a yes. We need to clear the toxin from your system. I'm going to depressurize the chamber. You're going to go to sleep for a little bit. Don't fight it."

Skye heard little hissing noises. The air felt like it was being sucked from her lungs. Her initial response was panic.

"Don't fight it," Char said.

It smelled of flowers. She relaxed her body and took a deep breath. Gardenia. Jasmine. Honeysuckle. She wasn't sure what flower it smelled like, but it was nice.

The sheets were the first thing she noticed. The softness and grayness of the sheets. The threads. The warmth. Her whole body ached when she moved. Her mouth was dry.

"Saba, I need water," Skye croaked.

A storage cubby overhead clicked. Skye followed the sound and found a box of packets labeled "water." She tore one open and drank the contents.

Her movement suspended with a brief, terrifying panic of a texture not associated with water. Jell-like beads rolled on her tongue, and her immediate thought was that she just consumed an ice-pack and poisoned herself. Looking inside, she saw remnants of clear pearls of liquid. Re-reading the packet, it most definitely translated to water. She popped the spheres, relieved as the taste of water quenched her mouth.

Saba spoke softly. "You have been ordered to rest until the event is thoroughly investigated."

She was now awake, refreshed, and alert, but could probably still take a nap. "What happened?"

"You were exposed to a toxin that robbed your body of oxygen. You made a significant recovery in the stasis chamber, and Char okayed the transfer to your room."

"Will I be okay?"

"The toxin is unknown. Long term effects on humans are unknown."

She curled on her bed. Pressure built in her exhausted and sore chest. Tears gathered in her eyes and wet her pillow. A knock on her door made her sit up and wipe her eyes.

"Davin is at the door," Saba said.

Skye moved to the small table. "Is it okay for me to be around others?"

"The toxin has been removed. It is not contagious."

"Come in."

The doors whooshed open. Davin peeked his head in and offered a sympathetic grin.

"I came to check on you. How are you feeling?"

"Thanks. I'm doing okay."

He sat across from her. The silence became awkward. They had not been alone in a room since he'd woken from stasis. They had spoken little and barely knew each other, mere strangers enduring a similar predicament.

"You are not alone. You should not have to feel alone."

The kind sentiment crumpled her resolve. She wiped tears from her face as they fell. She actively tried to force herself to stop crying. She took several deep breaths, but the tears kept coming. Davin reached a long arm across the table and rubbed her shoulder.

"It is okay to cry. It is okay to feel sad and angry and afraid."

She sobbed. Her eyes squeezed shut, but the tears continued to slip out. She was angry and afraid, and she despised feeling vulnerable.

He kneeled beside her and put an arm around her shoulder. He gently pulled her into a hug. Her head buried against his chest while he held her tight. His warmth was comforting. Though she barely knew him, the touch of another human being felt familiar. He felt like home. As horrible as things were, as horrific as they had been, the feeling of home was still a good one.

She pulled away, straightened her back. "Thank you." Her chin raised.

He sat back on his heels. "You've been very busy with your work. I just wanted you to know that I'm here if there's anything you need." The corners of his eyes creased when he smiled. "I have a lot of time on my hands these days."

"I appreciate that. And same to you. If you need anything, let me know. I'll try to help."

He blushed and looked at his shoes. He opened his mouth to say something then stopped. Instead, he smiled and stood up. "I'll see you around."

Skye narrowed her puffy, red eyes at him. When he left, she had food delivered by recruit Stabby and opened several reports. She focused on papers written by Kas, getting to know his writing style and major interests when researching new planets and species. She came across several guidelines for Alliance report writing and tutorials on conducting a proper study.

Kas was a traditionalist. It was a term they used. She could see a clear difference in his writing versus the writing of other scientists. Kas followed the guidelines with precision. His methodology was consistent and thorough. She expected, as his mentee, she should abide by his example. Until this point, she had not. Her notes were sporadic. Her report was informative but not well-structured.

She pursed her lips and saved the documents to her slate. Using the guide, she made a report template. Over the next few hours, she typed the reports of her observations and edited them to meet Kas standards. She rewrote her notes of Kepseli, breaking her heart with the memories. She took a moment to mourn.

After hours of writing, another meal, a short exercise break, and a nap, Skye was thoroughly bored. Cabin fever made her restless. She wondered how the others were faring.

"Saba?"

"Yes, Skye."

"What does the Alliance have for entertainment? Are there any videos I can watch?"

"Yes. There are a variety of entertainment choices from the Alliance territories. Several planet communities have industries dedicated to producing entertainment."

"Can you send some examples to my slate, please?"

"They are accessible through the InStar application on the slate."

"Thank you."

You can learn a lot about a culture from its source of entertainment. Skye felt like she had a new grasp on the characteristics and diversity of the Alliance community. Some of what she saw was mildly disturbing, some incredibly disturbing. Several recordings were captivating, hypnotic even. Others made her blush. Although she learned more each day, her conclusions about the Alliance remained the same. The more she learned, the more she realized how little she knew.

A blip on Skye's armband roused her from a deep sleep. She didn't remember falling asleep. Einar requested her on the bridge. Alert and well-rested, she bathed and dressed for a new day.

JEDRE WALKED out as Skye arrived on the bridge. He cast her a glance that would have suggested indifference, had it not lingered. Kas sat next to Einar in a cluster of lounging chairs. There was an open seat near them. Skye waited for an invitation before sitting.

Einar greeted her with the brightening of his ever-changing skin tone. "Welcome, Skye. How are you feeling?"

Skye genuinely smiled. "Much better, thank you."

"We have received your latest reports. I am impressed with the sudden improvements. What prompted the change?"

"I had some time on my hands, so I spent it researching."

Einar placed a gentle hand on her shoulder. "Do you know what happened? How you came to be ill?"

"No. The last thing I remember was hitting the floor in the crew deck."

His head tilted slightly. "Were you exposed to anything on Shehur?"

"Not that I know of. I was feeling more tired than usual the last few days," Skye said.

"Please notify Char when there are changes in your health." Einar turned to Kas. His skin darkened as if stepping in a shadow. "Kas, have there been similar changes with your health."

Kas remained quiet and still throughout the conversation. "No, not at all. I don't recall any exposures either. Perhaps there was a defect in Skye's suit. We should have the maintenance crew look into it."

"I will have them do that. I look forward to your reports." Einar nodded thoughtfully. "We have begun exit protocols."

Einar stood and gracefully crossed to his workstation. Kas stood and exited abruptly, leaving Skye. She hesitated, looking between Einar and the door before following Kas out.

Skye caught up to Kas in the hall. "Kas, is everything okay?"

He turned to her slowly. "Of course, why wouldn't it be?"

She took a step back and a deep, even breath. "Just checking. Is there anything you need me to do?"

Kas waived her off. "Your primary responsibility is to complete your reports. Aside from that, your time is your own."

A heaviness and nausea settled in her stomach as Kas walked away. She wasn't sure if she did something wrong, if she upset him, or if his mood had nothing to do with her. She returned to her room and finished her report. Her stomach rumbled. Rather than ordering food, she thought it would be a good idea to stretch her legs.

Joey, Davin, and Farren were in the canteen when she arrived.

"Hey. What have you guys been up to?"

Joey slurped a green smoothie. "Not too much. Einar has us doing some chores now that quarantine is over."

"Oh, what kind of chores?" Skye asked.

"I think they're like, basic recruit chores – not that we see or spend any time with the other recruits – but basically just wiping things down. I've been working with the others to write down everything we remember about Earth."

"That's good," Skye said. "We need to stay busy."

Farren ate a purple root. "Any news for me?"

Skye grinned. "Yea, it's been approved. We just need to meet with Char. Are you sure it's what you want?"

She visibly relaxed into a warm smile. "Yes. Absolutely."

Davin looked between the two women. "What is going on?"

Skye grinned and tapped a food order into the machine. Her gaze purposefully avoided the men.

Farren smiled sadly. "I want to be put back in stasis."

Davin's face dropped. "Why?"

Joey leaned in with sadness and concern.

"I don't want to –" she hesitated. The words she looked for were painful to say aloud. "I don't want to be alive right now. I miss my family. I would rather be put back."

"We've all lost people," Davin said slowly.

Deep sadness cloaked her face again. "Did you lose your children?"

Davin's mouth sealed into a tight line. "No. I never had children."

Farren straightened her posture and shook her head. "Then you can't even begin to understand."

"How old were they?" Joey said quietly.

"Evelyn was two years old. James was three months." Her face crumpled. Tears welled in her eyes.

They all offered condolences with broken hearts. Farren nodded but couldn't respond. Skye retrieved her plate of food and turned to see her least favorite human entering the canteen. Her face scrunched in contempt.

His lip curled in a snarl. "What is this one blubbering about now?"

"Ashwin, don't be rude," Joey said.

"I think I'll take my dinner elsewhere. Farren, would you like to join me?" Skye said.

She nodded and stood.

Ashwin pointed at Skye. "You need to tell the creatures that I do not work for them. I will not be subject to manual labors."

"Tell them yourself."

"I don't talk to the animals, and I am not letting them inject me with some tracker like a cattle."

Skye walked out without another word, and Farren followed. They sat quietly at Skye's table.

"Have you been eating okay?" Skye said.

"Yea. So far, it's been okay." Farren looked up from her fingernails. "Thank you. For doing this for me. It is what I want."

"No problem," Skye said between bites. "If it's what you really want, who am I to stand in the way?"

Farren smirked. "I think at this point, I'd like to be sent back just to get away from Ashwin."

Skye's poker face did not respond. "Is that his name?"

"Yea. He's horrible. You don't even know. You haven't had to be around him for the past week."

"Apparently, it's unethical to send people I don't like back to stasis. At least that's what Char said."

"She seems nice."

"She is."

"Is she okay?"

"Yes. She's doing well." Skye nodded thoughtfully. "Thanks for asking."

They spent the evening talking about Skye's job and the planets they'd been to. Farren told Skye about her family and the cute things her kids used to do. Skye genuinely enjoyed the company. She would be sad to lose the female companionship.

They met at the med bay the next morning. A vacant stasis pod occupied the center of the room, in place of the usual table. Char tapped away at her work station, spinning around when she noticed the women.

"Good morning." She sang cheerily. "Are you ready, Farren?"

Skye looked at Farren. "Are you ready?"

Farren wore a tight smile. "Yes. I'm nervous but ready."

Char gestured to the pod. "Climb in, dear."

Skye translated. Farren took a deep breath and bounced on the balls of her feet before getting in the pod. She rested her head and relaxed her muscles.

Char smiled warmly, almost pitying. "I hope your second awakening is better."

A numbing warmth swept over her body. Farren smiled, not understanding the words, but feeling the meaning. "Thank you."

Skye watched the process carefully. She felt a strong need to ensure her safety. Once the pod was sealed, it was transferred to the storage bay and parked alongside the others. Skye took a moment, scanning the frozen lives, and once again acknowledging the lost souls of Earth.

TWENTY-ONE

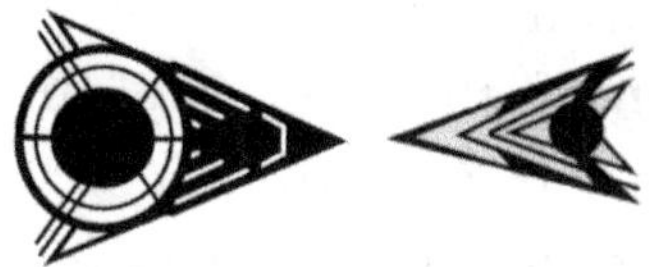

A SCREECHING ALARM BROKE HER MOMENT OF SILENCE. Unsure of what was happening or what to do, Skye raced to the bridge. Jedre nearly crashed into her in the hall. They entered together and stood near the back wall.

"What's happening?" Skye said.

He cast a sideways glance and hesitated before speaking. "We've been locked by a targeting system."

"Someone is shooting at us?"

He frowned. "Someone is threatening to shoot us."

Einar stood tall and serious at his helm. Zaima attended her station, eerily still. Char stood off to the side, nuzzled up to a support banister. Her crossed arms hugged her frame tightly, causing the skin of her fingers to whiten.

The communication screen flashed a man with odd, fluid features. His fingers steepled and perched over his mouth. "Crew of the Evander. We have our weapon system locked on your location."

His voice tickled a memory in Skye's brain. She couldn't put her finger on it.

"Why are you threatening my ship and my crew?" Einar said calmly.

"I am the captain of the Carasius. We are human. I demand the release of all humans on your ship."

"We hold no humans against their will. But we will not be releasing any of our crew to you."

His movements were erratic. "I will not hesitate to blast you to pieces. Send a shuttle with the humans, or die."

Skye stepped behind the shadow of Jedre. He noticed her movement and swayed to block her from view.

"What would you gain from destroying my ship and everyone on it, including humans?" Einar clasped his hands.

The man laughed. "I'd rather end their lives now than allow them a slow, tortured death at your hands."

"Should you not consult them first?" Einar said.

The man hesitated. "What do you care? Send them over in a shuttle, and we'll be on our way."

"When they came aboard this ship, they came into my care. I will not blindly release any of my crew to the hands of rebels. Especially, not to someone who hides his face behind a camouflage screen. However, I keep no prisoners. If any human in my care wishes to leave, they may do so. I will gather them and allow you to personally request their presence on your ship. We will reconnect in twenty minutes."

"We reconnect in ten." The man disconnected.

Skye felt the eyes of the room drift toward her.

Einar smiled gently and approached. "Skye, what is the cause of your fear?"

She hadn't realized she was trembling. "Death and torture seem like decent reasons." She laughed nervously. "It might just be adrenaline."

Einar nodded. "Our timeline is fleeting. Saba, alert the human crew members to join us on the bridge."

"Already done, Commander. They are on their way," Saba said.

The doors opened, allowing Joey, Davin, and Ashwin to enter. Jedre grumbled. Ashwin sneered and kept some distance behind Joey and Davin.

Joey immediately sensed the serious tone. "What's going on?"

"We are under attack from a rebel ship. The leader of the ship requests that we turn over all humans on board."

"What! We're under attack? They're gonna kidnap us?"

"No. I have persuaded them to speak with you and obtain your consent. If you wish to leave, you may do so. If you wish to stay, you may do so."

Skye calmed her nerves. "He claims to be human."

The familiarity bothered her. She was certain she did not know the face, possibly because of the mask he was using, but the voice triggered a wisp of a memory. She couldn't say for sure, but he sounded like one of the hunters from Shehur. The angry one.

"Really? How is that possible?" Davin said.

"Einar, when you say rebel –" Joey trailed off.

"They are not part of the Alliance, nor do they wish to be." Einar returned to the helm and faced the screen as it reconnected to the Carasius.

The man scowled. "Is that it? These are the only humans you have?"

"These are the only humans available to speak to you. They have your attention."

"My name is Rhys. I am the captain of the Carasius, a human ship. We've come to save you from your captors."

Skye's skin tingled. It was a lie. Her gut churned, certain this guy was not who he claimed to be.

"How did you get your own ship?" Joey said.

Rhys laughed. "It's a long story, one I'd be happy to tell you once you're safe. Prep for transport."

Einar motioned. "Prepare a shuttle for transport."

Skye watched the Evander crew and her human crew. There was a definite separation, one she hadn't paid much attention to before. A chill settled over her skin and gave rise to goosebumps. The uneasy feeling settled heavily in her gut.

"So, we just go with them?" Davin said.

"Of course!" Rhys boomed. "We need to support the last remaining members of our people. That's why we've been seeking out any human captives."

"I'm ready to go. How do I get to transport?" Ashwin said.

"You will be escorted to the flight deck." Einar motioned to the bridge exit. "Please show them the way, they opted not to have the nanotech."

A recruit Skye never saw before stood by the exit as the doors opened. Ashwin left immediately. Joey and Davin began to follow, then paused when they realized Skye was not moving. She felt all eyes on her once again.

"What are you waiting for, Skye?" Joey said.

The butterflies in her stomach fluttered. "I'm not going."

Davin stopped. "What do you mean?"

Rhys leaned toward the screen. "Hi there, Skye, is it? Nice to meet you. You should definitely get on that transport."

Skye stepped out from the group and held his gaze. "I don't know you, and I don't trust you." Her voice held solid and strong. "And I'm not going. The only one holding anyone captive here is you."

He scoffed. "You're choosing to stay a foreigner among aliens, as opposed to being with your own people. Get on the transport, Skye. It's for your own good."

Skye held eye contact. "No. I don't think so."

"How about this, if you don't get on that shuttle, no one gets on the shuttle, and we blow your little ship to pieces?"

"Skye!" Joey whined. "Come on."

Skye scoffed. "You're out of your mind. What happened to 'we need to stick together'?"

"Get on the transport, woman!" Ashwin stomped between the bridge and the hall. "I will not be stuck here!"

Skye's hands rested on her hips. Her eyes never left the screen.

"Go! You don't need me. And let's be honest. You were planning on blowing up this ship anyway. You're nothing but a terrorist."

Rhys glared through the screens. "You're right. I don't need you. But you need me more than you know. You should get on the shuttle, Skye."

"No."

Silence held the room while they waited for his response. He leaned back in his chair and crossed his legs, resting his ankle on his knee. His fist hid a manic, amused smirk. "Then stay. We'll be happy to take your friends."

Ashwin shuffled out the doors again. Joey and Davin hesitated.

"Skye, are you sure?" Joey said.

"Absolutely. I don't trust this guy. You guys can take the gamble, but I'm not," Skye said confidently.

"I'm staying with her," Davin said.

"Don't be like that." Rhys threw his hands up with a guttural protest. "Don't worry about your girlfriend. It's not worth it, man. Just leave her."

Davin stood next to Skye and shook his head. Joey looked at them one last time, then walked out the door.

"He's a smart man. You two should reconsider." His maniacal grin wavered.

"I'm good," Skye said.

The Evander shuddered as the shuttle displaced. It thrust across the gap.

Davin swallowed hard. "He is going to blow up our ship anyway, isn't he?"

Einar glanced at Davin and smiled softly. "He made no promises otherwise."

"Is there anything we can do? Is the Evander equipped to fight back?" Skye said.

Einar remained stoic at the helm. "We have some defensive measures, but against that ship, I fear they are irrelevant. We have done everything we can at this time."

An alarm sounded in the distance. Skye looked around. The crew of the Evander stood tall and proud. Everyone except Zaima. She was nowhere to be seen.

"Where's Zaima?" Skye said.

A grin crept across Jedre's face. "Do you hear the siren?"

Skye and Davin looked puzzled. The screen burst to life once again.

"This isn't over. We'll be back, and when we do, we're coming for all the remaining humans."

The screen shut off, opening the view of battle in front of the Evander. The Carasius evaded the attack of a small, swift vessel. The larger ship fired several rounds before jumping into the slipstream. The small vessel followed and returned almost immediately.

"Zaima, please retrieve the shuttle." Einar tapped his workstation and turned briefly to Skye. "The Evander has limited defenses against larger ships, but we're not defenseless. Most discovery ships have one or two tactical vessels for emergencies."

The little ship gathered the abandoned transporter shuttle and docked the Evander. Skye felt a gentle shudder. Within moments, a terrifying and exhilarated Zaima sauntered onto the bridge. Her smile seemed uncontainable.

Joey followed, significantly paler than when he left.

Skye rushed over and hugged him tightly. "Joey, are you okay? What happened?"

"We docked on the other ship. They opened up to let us on one at a time, then an alarm went off. Ashwin made it, but the doors slammed shut and they disengaged." His voice cracked. "They threw me away."

Einar approached slowly. "The other ship detected Zaima. I am sorry that it did not work out as you wished. We were merely trying to ensure our survival of this encounter."

Joey nodded. His lip quivered. "I'm going to return to my room. Is that okay?" His movements were rigid and hesitant.

"Of course, Joey. And if you are asking if you are still welcome on this ship, the answer is yes." Einar smiled gently.

Tears formed in his eyes. One slipped out as he nodded again. Skye moved to follow him when he left. Davin motioned for her to stay.

"I've got it," he said.

Skye turned. She found herself face-to-face with Zaima. Her startled response elicited a low purr. Her eyes were black saucers and locked on Skye with disconcerting intensity.

"Zaima?" Skye's voice cracked.

Einar darkened and stood stonily at the helm. "Thank you for your work, Zaima. You are to report to Char in the med bay, then retire to your chamber for isolation and decompression. You are dismissed."

Einar's directive snapped her attention. Her gaze lingered on Skye as she passed and exited the bridge. Einar did not acknowledge the interactions. Skye looked around for an answer or explanation and found most eyes averting her gaze. To her surprise, the only person to meet her stare was Jedre. He watched her with apparent amusement. His enjoyment of her confusion aggravated her more than the uncertainty itself. She left the bridge with more questions than answers.

Jedre locked eyes with Einar and received a nodding approval. It didn't take him long to catch up with Skye in the hall. His stride was significantly longer than hers. She slowed at his arrival and instinctively moved out of the way. He matched her pace and stopped when she stopped.

"What do you want, Jedre?"

"We need to talk," he said.

She sighed. "About what?"

He tapped several commands in his band. "Meet me here in an hour."

A notice blinked on her tech. The location was not the nursery or any part of the ship she'd been in. "What's it about?"

He strode off toward the marker on her tech. "I'll answer some of your questions. Just show up."

She was tempted to follow him, but her stomach grumbled, and she could smell herself. Instead, she opted for a shower and a meal. An hour was a short wait for answers.

TWENTY-TWO

SKYE FOLLOWED THE PAC-MAN DOTS TO THE LOCATION IN THE ship. After the third turn, the decor became more, well, decorative, and less utilitarian. She had a strange feeling that this was the nicer part of the ship. She stopped in front of large ornate wooden doors, but unlike any wood she'd seen before. The tech pinged, signaling her arrival at the destination.

She knocked. Though the doors slid open, much like any other, Skye eyed them carefully as she entered. The room was adorned with ornamental carvings and furniture best described as modern. Silky drapery hung floor to ceiling and twisted intricately above a plush seating area.

Jedre came out dressed in his usual crew attire. "Have a seat."

Skye continued to observe the space as she nestled into one of the cushions. "What is this place?"

"My room," Jedre said flatly.

A tingle spread over Skye's skin, sparked by sudden discomfort. "Kind of a lot of real estate for ship chambers. How'd you swing that?"

His head tilted. "I don't understand your meaning."

"How'd you get the nice room?"

"Its purpose is dignitary transport. We don't get many of those, so I claimed it."

Her eyebrows raised slightly. "Seems unfair."

"Jealous?" He smirked.

Skye frowned. "Why am I here? I'm sure it's not just so you can brag about your room being nicer than mine."

He sat across from her and leaned his arms on his legs. "You have made some very curious decisions while on this ship. I need to be sure you are honest. I need to be sure you are an ally."

She sat up straight, one eyebrow raised. Her mouth opened to respond, but only released an air of disbelief.

He studied her. "Your tendency to choose the well-being of the Evander to members of your own species... that is unusual."

She relaxed a bit. "Eh. I mean, it depends on the person."

He shook his head and leaned back. "Your casual demeanor is not helping. Why didn't you go with the Carasius?"

"Listen, I know you don't like humans. You've made yourself perfectly clear," her hands jabbed the air, "but I'm a member of this ship. I agreed to it when I agreed to be the apprentice to Kas. Speaking of, I should probably be having this conversation with him or Einar." She stood to leave.

He growled. "Sit down."

She glared at him and stabbed her finger at him. "You don't get to talk to me like that."

He huffed and tapped on his band impatiently. He read something that made his lip curl. They locked eyes. "I'm sorry. Please sit. It's important."

Her eyebrow raised with a downturned smirk. She sat, crossing one leg over the other and resting her chin on her hand. "I'm listening."

"Have you noticed a difference in Kas?" Jedre said.

"Maybe. I haven't been around him lately. I don't know if that's strange or not. I noticed he wasn't on the bridge." She fidgeted.

"No, he wasn't. I have noticed a difference since Shehur. What happened while you were on the planet?"

Skye recounted the days spent setting up tents, releasing droids, and exploring the caves. She mentioned the fog and the Carasius landing. "How do I review the footage from the droids?"

"You should have access to it from the reports."

"I'm still learning a lot about this. It's not like I was born using nanotech."

"No one is born with nanotech. It is banned in infants."

Skye cringed. "That's not – never mind."

He walked her through a grumpy tutorial on record keeping and information retrieval. She took notes on her slate while following his instruction on her armband.

"What is the name of the droid?" Jedre said.

"The droids have names?"

He growled. "These things should be noted in your reports. You should have assigned it a marker when you released it, or prior."

She sighed and stood. "Thanks for showing me all this. I have a lot to review."

"Why are you in such a hurry to leave?"

"Wow, Jedre, I didn't realize you enjoyed my company so much," she huffed an exasperated sigh. "Is there anything else you needed to talk about?"

He appeared confused and checked something on his band. "It is not as frustrating now as it was initially. But you are still a difficult creature. You did not answer the question."

She felt the heat in her skin. "It makes me uncomfortable to be here. I have trust issues. It's a survival skill. Besides, I actually have some work to do."

His body recoiled. The free-flowing appendages curled into themselves. "I will not hurt you."

"I appreciate that. I'm not saying you would." She rubbed the back of her neck and looked at the woven fabric above her head.

He watched her carefully. "What questions do you have?"

"Man, I got a lot of questions. You gotta be more specific."

"Ask anything." He rolled and cracked his neck. "Almost anything," he amended.

"Tell me about Zaima."

His brow raised in sync with the corner of his mouth. "Zaima?"

"There's something I'm missing. Something that everyone knows, but because I'm human and I'm not from around here, I don't know. These are the things I want to know." Skye stretched and plopped back down on the cushion.

"Ah." He smiled. "I understand. Common knowledge that is not common to humans." He watched her and chuckled. "Zaima is of the Lis of Hevoc. This should mean something to you. The Lis of Hevoc are known throughout the Alliance for their ruthlessness. They serve as guards, enforcement, and – unofficially – assassins for hire. Zaima is a particularly special case. She is well-known throughout the Alliance. She serves this detail as punishment for her crimes."

Skye leaned back into the plush couch. "She's a convict?"

Jedre visibly suppressed a growl. "Do not interrupt, and you will have more explanation. When the Alliance deployed discovery ships to the Soturi region, they had not imagined the horrors they would find. After several "lost" discovery vessels, they began to deploy battleships alongside the scientists. It was not until after a vicious and bloody rebellion did the Lis of Hevoc join the Alliance. Hevoc and Dodelig are the only two planets of the Soturi region that have representation.

When the scientists were finally permitted to observe the Lis, their findings continued to be astonishing. They are by far the most unforgiving known species. It was debated for a long time whether to allow them as a recognized citizen species. They, and their rebellion, are often the justification for quick trigger destruction of planets."

Skye gestured her hand before resting her face on it. "You're referring to Earth?"

Jedre grumbled. "Zaima, like I said, is a special case. She was born to the leader of the Lis. One of many children, but one of only two that survived. The Lis abandon their young at a very young age and force them to survive on their own. Most of them do not. The ones that do are welcomed into the Lis society and trained to be deadly. Zaima is notably one of the deadliest.

During the rebellion, her guardian Contra was the final barrier of the Alliance. Hevoc was given an ultimatum. End the resistance and join the Alliance, or the planet would be destroyed. Contra chose the latter. He would allow the destruction of Hevoc and the end of the Lis. They would not secede. The Lis follow their Alpha absolutely. They may disagree, but they do not defy."

"He was willing to let everyone die? And no one said anything?" Her eyes narrowed.

"No one, except for Zaima. As the GRANT system charged and death was imminent, Zaima killed her guardian. She immediately inherited the leadership and seceded the rebellion. Hevoc was not destroyed, and the Lis became part of the Alliance. However, murdering the Alpha is frowned upon, even by the Lis. Remember, I said there were two survivors of Contra's children. Zaima has a sister, Aris."

Skye raised an eyebrow. "Zaima has a sister?"

Jedre sighed. "Yes. Aris is the current sitting leader of the Lis and serves on the Alliance High Council. Zaima was sentenced by her people for her crimes. One, banishment from Hevoc for twenty Hevocian years. Abandonment with the intention of her learning to survive in the conditions she created. Two, servitude under the Alliance. She serves this ship as atonement. To the Lis, forced servitude is among the greatest insults to the essence of their race. It can be worse than death. Three, she may not accept any assassin positions until her sentence is fulfilled. Once the twenty years is done, she may return to Hevoc as an active citizen. Planetary history reports are in the Alliance record archives. You will need to speak to Zaima if you want more details."

Skye quietly let the information settle as she scrutinized Jedre. "What made you decide to help me?"

"I told you. I have noticed a change in Kas, one that I find concerning. You are his apprentice and in the best position to offer help. And if humans are offered placement into the High Council, they will require someone to accept the position. You will be the most likely candidate, and therefore, you need to be knowledgeable about the other species in the Alliance," he hesitated, "and you have not had access to the training most Alliance members learn over the course of many Jodra shift."

"You're offering to be my tutor?" Skye said.

He nodded slowly. "Conditionally. Yes."

She paused. "Okay."

They set up study times. Skye requested the classes to be open to other humans. Jedre declined. They would not be welcome until they were accepted into the Alliance. Skye was in a unique position. Her foot was in the proverbial door, and given time, she hoped to kick it open for others.

As she wandered the ship in the general direction of her room, she smiled at her newest revelation. Her meeting with Jedre produced many answers and the opportunity for a great deal more. She recalled the moment on the bridge when she suggested Zaima come with her instead of Jedre. Only an ignorant human would think Zaima less terrifying.

Although she had this new information, it hadn't truly swayed her opinion of Zaima. At no point in their previous interactions did Skye think she was safe. It only confirmed her assumption that the woman could destroy her if she so chose.

Zaima swirled in her workstation chair and rubbed her ears. Their sudden itchiness did nothing to improve her irritable mood. A blip on the screen notified a transmission from Jodra. The little blips that danced across the screens rarely caught her attention, but this one was unusual. How odd to get a communication prior to docking at a waystation. Usually, they followed the uploading of reports. She read it and relayed the message to Einar.

Her eyebrows raised. "We have been summoned back to Kepseli. A group observed strange behavior among the Enatomo. We have been accused of disturbing the life cycle of the species."

Einar tapped a summons to the pertinent crew. It was a short message, as were most sent by Einar. One by one, Kas, Jedre, Char, and Skye reported to the bridge.

Einar made the announcement when they arrived. "We have been summoned to Kepseli."

Kas scrunched his face. "Why would we be returning to Kepseli? I need to go to a way station!"

An awkward silence followed Kas's outburst.

Einar shifted slightly, keeping Kas within sight. "In due time. We have our orders. We will return to Kepseli."

Skye approached Kas. "Are you feeling alright?" She whispered.

"I'm perfectly fine." He huffed. "Are you daft? To question me in front of the Commander!"

Jedre's looming figure cast a shadow over Kas. "That's enough."

Kas diverted his attention to the large man. "Jedre, did you harvest any of them?"

"The enatomo? No. Should I have?" Jedre said.

"NO. Zaima said, – never mind. No. Do not harvest the enatomo. There is only one explanation to account for the change." He glared at Skye. "Your interactions have tainted our studies. It was a mistake to make you an apprentice. This time you will stay on the ship!"

She steeled. Only a single quiver of her lip escaped. Her adrenaline and blood pressure spiked as she forcefully regulated her breathing and cemented her lips. Her defiant eyes, however, were murderous.

Kas turned to Einar, who was the only crew member to keep a neutral face during the tirade. "May I be excused, Commander. I need to plan my time accordingly to prevent further disruption."

"Certainly," Einar said.

An uncomfortable, deafening silence followed the departure of the scientist. Skye remained stoic, though her respiratory rate increased, and tears formed against her will. Her voice only wavered slightly when she spoke. "May I be excused?"

"Yes, Skye. But please return, at your convenience, prior to our arrival on Kepseli." Einar nodded.

She escaped the bridge with her face intact. The walk to her room was forced and made increasingly difficult with trembling limbs. A sob caught in her throat as she reached her door, which mercifully opened and sealed behind her.

TWENTY-THREE

SABA CHIMED WITH AN UPDATE AS THEY ENTERED THE LAST slipstream before Kepseli. Skye sent a message to Einar and headed toward the bridge, leaving the solitude of her room.

Her puffy eyes critiqued her environment and picked up small details. The texture of the wall split into a diamond wainscoting pattern as she neared the controls. A barrage of unending questions seemed to flood her mind daily. Perhaps she should pay a visit to Char and Kuza. If she could win over Jedre, they would certainly be more forthcoming.

She had time to decompress and reevaluate. She was determined to remain professional, even if she had to suppress the bitterness that clouded her thoughts of Kas. It would pass. It was a temporary circumstance, not the end of the relationship. At the very least, she doubted it would be so easy for him to disavow her as his apprentice.

Einar was a shadow of gray when the doors opened. He brightened noticeably when she approached, both in expression and color. "How are you faring, Skye."

Her cheeks lifted in a pseudo-smile. "I'll manage."

"We need to discuss the changes of the enatomo," Einar said.

Heat flushed her face. Her stomach turned, and the familiar feeling of guilt settled. With her eyes cast down, she nodded.

"And of Kas," he said more gently.

Her head perked up. She met his eyes.

Einar's eyes pleaded. "What happened on Shehur?"

"I'm not sure, Einar. We split up. I need to review the tapes," Skye said.

"I have already reviewed the images captured by the droids," he said, bringing up the images on the large screen.

Skye watched herself interact with the fog replica. She saw when it tapped its face, and when she shook her head. The screen switched to the recordings of Kas. He also had an interaction with the fog figure. It surprised Kas, taking his form and mimicking his movement. Kas's fear quickly turned to excitement, and when the figure tapped its face, Kas quickly mimicked the movement. His mask receded, shocking Kas with the accidental exposure to the elements. Luckily, Kas tapped the mask again, almost immediately, rectifying the error. The fog figure dissipated.

Einar opened and clasped his hands. "Please update your report accordingly. It appears both you and Kas have had a significant interaction on Shehur. I fear the toxin that rendered you immobile has affected Kas differently. I think it prudent to submit him to a stasis pod, but it would put us in a precarious situation."

"How so?"

"There will be another crew on Kepseli when we land."

"Oh." Skye's head dropped.

"We are already known to be harboring humans. Your presence during the observation will solidify certain rumors."

Skye nodded. "I should remain on the ship."

"I was thinking quite the opposite." Einar grinned at her surprise. "You should take the lead on this site. Besides, Kas will likely be indisposed until the toxin is removed."

"If you think that's best, Commander." She bowed awkwardly.

"I do. And I may need your assistance getting Kas to the med bay. Zaima tells me you are a decent performist." He smiled sweetly.

Joey was bored. He thought the human ship would have provided some new comradery or at least a few new people to entertain a conversation. It was incredibly lonely to have no one with the same interests. Not truly. Davin had music, but no instrument to play. Ashwin had unrelenting anger, but no willing audience. Then again, maybe now he did.

Skye had an actual job and a developed purpose in this new world. He used the term world loosely. He wanted that, to find a job and a purpose.

Joey wandered the ship, as he did most of his days, drawing schematics in his slate. He was grateful that Skye thought about him and the other humans from time to time. She had managed to get him the slate, and he used it as his personal journal. It was a shame that it was only accessible to people with the nanotech. He thought Davin would have liked to write music. He assumed Ashwin would have used it to make a hit list.

Which made him pause because he also assumed that everything he scribbled was recorded. Although he was sure an intelligent and vast alien alliance would care very little about his doodles. He walked most of the ship at one point or another, all the places with open access. He assumed whichever doors did not open were not meant for him.

The maze of halls and ladders, elevator systems, and rooming quarters was an engineering marvel. At least, it was to him. He assumed it must be standard for whoever built the ship. He descended an elevator disc until it stopped in a large, pipe-like tunnel. It was the first time he'd ever explored the bowels of the ship.

He assumed the more mechanical parts would be off-limits, so it took him a moment to recognize that the colossal structure in the room he wandered into was the ship engine. It puffed and pulsed, swirled and buzzed with life. While entranced by the symphony of mechanics before him, he failed to notice the crew member in the room watching him with equal fascination.

A strange trilling noise made his hair stand on end, followed by an unmistakable, "H-hello." Joey wailed a high pitch scream from his insides and threw himself to the ground before succumbing to fear paralysis.

"I am Kuza," he said.

Joey hesitated, then slowly brought himself to his feet. He paused every time Kuza mimicked his movements.

"Hi, I'm Joey."

"Did Einar send you?" Kuza slowly tilted his head.

"Uh, no."

Did Skye need something?"

Joey gave a strange look at the mention of Skye. "No. Wait, you've met Skye?"

"Yes. I told to visit again, but she has not." Kuza's shoulders dropped with a pout.

Joey shifted uncomfortably. "Yea, she's been busy. Sorry to disturb you. I was just exploring the ship. I don't have much to do."

"You are in search of work, Joe-ey?" Kuza's mouth spread widely into a grin with the pronunciation of the name.

Returning fear crept over Joey, followed by curiosity. He let out a gurgle while the two emotions battled.

"I do not understand," Kuza said.

"Y-yes, I guess. It depends on what it is, but I'd definitely be interested in helping out more around the ship or learning something new. I used to work in technology back home, but I suppose that's all outdated here."

"There is always something new to learn. I saw you staring at the main energy station. Would you like to know how it works?"

Joey brightened. "Yea."

Kuza purred with delight. He ascended the walkway to the power station and waited for Joey to follow. Joey was almost sure he saw sparks on Kuza's fingertips. With as fast as he moved, Joey wouldn't have been surprised.

Skye sat in the med bay and concentrated on her breathing. Skye watched Char with only partial attention - she was reorganizing again. To Skye, all the supplies looked like plain, unmarked silver metal cylinders.

The doors whooshed open, taking Skye's breath away. Kas thundered into the bay. Skye sent him a message only moments before, letting him know they needed a health check for the next Kepseli excursion. She expected he'd be confused, upset even.

He motioned wildly and spewed like a rabid beast. "SKYE! What are you doing? What are you thinking? Are you so daft that simple instructions are beyond your comprehension? You. Are. Not. Going. To –"

Char pressed an unmarked silver rod to his neck. Kas dropped to the floor in a heap.

"Skye, be a dear and help me get Kas into the stasis pod." Char smiled.

Skye took a deep breath and slid off the table. She aided Char in moving Kas's dead weight.

Char placed a hand on Skye's shoulder. "He'll be back to his old self soon. Don't worry."

"I hope so." Skye said flatly.

"You didn't deserve the nasty things he said, Skye. You're doing a fine job and learning things very quickly for someone who hasn't ever been instructed by the Alliance. I like to think that I have some keen observation skills myself, but you and Joey are the first humans I've met, so sometimes it's hard to read you two. Have his words affected you?" Char said.

"Just a bit," Skye said, raising her cheeks in a default smile.

Panic bubbled in her chest. A blip on her band notified a meeting with Einar. She waved a goodbye as she exited, pushing her emotions aside and sealing them away.

EINAR BRIGHTENED when she entered the bridge. "We will be arriving on Kepseli momentarily. Are you prepared to run an observational encounter?"

Skye took a deep breath. "Honestly, no. But I'm sure I'll figure it out."

Einar wagged a long finger in the air with each word. "Observe. Record. Report. Those are the fundamentals of the scientific community."

"I can do that, and um," she searched for the words, "what interference might I expect?"

Einar faced her and tilted his head. "Interference?"

"I don't know. That might not be the right word. You said there would be another ship on Kepseli. It seems more complicated than our previous excursions." Skye tumbled through her thoughts.

"It is more complicated."

"And with Kas indisposed..." She trailed off.

"That is part of the complication."

Skye's worry scrunched her forehead. "Who are they?"

"They are a scientific discovery ship similar to our own, formally known as the Llowei." Einar answered matter-of-factly.

Her eyes narrowed while she straightened her back. "Einar, I feel like you are purposely keeping something from me."

He walked leisurely to his main workstation. "I have my own opinions about crews that I have encountered. I will not freely discuss those opinions until you have had a chance to form your own.

If you were going to be in danger, I would alert you. I do not anticipate the crew of the Llowei to be a danger."

Skye stared at Einar.

He smiled pleasantly. "You're dismissed."

She slowly exited the bridge and stood outside the closed door. She tapped a message to Joey and Zaima, requesting a meeting on the crew deck.

TWENTY-FOUR

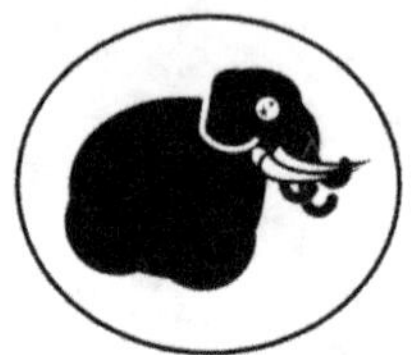

SHE CHOSE TO DRESS IN HER SUIT, THOUGH NOT NECESSARY FOR the terrain. It gave her more confidence. Joey didn't return her message, and she couldn't find him on the ship. She was on her own for this mission.

Skye was as ready as she'd ever be. When the hatch opened, she walked out with the Evander crew but stayed on the platform to survey her surroundings. The Llowei welcomed the new ship cheerfully. Jedre greeted a large man with an embrace and a hearty slap on the back. Zaima set up carrier transport.

Skye headed toward her crew with her head high and an air of purpose. The other crew stopped their work and stared as she approached. She walked up to Jedre and the man he greeted as a friend.

"Do you know where the scientist of the Llowei is? I'd like to introduce myself before starting the observation," Skye said confidently.

Jedre stared at her with mild amusement. "This is Skye. She's Kas's apprentice scientist. Skye, this is Vox, the botanist of the Llowei."

Vox's expression was of far more amusement. "Kas took an apprentice! And if I'm not mistaken, a human at that."

He laughed heartily, causing a smirk from Jedre.

"Nice to meet you, Vox." Skye nodded her head.

Vox abruptly changed from hearty laughter to a calm, serious demeanor. "Where is Kas?"

Skye observed him with piqued interest. "He's indisposed."

This caused a burst of raucous laughter from Vox. "He hasn't even had my famous sap-tipple yet." He nudged Jedre and spoke from the side of his mouth. "Speaking of, I have a nip for you to try."

"He might be better off," Jedre put a hand on Vox's shoulder. "Let's introduce Skye to Pettr."

When they entered the tent, Vox was calm and serious once again. Large totes crammed the tent space, some stacked while others scattered and open across the floor. Equipment cluttered the surfaces.

"Pettr! You have a visitor," Vox said.

A lanky man popped his head up from behind a stack of boxes. He scanned the group.

"Hello, Jedre. What can I do for you?" Pettr said.

"I'd like to introduce you to Skye, Kas's apprentice. She's going to be running the observation in his absence," Jedre said.

Pettr stared blankly. His eyes fluttered and flitted back and forth between them. "Hello, Skye. I am Pettr. From where do you hail?"

Skye raised an eyebrow. "I am a human from the planet formerly known as Earth." His brows twitched upward on his face. Her cheek tugged her lips into a smirk. "From where do you hail, Pettr?"

He seemed genuinely taken aback as if it should be obvious. "Gafur."

He tapped a disc attached to his shirt. Skye leaned in for a closer look. The shining royal blue disc was engraved with the image of a spaceship and a sun. Sure enough, her nanotech translated the image: *Gafur, Llowei – Scientist.*

Jedre coughed to hide laughter and excused himself. Vox

followed. Perhaps it was obvious to everyone else. Skye took a mental note for her and Jedre's next tutoring session. Skye wasn't oblivious to her ignorance of the Alliance races. There was no point in dwelling on information she had yet to learn.

"We were summoned here because of a change in the enatomo. What happened?" Skye's poker face masked her thoughts.

"That is precisely my question for you. I've read the report and notes submitted from your previous encounter. There were several unusual interactions." Pettr stared at her pointedly. "Previously, the enatomo barely acknowledged the presence of discovery vessels – aside from avoiding them. Their patterns have always been the same. Their mannerisms have always been the same. This was supposed to be a routine observation." He huffed.

"So, what changed?" Skye said innocently.

He sneered. "You could not tell?"

Skye narrowed her eyes to match his contemptuous tone. "We've just arrived. I thought it prudent to make an introduction before setting off on an observation. If it's not necessary, then I won't waste any more of my time."

He scoffed. "They have been observing us. When the new generation burrowed out of dormancy, they resumed normal patterns. However, when our ship landed, they briefly approached." He huffed and flailed his noodly arms. "An enatomo approaching a discovery vessel is unheard of! Ever since, they have had scouts on the ridge, keeping an eye on us. It is unnerving."

"And you blame the Evander?"

His mouth opened and closed like a fish on land. "Yes! The species behavior drastically changed since its last life cycle."

"But it began with your arrival," Skye said.

He snorted. "You have so much to learn, *apprentice*."

Skye smirked. "I'm going to head out. I'll send you my notes."

Pettr stumbled and clamored after her as she left the tent. Jedre and Vox watched the commotion from afar.

"You will not go alone!" Pettr said.

Skye smiled calmly. "Of course not, Zaima is driving."

Zaima appeared, smiling over Skye's shoulder. Skye hadn't seen her when she exited the tent. The assumption that Zaima would make an appearance with the mention of her name proved true. Pettr visibly shrank and disappeared into the tent.

Skye heard the familiar rumble and song of the enatomo as they climbed into the carrier. The scouts perched like towers on the ridge crest, keeping a watchful eye on the intruders. When the carrier zoomed off, one of the scouts disappeared and reappeared – perhaps a changing of the guard.

As they got closer, the differences became even more apparent. The scouts were slow to retreat but gave a wide berth to the carrier. The ridge provided a panoramic view of the enatomo cluster and the campsite. The first difference Skye noticed was the scouts. The second was the patterns. No longer wistful and joyful, they now moved in slow, gloomy formations with long, statuesque pauses. During one of the pauses, a murmur spread through the enatomo. A slow purr rumbled across the masses, and the formations began moving again. Skye watched in awe. It broke her heart to see them again.

Zaima furrowed her brow. "What is wrong with them? They are broken."

"I don't know," Skye said, trying to keep the emotion out of her voice.

Zaima shrugged. "Eh, they will respawn again."

Skye watched them quietly. "What if they don't, though."

"What do you mean?" Zaima examined her fingernails.

"What if something really is wrong, and they never come back?"

Zaima watched Skye's expression from the corner of her eye. "Like your little pet?"

Skye bit her lip.

After several hours of observation, Zaima whined and begged to go back. Skye obliged. Chatter, laughter, and music radiated from the largest camp tent. Skye was pleasantly surprised by the lively atmosphere.

"It is not usual to have two crews on a planet at once. Take advantage of the comradery," Zaima said as she disappeared into the crowd.

Skye stood quietly to the side of the entrance and observed the room. The diversity among the two ships was remarkable. Sadness brushed over her like a warm breeze. The variety in this room, though unique, was nothing compared to what Earth lost. She was thoroughly lost in thought when Vox sidled up next to her.

"You're looking awfully serious. Maybe that's why Kas thought you'd make a good apprentice," he said.

Skye blinked. "What?"

Vox smiled ruefully. "You're quite the topic of conversation among my crew."

Skye eyed him carefully. "How so?"

He swayed slightly and rocked on his heels. "For one, obviously, you're human. These days, that's not a common trait from what I hear, not that humans were ever common in Alliance dealings. And two, Kas made you his apprentice. The fact that Kas finally made anyone his apprentice is one thing, but to name a human as an apprentice." He whistled. "That's something else."

"I'm aware I have a lot to learn about the Alliance and its people," Skye said diplomatically.

His square jaw clenched and twisted into a lopsided grin. "If you ever need a lesson, I'll be happy to show you a thing or two."

Alarms flooded her system and ran fire across her skin. Her jaw clenched as she locked eyes with him and frowned. She was about to respond when a long, slender arm wrapped her in a hug. Zaima rested her head on Skye's shoulder and grinned a full toothy smile.

"Skye has a sufficient teacher. Thanks, Vox."

Vox flinched. "Well, the offer stands." He shrugged and retreated into the gathering.

"Thanks, Zaima," Skye whispered.

She cocked her head. "For what?"

Skye blushed. "For being my friend."

Her eyes widened, and her bright, toothy grin creased her face. "We are friends?"

"Well, yeah. I think so." Skye nodded and smiled.

Zaima's head bobbled slightly as she turned away. Her eyes caught a monster of a man in the far corner, hiding in the shadows. "I'll see you later, my friend."

Skye kept her head high, exuding confidence she did not feel. She perused the platters of food and helped herself to a light dinner of things she recognized.

Pettr made himself a plate. He did not look at her when he spoke. "Did you make any keen observations?"

Skye glanced at him briefly. The corners of her mouth pulled into a tight smile.

He looked at her, astonished at her lack of response. "Has your nanotech malfunctioned? Did you not understand me?"

"I understood you perfectly, Pettr," Skye said.

"And?" His head bobbled, aghast.

Skye picked up a yellow shrimp-like appetizer. "It will be in my report once my observations are complete. Have you made any new observations you'd like to share?"

Confusion flabbergasted his face. "I will not be conducting core sampling until tomorrow. I will let you know the data then."

Skye nodded and moved to another corner of the tent. She saw Davin in a group of Llowei recruits. He waved her over. It seemed that everyone wanted to meet the humans. Joey joined them soon after. They mingled between the two crews, answering questions about themselves and their former planet.

Davin was naturally charismatic. He wanted to know all about the music from their planets. They took turns singing little numbers and discussing instruments. Joey translated the conversation. Skye's heart warmed to see them doing well.

When she'd had enough of the barrage of questions, Skye found her way to the tent exit. The laughter and chatter dulled. Night on Kepseli was quiet and dark. Skye stared off toward the enatomo. She couldn't see them, but occasionally heard the soft moan of their song.

"Turning in, scientist apprentice?"

Skye searched for the voice in the dark. A tall creature, assumedly female, stepped out from the shadow of the tent. Her arms hung disproportionally long at her sides. Her head mounded on her torso, wearing rings of skin as necklaces. Skye froze. The hair on her arms rose, despite the suit being perfectly temperature regulated.

"Soon, perhaps. I just stepped out for a break." Her voice seemed far away and surprised her with its evenness.

The creature chuckled. "I mean you no harm. I am Llewe, Commander of the Llowei."

Skye dipped her head. "It's nice to meet you, Commander. My name is Skye."

"You have never met most races of the Alliance. Am I correct in the assumption?"

Skye grinned. "Yes. Every new race I encounter is a first."

"You, and your compatriots, are the first humans most of the Alliance will meet, if ever. Please forgive the stares and multitude of questions." Llewe bowed her head.

Skye mimicked the bow. "Please forgive ours as well."

Llewe chuckled again. "I look forward to reading your work. Welcome to the Alliance, Skye."

She decided to end the evening on that note. She was here to work for the next six days. That wasn't a great amount of time to determine the cause for the enatomo behavior change. Everyone assumed she did something, but no one knew what exactly caused the change. From what she read and learned of the enatomo, they had no memories. They lived a short life and respawned a new generation every cycle. Yet, here they were. On her way back to the ship quarters, she thought of Ollie. Her heartstrings tightened and strummed with the moan of the enatomo song.

TWENTY-FIVE

The next morning Skye checked on Kas. He was still unconscious in the stasis chamber. Char said his vitals were good, and he would be waking up within the next few days. After grabbing a light breakfast and dressing in her suit, she found Zaima in the carrier. She spread across the back seat and peeked her head up when Skye approached. After a full-body stretch, she hopped into the front.

"Good morning, little scientist."

"Good morning Zaima. You seem in a good mood this morning."

Zaima flashed a pointed look. "You are mistaken. I would rather be sleeping."

Skye got in the carrier. "Why don't you sleep once we get to the ridge?"

"I am tasked with watching you." Zaima yawned a silent roar.

"So, you're saying you can't detect danger when you're asleep?" Skye smirked playfully. "Good to know."

"Once again," a predatory smile tugged at Zaima's lips. "You are mistaken."

The carrier lurched forward and sped across the dunes. They rode in silence while the wind whipped their skin and blew their hair back. The suns broke the horizon and drifted up above the ridge. Skye never tired of seeing the Kepseli sunrise. It was so different from anything she'd seen before. The speed of their movement – faster than Earth's sun – reinforced the surrealism.

The enatomo huddled en masse as they slept, just over the big ridge. Skye quietly descended and sat on the ledge. She tapped her tablet and watched the creatures sleep. As the suns rose higher and warmed the planet, the enatomo woke and rolled into formation. They spread out in a spiral and collapsed together. One called out and started a murmur of song. Two of the littlest enatomo broke off and rolled toward the ridge. They paused when they noticed Skye and the carrier.

Zaima peeked her head over the side, eying the creatures. One let out a chirp, then the other. The hoard of enatomo stopped and looked to the ridge, chirping an alarm. When Skye and Zaima did not retreat or move at all, the chirping quieted. They slowly resumed their patterning, and the two littlest enatomo rolled cautiously forward.

They kept distance and trained an eye on their observers. Skye noted their curiosity and mannerisms. They swayed gracefully, encircling one another in a playful dance. She noted the tuft of hair behind their ears and matching patches of gray on their curled trunks. She questioned the breeding patterns of the enatomo. These two could be twins.

They slowed their roll as they came closer to the carrier, curiously swerving and ducking. Skye stood with her palms out and walked closer to them. They were slightly larger than Ollie, but not nearly as large as the other enatomo. They inched toward Skye, keeping a watchful eye on the carrier and Zaima.

"Do not get too close," Zaima said.

The twin enatomo skittered away and resumed their dance further down the ridge. Skye huffed and placed her hands on her hips, twisting to look at Zaima. Her head lolled on the edge of the carrier before slipping down into the back seat.

Skye huffed. "They weren't going to hurt me."

"You will not like the feeling of being gored," Zaima said dryly.

Skye dropped her frustration. "Has that ever happened?"

"Yes. The first discovery crew on Kepseli had a fatality."

Skye tapped her band. "I don't remember reading that."

"Their scientist wandered into the enatomo herd during patterning. His bones shattered beneath their weight. Their tusks shredded his innards." Zaima made a squishing sound.

Skyc forced herself not to react to the graphic visual. She suspected Zaima often phrased words for the reaction of others.

"Why did he wander into the herd?" Skye flipped through past Kepseli reports.

Zaima peeked her head up and raised one brow. "He did not record his thoughts prior to his demise, or after, for that matter."

Skye resumed her observation of the enatomo. She also continued to search the report archives for the first discovery ship on Kepseli. After sifting through several hundred reports, she found the one she was looking for. The Uvarovi was the first discovery ship assigned to Kepseli. The scientist, Sakh of Gafur, died at the hands of the species he discovered. The report linked the accounts of the other crew members, but nothing of note.

The enatomo continued with their structured patterning. They continued into the night, long after Skye and Zaima headed back to camp. A drone, left by Skye, watched silently on the ridge. When the Kepseli suns were completely hidden – and the spongey ground lost its warmth – the enatomo huddled together and hummed a lullaby.

The two crews developed a routine of evening celebration. Skye ate in her room while reviewing the drone recordings, but eventually joined the group. She felt a sensation of déjà vu, but could not place the exact moment. Joey and Davin made new friends among the Llowei. Jedre often played some sort of card game with Vox and others. A holographic tally kept track of the gambling. Receptivity to the humans warmed significantly. Skye assumed Commander Llewe had something to do with the change.

Each day, the moment they returned from the assignment, Zaima distanced herself from Skye. At first, it grated Skye's feelings. Not enough to say something. She assumed Zaima had more than enough of her company for the day.

When she saw Zaima slip out with a Llowei crew member, Skye suddenly understood. With piqued curiosity and a healthy sense of danger, Skye casually followed Zaima out of the tent. Zaima and the Llowei man stood closely near the crew deck of the ship. The man did not shy away from Zaima's predatory grin. On the contrary, he leaned in with his own.

Skye stayed out of direct sight. She examined some of the stacked crates, keeping watch out of the corner of her eye. Zaima and the man noticed her but paid her no attention. His appearance shifted briefly as he spoke with Zaima. As quickly as it happened, it changed back, but Skye saw it. He was like Zaima – the Lis of Hevoc. That meant something to her now.

However, she wasn't sure what his presence meant. It could mean nothing at all. Maybe every discovery ship had Alliance diversity, and Hevocians were as common crewmates as any other. Skye reminded herself of how very little she knew about her new universe.

And they were gone. Lost in her thoughts, Skye also lost track of the pair. She slowly reentered the tent, unsure if they disappeared into the ship or into thin air. A chill raised the hair on her arms.

The days passed without much progress. The observation continued. Eventually, Pettr joined the excursions, but from a distance. He did not warm to the humans like the other crew. The twin enatomo continued to watch the ridge, and the enatomo herd continued their rigid patterning. Skye made notes on the curiosities of the two creatures.

On the last full day, Skye woke up late. She planned on getting a solid breakfast and cleaning her suit. She forgot to shove it in the cleaning chamber. She'd have to choose one over the other. She opted for breakfast. She shoved the suit in the cleaning chamber. At least it would be ready for tomorrow. It dawned on her that she didn't have many additional clothing options. She looked around the room and opened the little cabinet. A clean and pressed tunic set was folded on the shelf.

When she changed clothes and put on the outfit, memories of Ollie flooded back to her. This was the outfit she wore when they last saw each other. It was probably the last time she wore it. Her eyes watered, and she took a deep breath. She only had two more days on this planet. Only two more days with the enatomo before she would have to relive the crater. She concentrated on the tasks at hand, pushing her emotions aside and sealing them away.

She grabbed the slate and slung the strap across her body. Zaima was sitting cross-legged in the bed of the carrier when Skye arrived. The crew deck was unusually quiet.

"Good morning Zaima."

"It is not morning."

Skye got into the carrier and tried not to be awkward. "Are you ready to go?"

Zaima raised an eyebrow and frowned. She wordlessly slipped into the driver seat. Skye felt the tension rolling off Zaima. Her heart pulsed in her ears. The feeling of being watched caused her to glance repeatedly at Zaima, though she never caught her eye.

Zaima sat stiffly while Skye observed the enatomo. Pettr already set up at the ridge. Skye greeted him but did not interrupt his studies. It wasn't until he spoke, did Skye notice the man with Pettr. His ability to go unnoticed made her hair stand on end. The Lis had joined them today.

The twin enatomo scouts kept distance from the group, as usual. Skye felt uncomfortable. The tension of the herd, the tension between Pettr and Zaima, and her – it all gave her anxiety. She walked along the ridge and sat in the shade of several large trees.

She noted in the slate that she hadn't paid much attention to the vegetation previously. Kepseli had a variety of different flora that reminded her of some plants from home. The trees were tall with sprawling limb extensions that carried dense tufts of leaves. Skye took a sampling of the leaves and scanned it into the slate. The leaves resembled feathers in their appearance and texture. She tickled her palm with the softness.

"Skye, don't move," Zaima said.

Naturally, Skye's head snapped in the direction of the voice.

Zaima flashed her teeth. "Do not move."

The deep moan of the enatomo song rumbled, vibrating through her right leg and into her chest. Frozen stiffly in place, Skye slowly turned her head to the creatures at her side. The twin scouts flanked her. Adrenaline spiked her veins, urging her to run. She relaxed and gently reached a hand to the quivering trunk of the large creature. They were much larger than Ollie, and their tusks formed longer spears of seemingly advanced age, but familiarity warred with Skye's sensibility.

She didn't feel as if she was in danger. Her mind urgently reminded her of the scientist who died. She felt like they recognized her and were showing her affection. Her memory reminded her that these creatures were not known to have short- or long-term memories. It also reminded her that Ollie was dead, and these two creatures were not him.

With a heart of sadness, her mind of reason won. These were wild and unpredictable animals, thus the reason they were being observed. Skye slowly shifted her gaze toward Zaima. She saw the terrified look on Pettr's face, and his crewmember uninvested in her fate.

Zaima slunk toward Skye and the enatomo like a predator on the hunt. The enatomo kept a close eye on her. They shifted and trilled angrily whenever she moved closer. For an excruciatingly slow and lengthy time, Skye stood frozen between the enatomo scouts and an advancing Zaima.

The smaller of the two rubbed against her leg and wrapped one of its trunks around her arm. It tugged gently and rumbled. Skye could feel its discomfort with Zaima. However, she couldn't understand why it so confidently touched her. If it was trying to kill her or drag her into the herd, it was doing a very gentle job.

"Zaima, stop," Skye said.

Zaima slowed but did not stop. "I'm not supposed to let you die, human."

"Give me a minute," Skye said more gently.

Zaima looked deeply troubled and somewhat constipated. Skye cocked her head sympathetically, pleading for trust. She moved slowly and with purpose, steadying her breath, and gently placed a hand on the trunk of the enatomo. It trilled and nuzzled her, squeezing her arm. It set Skye's already frayed nerves on edge, but it wasn't so tight to hurt, so she took it as a good sign.

The weight of the enatomo pushed Skye off balance, and she slowly lowered herself to the ground. As it leaned against her and rolled, Skye held a hand up to Zaima.

"Do you wish to die?" She hissed.

Skye did not respond. She sat with the large creature, clumsily rolling its body against hers until its head gently rested in her lap. Its tusks placed alongside her leg, not once goring her flesh. The second enatomo watched intently during the entire interaction. Skye felt its reluctance and uncertainty as much as she felt Zaima's.

With a smirk and a careful glance, Skye nodded to Zaima. So far, so good. She also noticed a frozen and terrified Pettr. The Lis crewmate seemed to show slight interest in the show, but just barely. Skye looked back at the creature on her lap.

Dark, dark blue, and black eyes with shining flicks of light that hinted at shades of green and purple stared up at her. Her heart ached.

"You remind me of a little friend I once had," Skye said.

The enatomo trilled in delight and wiggled, nuzzling her lap. Skye chuffed at the enatomo's response. A familiar scent of mint and baby lotion wafted through the air.

Skye gently stroked the cool skin of the creature. The velvety, silky smooth touch brought back memories of the night in the tent with Ollie. The creature rolled off her lap and wrapped its right trunk around her arm, pulling her up. Skye obliged and stood. Its intelligent eyes met hers, desperately tried to tell her something.

"What do you want, buddy?" Skye whispered.

The enatomo trilled insistently. It shifted its weight and circled before locking eyes with her.

"What does it want?" Pettr said.

Skye looked over her shoulder to find Pettr and his Lis standing closer to Zaima. "I'm not sure. I'm trying to figure it out."

"It is very strange for enatomo to react this way. What did you do?"

Skye opened her mouth to respond when a thin white line caught her eye. It was a scar above the enatomo's right shoulder. She gently reached her hands to the spot and traced it with her fingers.

"Ollie?"

The creature trilled.

"Who is Ollie?" Pettr whispered.

"Her pet enatomo. It died." Zaima answered Pettr and called out to Skye. "Skye, it died."

"I know, but –"

"Creatures who have tusks have scars. All creatures fight," Zaima said.

Skye looked more closely at the creature. It was larger than Ollie, but with the same eyes, the same scar, the same overall markings.

"How is it possible?" Skye whispered.

"It's not," Zaima said. "Now get away from it. Get back in the carrier."

Skye took a step back from the enatomo. It shuddered and slowly released her arm.

"I got to go, buddy. I'll see you later."

"Does it understand human talk?" Pettr asked, scribbling on his slate.

"Skye, get back in the carrier. We are returning now," Zaima growled.

Skye did as she was told. They quickly packed up for the day and headed back to the ships. Skye watched the enatomo scrutinized them from the ridge. The scout pair did not approach the group. When Skye retreated, they did not follow.

Zaima parked the carrier abruptly and gripped the steering column. She huffed and turned to Skye. "You are a foolish, selfish creature."

Skye remained seated as Zaima stormed off. It all worked out fine. Nobody died. If anything, they may have found something new. Skye quickly returned her thoughts to the enatomo encounter. Before she could forget the details, she went to her room and began her report.

Recruit Stabby showed up with food several hours into her documenting. She hadn't stopped writing since their return. The initial draft was almost finished. Halfway through her meal, Saba notified her of a guest at her door. With her approval, the door opened.

To Skye's surprise, Einar stepped in and quietly surveyed the room.

Skye stopped eating and stood up. "Hi, Einar. What can I help you with?"

He seated himself in a chair across from Skye. "I have a personal request."

Skye's eyes widened while she sat. "Yea, sure."

He glowed as if he were looking at an adorable puppy. "You don't know the request yet."

Skye shrugged. "I can't imagine it would be too outrageous."

"I'm glad you have such trust and confidence in me," Einar clasped his hands on his lap. "There has been notice from the Jodra Core, the Alliance central command. We have been requested for an immediate interview following this research cycle. I would like you to be more careful. Your death following this request may be viewed as suspect."

"Oh. Is it something to be worried about?" Skye straightened.

"Not necessarily. I have been expecting the command," Einar tilted his head with a tight smile.

"Okay," Skye said. "Anything else?"

"No, that is it." Einar rose and left as gracefully as he entered.

An unease settled on her nerves. Skye continued writing her report, albeit more slowly. When she finished, she joined the regular festivities in the communal tent. She saw Pettr sitting alone, seemingly lost in thought, and opted to join him.

"Evening, Pettr," Skye said, pulling out a seat.

"Skye!" He looked up, still dazed.

"Are you okay?"

"I gave in... and tried some of Vox's – hic – sap treacle," he said.

"Ah," Skye smiled. She successfully avoided the multiple offers and planned to continue her refusal. "I wanted to ask you about the enatomo."

"Yessss," A bubble of spit floated from his mouth. "Hmm."

"Have you done any scans of the creatures?" She asked.

He gestured, flicking his fingers from his palm several times. "Of course. I scanned the enatomo for chemical composition, and have planetary samples as well. – hic – My reports are already linked to your reports in the InStar library."

Skye brought up her report library and found the links. "Thanks, Pettr."

TWENTY-SIX

On the last day of the observation, Skye interacted with the scout enatomo under Zaima's close supervision. They even let Pettr get close. Not too close, but closer than they had previously. She spent most of her time on the ridge, petting the enatomo while its head rested on her lap. They watched the patterning of the herd. It changed again. The rigid, abrasive patterning converted to the fluid, rolling pattern of their previous visit. They were joyful again.

"Pettr, what happened between the time we left Kepseli last and arrived this time? How many other observations occurred?"

He shot her a side glance. "You should have reviewed this before your observation started."

She raised an eyebrow.

He sighed. "None. We were the next scheduled study."

"What happened when you arrived? Did you observe the previous patterning, the one you see now? Or was it always the more rigid pattern?"

He was quiet. "What are you asking?"

"I want to know what caused the change. I want to know when exactly it happened."

"I observed the softer pattern when we landed. When the enatomo saw our ship, they came close to the camp." He paused in the memory. "When they saw the crew, they retreated over the ridge and began the rigid patterns."

Skye quelled her frustration. "I was under the impression the change was attributed to my crew's last visit."

"It is," Pettr said.

"How though?"

"Your report details the odd encounter of your previous visit. When the next study vessel landed, the behavior of the enatomo significantly altered. You either disturbed the planetary conditions or the life cycle of the creatures."

"I was under the impression they have no memory. This behavior clearly suggests otherwise."

Pettr stared at her. She could see the wheels turning.

"Why was it ever assumed that they lacked memory?" Skye said.

"The initial and continued lack of response to stimuli – until now," he sighed. "During initial encounters, they were completely oblivious to Alliance interactions. They were sourced! Yet, they did not respond. Most species recognize danger and flee from it. The observational crews eventually left. Enatomo were labeled low-grade sourcing material. There's very little nutritional benefit."

"I think the initial observations were mistaken." Skye stroked the purring enatomo on her lap.

Pettr scoffed. "Put it in your report."

The change came quickly. The crater formed, and the enatomo cried a summoning. Her chest tightened. The enatomo on her lap rumbled and answered the cry. Skye's arm fell from its trunk as it stood. She stayed perfectly still. It cocked its head sympathetically and touched its face to hers. And then it left.

"Time to go," Zaima said.

Skye did not cry this time and got in the carrier without protest. Zaima drove back to the ship. The crews packed up their respective supplies until the camp was as bare as they found it. Skye went to her room to polish and finish her report. Thoughts nagged at the back of her mind that she could not yet put into words. What she observed – she didn't know yet – but it was different from the initial studies.

The crews said their goodbyes, and the ships departed. A tense and heavy atmosphere weighed on the Evander. Skye knew something was very wrong, but she didn't bother to comment until she finished her work. She kept to herself and stayed in her room. The other humans felt it too. They visited occasionally, but left quickly when faced with Skye's cold demeanor. She didn't mean to be hostile or cold, but she'd rather bury herself in her work until she finished. The stress of her first solo mission – and the irksome missing piece – grated her nerves.

Her armband pinged. She'd been so deeply concentrating that the noise startled her. She tapped it. Jedre requested her in the nursery. They hadn't met since the Kepseli observation started, and she didn't feel like having a tutoring session right now. She declined and returned to her work.

Her band pinged again. She glared at the tech. It was a more insistent message from Jedre. She declined again and stared at the band for a moment before returning to her work.

Pounding on her door made her jump.

"Jedre is at your door. Should I open it," Saba said.

"No," she walked to the door. "Go away."

After a pause, the pounding resumed.

"Jedre is at your door. Should I open it," Saba said.

"Yes," Skye growled.

The door opened to a snarling Jedre and a snarling Skye. He pushed past her, into her room. She walked out, leaving him there by himself. Halfway down the hall, he caught up with her. He was still fuming, but considerably calmer.

"Would you care to explain yourself?" He said.

"If I did, I would be in the nursery right now, instead of walking around the halls of the Evander wasting time," Skye snapped.

He stopped momentarily, then caught up with her again. "What's wrong with you?"

"What is wrong with *you*!" She said. "I'm working on something. I just need some time to figure it out! I would really like to be left alone."

She made a conscious effort to avoid the nursery and his chambers. As she motioned to turn down an unfamiliar hall, he firmly grabbed her arm and threw her into an open room. It was dark. She could feel the snarl reverberate through Jedre's hands. They were firmly placed on her upper arms, pinning her to the wall. His appendages pinned her body. Her eyes began to adjust to the lack of light.

"What is wrong with you?" He hissed.

Skye did not answer.

"Don't pretend to be asleep, human. I can still see you."

"Let me go."

"Answer me."

"Let me go," Skye insisted.

His hands loosened their grip. She felt his other appendages slide across her stomach, chest, and legs. She was free.

"Saba turn on dim light," Skye requested as the low light adjusted.

He watched her intently, arms crossed. She matched his stance.

"The Jodra Core has requested us," he said.

"I know." Skye rubbed the bridge of her nose.

Surprise flashed and disappeared from his face. "You know, but you don't understand."

"Then enlighten me, Jedre. What is so important that you can't take no for an answer?"

He snarled. "You have put this entire crew in danger. All of our lives are at risk, and you have the audacity to behave like a child."

She glared at him.

"I'm done with you." He stormed out of the storage bay.

Skye immediately felt guilt for her treatment of Jedre. Then, she reminded herself of all the times he was a complete jerk – and then all the help he'd been giving her lately. Her emotions sprinted between anger, guilt, and grief. The emotional parade exhausted her mentally and physically. Eventually, she found her way back to her room, where she planned to remain for the foreseeable future.

Joey hung from the upper level of the engine room, suspended by a custom harness. He never planned on testing his fear of heights. While he spun slowly over a chasm of energy, he acknowledged that his curiosity outweighed that particular fear. Thus, his current predicament, for better or worse.

Kuza appeared upside down, drifting in and out of Joey's eyesight. He snatched the straps of the harness and thoroughly jostled the human. Joey let out a yelp – his grip petrified to the straps. A wide terrifying grin creased the creature's face.

"It holds well," he said, clearly impressed with his own work.

Joey wavered. "Did you have any doubts?"

"Rarely do contraptions work perfectly on the first design," Kuza shrugged, "for most."

Joey took a deep breath and questioned his life choices. His contemplation of death was cut short by the booming commands of Commander Einar.

"Kuza. Please remove our human crew member from your device."

Disappointment colored Kuza's face. Without protest, he unstrapped and deposited a terrified Joey on the floor of the ship. He stood at attention, awaiting the purpose of Einar's visit.

"We will be intercepted by the Jodra Core for questioning. Please make sure the Evander is properly maintenanced." Kuza and Einar exchanged nods before Einar shifted his gaze to Joey. "And please refrain from damaging the human crew members, on accident or otherwise. It may appear suspicious to the Jodra crew if there are rumored humans missing."

Kuza flushed and nodded. Einar left as suddenly and gracefully as he arrived.

Joey looked at Kuza openmouthed. "Were you trying to kill me?"

He scoffed. "No, you were perfectly safe." The thoughtful tilt of Kuza's head left Joey unconvinced. "However, Einar is correct. We shall resume any curiosity studies once the Evander has been cleared by the Jodra Core."

"Is this a routine check? Does this happen often?" Joey said.

"No."

Joey waited. Without further explanation, Kuza scampered away.

"What do you mean NO!"

JOEY KNOCKED on Skye's door. There was no answer. "Skye?"

"Skye is not accepting visitors at this time," Saba announced.

"I need to talk to her," Joey said.

"You should find something else to occupy your time. I advise you to try again in approximately seventy-two minutes," Saba said.

Joey reluctantly left. The meeting of ships weighed heavily on his mind. He thought of whom else he could ask that might actually give him an answer. Einar would have mentioned it to him if he thought it necessary. He didn't want to bother Einar. Kas was still indisposed. He found his way to the med bay.

Joey popped his head in the room. "Char?"

Clanging in the storage cabinet followed by a muffled cursing led him to the resident medic.

He called more softly. "Char?"

"I'll be right there, Joey!" She sang.

She exited the closet with a tote of bio wrapping and disorganized metal cylinders. "Just doing some supply refreshing and cleaning. What can I help you with?"

Joey watched her move around the room. His voice seemed to be lost. His mind scrambled for the correct words.

Char slowed and focused her attention on Joey. "What is it? Is someone hurt? Are you hurt?"

"No," he said. "Not yet."

She perched on a hovering stool and scrutinized his movements. "Not yet?"

He took a deep breath. "I'm concerned about the meeting with the Jodra ship."

Her eyes softened with understanding. "That is to be expected. I'm honestly surprised by the overall response from you humans. You really are such an assorted bunch – resilient, adept," she faltered, "and unpredictable."

Joey looked at his shoes. "I'm sorry for the bad experiences you've had with us. I'm sorry for the trouble we've caused you guys."

Char laughed. "There's no need for apology, Joey. Though it is appreciated and warms my hearts. We knew this was coming when we brought you aboard the ship. We quite literally brought this on ourselves. And regardless of the outcome, I would not change it."

"What should I do? What should I be doing?"

Char chose her words judiciously. "Spend your time doing something you enjoy. When the Jodra Core arrives, comply with any orders you receive and greet them as friends. They are not your enemy. We are not your enemy. You are a member of the Alliance. Can you do that?"

His brows furrowed. "Well, yeah."

"They will ask you about the human rebel ship. You should be honest and forthcoming."

Joey nodded. They locked eyes for a moment, acknowledging omissions of information.

Char's face lost its softness. Her back straightened. "While you are a guest on the Evander, while you are recruits of the Evander, we will protect and defend you."

TWENTY-SEVEN

THE ALMAS WAYSTATION DIFFERED GREATLY FROM THE ONE IN Ziet. Skye watched from a port window as they approached. It was a quiet sphere. She found the liquidity of its appearance both fascinating and alarming, like most things she didn't understand. The moments of quietude leading to their arrival gave her time for introspection.

The Evander landed gracefully on the shining black deck. A brigade of Alliance police stood in tight formation with a mountain of a man front and center. They did not approach the ship. They did not move at all.

Light footsteps in the hall drew Skye's attention from the window. Zaima stopped several meters away and waited quietly with her arms crossed. Skye followed her down the hall to the crew deck. Einar already stood on the platform, greeting the Alliance guards. It was just Einar, Zaima, and Skye.

"Where are the others?" Skye whispered.

Zaima did not look at Skye when she spoke. "Keep your mind clear, and your answers short."

Anxiety wiggled through her nerves and raised the hair on her arms. She took a deep breath and focused on the smell of her smart suit. It was clean and warm. The way it hugged and compressed her body without being restrictive was comforting. It gave her confidence. She adjusted her chin and her eyes, raising them to meet the confidence she created. She cleared her mind to only the task at hand.

Einar glanced back at the ship. Zaima took the signal to approach, and Skye followed suit. The walk to the brigade was slow and agonizing. At one point, in her careful, measured pace, Skye felt as if she forgot how to walk properly. Her eyes drifted to Zaima and mimicked the sway in her step and the straightness of her spine. They stopped slightly behind Einar. He turned and greeted them with a washed-out smile. When he began speaking to Skye, some of the brightness returned to his face, but Skye noted that it felt forced.

"Skye, welcome to the Almas waystation. This is Lieutenant Guilem." Einar gestured to the mountain. "He will be escorting you to a private office to have a discussion. You are in good hands. Please answer any questions he may have."

Zaima's words repeated in her mind. *Mind clear. Answers short.*

Skye nodded. "Of course, Einar."

Skye may have imagined it, but she thought the lieutenant's head twitched ever so slightly. When she looked at him directly, he was still as a statue. Skye had so many questions. The words sat heavy on her tongue behind a steely trap. The thick tension and stiff body movements of the group advised her to remain silent and observe. She was certain the anxiety would burst her heart.

"This way, apprentice Skye."

The lieutenant was an enigma. His voice rang smooth and gravelly in the same breath. He commanded attention and respect, but could easily fade into the background. The lines on his face and his uniform were sharp. His movements were fluid and silent, but each step reverberated tremors through the ground.

Skye quietly followed the other six members of the Alliance Patrol. They were nondescript and uniform. Simply for show.

Perhaps, babysitters of convenience. After all, it's unreasonable to assume one person to be responsible for another twenty-four hours a day, or however many hours constitute a day on this planet- station. Either way, in her opinion, it was overkill for a single human.

An opening presented in the central dome building. Three uniforms waited on the ground, while the others joined Skye and the lieutenant on a rising platform. It whirred smoothly to an upper bubble. The entire building was a cluster of bubbles in one large bubble, though admittedly stronger in substance. She followed the lieutenant to another chamber while the other uniforms waited outside. The little bubble room opaqued when they entered.

It reminded her of the living chambers on the Evander – utilitarian and minimalist. There was a single rounded table in the center of the room and two seats of drastically different sizes. She stood by the smaller of the two and waited.

"Be seated," he said.

She obliged, maintaining good posture with hands folded neatly in her lap. She appeared composed and professional, on the outside. Internally, her heart raced. Her hair stood on end. Adrenaline flooded her veins. Since she was summoned from the Evander, she had been on high alert.

She took a deep, even breath. *Mind clear. Answers short.* "How can I help you, Lieutenant?"

He stared at the human. "I have questions for you to answer."

He opened a holographic tablet over the table and flipped through several screens. Skye sat back and looked around the nondescript room. Patience had never been a strength of hers. She took a deep breath and calmed her simmering temper as the quiet reading and flipping carried on.

Skye sighed and leaned forward on the table. "Why am I here?"

"The Alliance has unanswered questions regarding the destruction of Earth and its inhabitants," he answered flatly.

She struggled to keep sharpness out of her tone. "Then, ask me your questions."

He paused the flipping of pages and stared. "It is known that several Alliance ships broke protocol and ventured to Rojje. How did you come to be on the Evander, apprentice Skye?"

"I woke from a stasis pod. I do not know how I came to be there."

"Where did you come from?"

"I'm from Earth. I traveled around quite a bit, but the last place was northeast Ohio."

"How many regions of Earth were there?"

"Many. More than I can name. Hundreds. And they were broken down into continents, countries, cities, even tribes in some places."

He scribbled on his slate. "When did you arrive on the Evander?"

"I don't know when. I woke up in a stasis pod. I don't have a clear understanding of how or when or how long. You're asking the wrong person."

"I assure you, apprentice Skye, we are asking everyone involved."

A chill ran over her skin. She thought of the crew of the Evander and the trouble they might be in for saving the people of Earth. Pressure built in her chest and throat.

"What is the last thing you remember prior to waking on the Evander?" he asked.

Skye searched her memories. She scowled. "I don't know. I remember walking. I was listening to music. It was warm. It was summer." Her heart squeezed.

The lieutenant scratched notes onto a slate. He asked question after question about Earth and the Evander, about the Evander crew and the planets they visited. It was nonstop. It had been hours. Skye was tired and hungry, and she grew irritable and impatient with every additional minute.

"Why were you chosen to be an apprentice scientist?" he continued unfazed.

Skye sighed and groaned. "I don't know."

"How are we to determine the good humans from the bad humans?" Lieutenant Guilem said.

"I don't know." Skye threw her hands in the air. "How do you determine the good Vanzkelgans from the bad Vanzkelgans? Or the bad Hevocians from the good Hevocians? Some people are good, and some are not. Some people make better decisions than others, but I think it depends heavily on your perspective. A lot of good humans were murdered by a few bad Vanzkelgans, but I'm not about to blow up their planet for it."

He straightened his back. "There seems to be a lot you do not know."

Skye sat back in her chair and crossed her arms. "I could say the same about you."

Lieutenant Guilem scribed notes. For the first time since the interrogation started, he adjusted in his seat. He stared at Skye. His head cocked slightly to the side, then he scribed more notes. Silence did not normally disturb Skye, but there was something in his movement that piqued her interest and flared her irritation.

"Why did we meet on a waystation? Like, can't the two ships just connect?" She touched her pointer fingers together.

He stared at her. "Waystations serve as meeting locations and report transmission centers. But ships need to restock and refuel, on occasion. Ship fuel is not made from nothing, though most Alliance systems are self-sustaining and regenerative. Do you know of any ship that does not have to refuel?"

"No, that's a fair point." She painted the sweetest grin on her face and leaned in. "So, is there anything else I can help you with, or can I go?"

He locked eyes with her – his stare more intense and meaningful than before. "You have not been dismissed. At the very least, you will need to learn the hierarchy of Jodra. You have not yet earned this level of dissension."

"Because I am human?"

His chin lifted. He viewed her with narrowed eyes. "Because you are an *apprentice* scientist of the Interstellar Alliance, and I am a lieutenant. Your status as a human in the Alliance is undetermined, but your status as an Alliance recruit is official. Your situation is unprecedented."

Skye straightened in her chair. They locked in a staring contest, attempting to better understand one another. The human blinked first, as would anyone who engaged in a staring contest with a member of the Elian race. She looked away and adjusted in her seat.

"Is Kas going to get in trouble?" She said quietly, not expecting an answer.

"Kas will be disciplined for his actions in accordance with Alliance guidelines."

She sat perfectly still. "What will happen to him and the crew?"

"The High Commander will confer with the High Counsel and determine the consequences."

A wrenching feeling of guilt settled in her stomach. Worry crept into her facial features.

The lieutenant tipped his head slightly. "You are concerned for their well-being?"

"Of course. Kas, Einar, Char, Zaima, even Jedre, they're my crew. They're as much my friends as any human I've met – more so in some cases. I don't want anything to happen to them."

He tapped his slate. "There was a report of you threatening another human."

Skye huffed and rolled her eyes.

"Curb your insolence. It is in your best interest to give your version of events," he said sharply.

She straightened her back again and clasped her hands on the table. "He woke out of stasis to a stressful environment. I threatened him because I didn't want him to hurt Char."

"You admitted to not intending on following through with your threat. Do you do that often, make threats you do not intend to carry out?"

"No, I don't think so. Maybe. It depends on the situation."

The corner of his mouth twitched. "That is not an answer."

She smirked. "I don't have enough observational data to make an accurate report."

His eyebrows raised. "Perhaps you should engage in self-reflection."

Skye genuinely smiled. "I'll work on it."

"Do you hold any connections to the Carasius or its crew?" Lieutenant Guilem continued.

Her lips pursed. "No, but I've encountered them twice."

"Who specifically?" He asked.

"I've seen the ship. I don't know the crew." She shook her head.

"Crew members listed include humans Rhys, Richard, Victoria, Aleah –"

"The guy who was holding the Evander hostage for humans, he called himself Rhys. Him and another of his crew were on Shehur. They mentioned Victoria."

He began to scribe. "You know Rhys?"

"No, I don't know him, but I've encountered him while he was threatening to blow up the Evander. Me and a whole room full of people."

Lieutenant Guilem scribbled in the tablet. "Describe the encounter on Shehur."

Skye recounted the mission. "I was in the caves. There was a ship that approached our camp. I later found out it was the Carasius."

"It was. And you made contact with the crew?"

"Uh, no. I hid from them."

He looked up from his scribblings to read her expression. "You hid from them?"

"I didn't know they were humans. I had no idea who they were."

"Okay. What happened?"

"I hid in a crevice in the caves. They called out to me. They were looking for humans. At the time, I thought they were hunters."

"Hunters?"

"Yea."

He scribed. "Who has been hunting humans?"

"No one, that I know of, but our planet was just destroyed, so I assumed..."

"Okay. Continue."

"There were two guys. The other guy, not Rhys, said they needed to go because our ship was coming – that Victoria said they needed to go."

"Your ship, the Evander?"

"Yes. When I saw them around our tent, I hit my alarm. But they saw my alarm too, so I shut it off. Kas and the Evander came in response to the signal."

"Why didn't the Evander come when the Carasius broke atmosphere?"

"I don't know. My band didn't even register them, but communication was shoddy on Shehur. Their ship didn't show up on my band, and then I couldn't hear Kas until I left the cave."

"Shoddy?"

"Kas was trying to reach me after I hit the alarm, but I didn't hear anything until I came out."

The lieutenant scribed. "Did you make a report?"

"Yes."

Lieutenant Guilem scrolled through the holographic records. "It is not in the database." He stretched his massive arm on the table. "Send it to me."

Skye looked at him quizzically.

His eyebrows raised again. "You do not know how to send a direct transmission?"

Heat flushed her cheeks. "No."

"Select the report from your band log. Then, touch your band to mine."

Skye complied. She gently laid her arm on the gigantic arm of the inquisitor so their bands aligned. She had to stand and lean over the table. A message flashed in her vision, causing her to startle; *Transmission open to Lieutenant Guilem, Jodra Core Central Command. Send report?*

Send the report, she thought.

The notice was replaced by another message; *Transmission sent.*

Lieutenant Guilem remained still while she removed her arm. “We will reconvene at a later time. The recruit at the door will escort you to your chambers.”

Skye rose and headed to the door. She turned back and locked eyes with the giant. “Thank you, Lieutenant Guilem.”

He nodded his head in acknowledgment.

TWENTY-EIGHT

The crew of the Evander stood shoulder to shoulder, bound in carbon cuffs. They did not resist the Jodra Core officers. As esteemed members of the Alliance, to resist would be social and physical suicide.

Zaima was half-tempted. It was in her nature. But it was also her nature to keep her word, and she had given a promise of survival to two very important people.

Jedre silently recounted the choices that brought him here. He weighed each one and visualized alternative outcomes. Many versions included the death of humans, more than already had been destroyed. Time and time again, he settled on his current choices, much to his dismay.

Char gave herself a sedative before leaving the Evander. She was pleasantly dreaming. Occasionally, she would jostle in her carbon cuffs, momentarily confused at their presence before drifting back to thoughts of accolade and nebula beaches.

Kas's fingers tapped nervously while his gaze searched for his apprentice. The anxiety twisted his insides and blasted his emotions.

It was exhausting. He regretted turning down Char's offer to be medicated. His last memory before waking in the stasis pod was on Shehur. Char gave him a brief and embarrassing explanation of what he missed. He knew this meeting with the Jodra Core was inevitable, but he lost considerable time to prepare.

Kuza did not like the bright lights of the Jodra core. His eyes remained closed while he purred in deep meditation. The carbon cuffs were merely a formality on the Wella race. He could have easily dismantled them with his fingertips – not that he ever would. A Wella never disobeyed a superior.

Einar stood as the imperial statue of a discovery ship commander. The Jodra Core officer apologized when attaching his cuffs – averting their eyes from his gentle smile. His mind remained unreadable, typical of the Kharahk.

"Crew of the Evander," Commander Jarlat said. "You have disobeyed the Alliance quarantine of the planet Earth. You will serve trial in the Harta Court with the collection of other dissidents. I trust you will behave as guests while in the confines of my ship. Further disobedience will not be tolerated."

Kas cleared his throat, wavering under a glance from Einar. "Commander? Wh-what will become of our human crew?"

Commander Jarlat approached the scientist. His tapping ceased into trembles.

"Your human crew," Commander Jarlat sighed and shook her head. "Scientist Kas, your humans remain in sealed guest quarters. Your apprentice scientist will be sequestered and questioned. Whether intentionally or inadvertently, you have turned a complicated situation into a clustered imbroglio. Do you have anything to say for yourself?"

Kas straightened his back and raised his chin to the High Commander. His voice did not waver. "Skye of the planet Earth is an exceptional scientist apprentice. As my first and possibly only apprentice, she has been resilient and pragmatic and offers a unique perspective on every new encounter. I did not make the choice superficially."

Commander Jarlat straightened to her full height. Her lips curved to a rare glimpse of a smile. "You stand by your decision. We will see how that decision serves you in high court."

Kas gulped dryly as the High Commander departed. The Alliance officers escorted them to the sealed chamber they would share until sentencing.

"Saba?" Kas called.

"Saba is dormant at this time," the voice of the Jodra Core responded.

"Are the humans okay?" Kas asked.

"The humans are intact."

It was not the answer he was looking for, but it was reassuring.

SKYE'S ROOM on the Jodra Core was almost identical to the one on the Evander, except for the officers outside her door. They gave her dinner and left her alone for the evening. While her nerves bristled from the lack of communication from her crew, she worried most about Davin and Joey. Her sleep was restless, and bathing in the morning left her unsatisfied. She scoffed. What she wouldn't give for a real Earth bath.

"Apprentice Skye," the Jodra Core ship said, "your escort has arrived."

The door slid open to a sharp-dressed recruit with pit stains. "Good day, apprentice Skye. My name is recruit Halden."

Skye waved a greeting. "Hi, Halden. Where are we going today?"

His movements hesitated and jerked. "I will escort you to a room for questioning."

Skye watched him cautiously. He looked different from the others she'd met so far. His broad, flat nose extended from a large forehead. His wide-set eyes rested on the sides of his face, rather than the front. Under his mop of curls, she noticed long ears tucked away. She memorized his appearance, labeling the likeness to a rabbit-elf hybrid. Though, despite a small mouth, he did not appear to have buck teeth. The rest of his body appeared human-like.

She stood slowly and smiled. "Can I get some breakfast?"

His eyes widened. "Yes. Yes, of course. Once you're settled in the meeting room."

The guards remained at the door and followed behind when Skye moved down the hall. It was a short walk. Halden gestured her through open doors. She obliged cautiously, taking a seat at the table.

He gulped. "W-what do you eat?"

She smiled and shook off some of his infectious anxiety. "Is there a menu I can pick from? If not, a vegetable mix from Ahila is good. I could go for a salad."

He straightened and visibly relaxed. "I can do that."

Skye sat alone in the room. She leaned back in her chair and looked around. It was another minimalist, nondescript four walls and a table. Halden returned quickly with a bento box of food. He sat across from her and watched while she ate.

"Why are you watching me eat? It's weird," Skye said between bites. She was hungrier than she thought.

Halden blushed. "Oh, I didn't know. I do not know the customs of Earth, just what I've read."

"What have you read?" Skye said, slicing a root vegetable.

His eyes met hers, and he hesitated. "The last Earth study, before the death of Yar Tukk, mostly, but there were a few others."

"Where do you find these reports? I've searched the InStar library, but you know, there's a lot to sort through."

"You may not have access." Halden frowned. "All reports are available to Alliance citizens. Shared knowledge is shared power, or so the saying goes," he chuckled.

Skye watched him while she chewed. Her gut told her he wanted something from this meeting, but she couldn't quite gauge what. "So, what do you do, Halden?"

"Oh, I'm just a recruit. I usually work in the records acquisition office. We receive transmissions from scientists, like Kas, and you, I guess." He smiled cheerfully with an anxious undertone.

Skye narrowed her eyes and grinned. "So how did you get stuck with me? Slow day in the records office?"

His breathing quickened. "Not exactly," he laughed nervously. "I volunteered for the assignment when I heard you were on our ship."

"Why?" Skye sat straighter.

She eyed the metal disc on his shirt. It was navy blue with a white stripe down the center and an engraved ship. Her nanotech translated the image: *Razvedka, Jodra Core – Recruit.*

He fidgeted and smiled meekly. "Curiosity, perhaps. The reports are fascinating."

Skye sensed he wasn't telling her the whole story. "Can you send me the reports on Earth?"

His breathing increased. "I don't think – I don't know if I can –"

Skye smiled sweetly and extended her arm across the table, presenting her band. "Shared knowledge is shared power, or so the saying goes."

He smiled nervously. "I suppose. I mean, you are an apprentice scientist." He shook his head. "Of course, you should have no issues. Right?"

He rested his arm over hers. She reflexively grabbed his arm, startling them both. Her fingers paused on the chill of his skin. He jumped, eyes wide, heart beating out of his chest. The transmissions sent immediately in rapid succession. He hesitantly pulled his arm away while she recoiled from the nano assault.

Skye smiled. "Received. Thanks, Halden. I look forward to reading over these. I'm sure it'll be fascinating."

"Of course," he said and stood from the table. "Lieutenant Guilem will be in soon to ask you more questions. Um, I look forward to receiving more of your reports."

Skye grinned. "I look forward to sending them."

He left quickly, leaving Skye staring at the door in his absence. The awkward encounter spun the gears in her mind. It spurred a battle of logic and curiosity, quickly drawing and stifling conclusions. Her eyes remained glazed in thought until Lieutenant Guilem walked into the room.

"Good morning, Lieutenant," she stood, unsure whether to salute.

"Be seated," he said, producing a large chair from the wall for himself.

She obliged and waited for the questioning to begin. He opened his slate and flipped through some notes. Skye observed the purposeful movements of the large stone man. He looked up, catching her eye.

"You seem to be in good spirits for someone about to stand trial," he said.

Her stomach dropped. She tried not to show her surprise or the turmoil stirring her insides and plastered a smile on her face. "Well, I wasn't aware I was going to trial, Lieutenant. I just thought you had a bunch of questions, and I was being helpful and forthcoming. What are the charges?"

"We are headed to the High Council to determine the fate of humans in the Alliance."

She sighed a stiff breath. "Well, I don't really know what I can do about that."

"You are in the best position to represent the human race," he said, "Unless there is someone else you would recommend to represent your species."

"That's not exactly a job for one person." She huffed. "I mean, do you have one person who is in charge of the entire Alliance?"

"Yes," he said flatly.

"Really?" Sky frowned. "Who?"

Lieutenant Guilem's jaw clenched, making a quiet grinding

noise. "You will be in the presence of the High Council. Premier Entu, ruler of the Alliance, may choose to be present for such a controversial decision. Not all species are offered a seat in the Alliance as citizens. Your species has a good chance," he paused, "if it is represented well."

TWENTY-NINE

High Commander Jarlat returned to the High Council hall of Opes. It was unusual for more than one meeting in a Jodra shift, but changing times were upon them, and the humans of Earth proved to be causing shifts of their own.

The council members stood as Premier Entu entered. Tension crackled as the weight of the matter settled.

The Premier's voice boomed. "Commander Jarlat. This is the second time we've convened on this issue. What is being done?"

The Commander remained standing while the others sat. "We have rogues in our Alliance, my Premier. The Vanzkelgan insurgents responsible for the premature termination of Earth are in stasis."

Khorsol stood. "They turned themselves in, my Premier. I request leniency."

"Denied."

Khorsol's head dropped as he took his seat.

Commander Jarlat continued. "Several Discovery ships preserved the human species prior to the destruction. Most of them are quarantined and under questioning."

"What is being done with the humans?" Eudia of Mencuri asked.

Jarlat nodded. "That is the debate for today's meeting."

"They have no home planet. They should be turned over for study. There are already programs in place to harvest the species," Anevay of Enantios said. "Our main concern should remain with the rebel humans and the stolen discovery ship. Efforts should be directed at their destruction."

Arwel of Kharahk narrowed his eyes. "Why wipe out the species, Anevay?"

Anevay raised his nose. "Threats to the alliance are best eliminated."

"That sounds dangerously like the reasoning of the Vanzkelgan insurgents," Shivali interjected. "There were whispers of honorable benefactors –"

"I will not entertain unmerited accusations or simpleton rumors. This is a high council, not a brothel," Anevay hissed.

Shivali glared and chuckled dangerously.

Nhan of Ahila stood and shifted the room's attention. "What of the human Skye?"

The council quieted. Premier Entu waived a hand for elaboration. "The human Skye? What is special of this particular human?"

"She is the apprentice of scientist Kas Liska, of the Evander," Lieutenant Guilem said.

"How is that even possible?" Khorsol said through gritted teeth.

Lhu of Razvedka waved a clawed hand. "A scientist has the autonomy to name any being their apprentice or successor."

Some high council members engaged in passionate discussion, talking over one another and slowly raising their voices. Others remained stoically silent and watched.

"How can we accept an outsider to such a distinguished position, without any training, without any vetting?" said Anevay, "and if the scientist Kas dies? Are we to accept this human recruit as an untrained scientist? She would assume his roles and responsibilities as his successor."

Thyst of Gafur scoffed. "But humans aren't even members of the Alliance."

"So we accept one? Does that mean that we accept them all?" Asho-Pani of Ula asked in earnest.

"The scientist Yar Tukk, revered by the Vanzkelgans, named a statue of himself his only successor," Lhu said dryly.

"That is different," Khorsol hissed.

"The actions of the scientist Kas are traitorous. He should be terminated immediately. How can one scientist force the Alliance to adopt an entire race? They should both be eliminated," Anevay huffed.

"What are her crimes?" Eudia said.

"Impersonation!" Khorsol gestured erratically.

"She maybe accepted a position for which she was not qualified, but has broken no rules," Lhu said.

"She is bound by Alliance regulations. She already endangered her crew!" Khorsol argued.

"If so, that disciplinary action is under the jurisdiction of her immediate supervisor," Lhu said.

"Who is a traitor!" Khorsol said.

Arwel held up a hand to stop the exchange. "Though we may not like his actions, he has broken no Alliance rules. You are too quick to destroy these lives, Khorsol."

Premier Entu stood and sufficiently quieted the room. "They will stand trial and provide explanation. They may not have broken any rules, but their actions have put the Alliance in a precarious situation. The scientist Kas and his apprentice will have the opportunity to defend their actions and their lives."

The hall remained quiet as the Premier left. The abruptness of the edict – decided without council vote – left a bitter tension. Whispers resumed as council members shuffled out. Commander Jarlat and Lieutenant Guilem did not speak until they reached their ship. The Jodra Core left Opes and docked on Harta while its cargo awaited trial.

SKYE READ the reports sent to her by Halden. She found the account by Yar Tukk both infuriating and hilarious. He made so many mistakes and so many completely unfounded assumptions. In the short time she'd been apprentice, she'd learned the importance of evidence and unbiased observation. Of course, she'd learned that in science classes on Earth, but she never really paid attention. Now that it was relevant, she truly understood it.

More importantly, she understood how they came to be here. She listed the series of events. Yar Tukk didn't just go to Earth and observe humans. He integrated. He pretended to be one. He found a human to mimic, made friends with him, and then slowly changed his appearance and behaviors. Anybody would find it concerning. It was stalker-level creepiness.

Her thoughts left her exhausted, though she couldn't possibly sleep. She paced, counting the hours since her last interaction. She had her slate, but couldn't communicate, which left her to finish reports and read. Normally, this wouldn't be an issue. Right now, she was restless. She didn't want to sit and work, but she forced herself to keep busy.

She needed more information on her current situation. She searched for the Alliance court system and sorted through history and reports, geography, and title appointments. The three planets of the Torrens planetary train – Opes, Harta, and Anour – cycled together on the same orbital pathway. Opes hosted the High Council – one representative of each planet or cluster in the Alliance community. Harta hosted the Khigh– a collective of judges appointed to decide what is ethical and right. Anour offered residence to dignitaries, high council members and their families while they served the Alliance in the galactic core. The only other planet in the galactic core was Jodra, which served as home to Premier Entu.

Harta Court decided the greatest threats to the Alliance and violations of the Alliance Accords – the rules that govern. The Khigh serve the Alliance to determine the fate of those who seek court or are brought to court. While there are monasteries for the Khigh on every planet, only one may be appointed when a sitting Khigh chooses their replacement or dies. They are crafted into pillars of conscience who seek truth and justice, without sway from cultural or political intervention – their decisions based on ethical standards, not societal acceptability.

Lieutenant Guilem's presence broke her concentration. He stepped inside, ducking below the door frame. "Are you ready?"

She hopped up and took a deep breath. "I have so many questions for you."

He held up a massive palm, stopping her excitement. "They will have to wait. You have been summoned. You will need to leave the slate here."

Carbon cuffs dangled from his other hand. Her stomach dropped as she complied and set the tablet gently on the table. Without being asked, she held out her hands. His eyebrow raised as he attached them with a surprisingly gentle touch.

"You will stand before the Khigh court, and you will be judged. You will have an opportunity to speak, but not before you are permitted. Please keep that in mind. If you attempt to speak out of turn or cause disruption, you will be silenced for the court to proceed."

Skye's heart raced. "I understand."

She focused on her breathing as they walked through the tunnel system. They took their place on an opaque cylinder and waited. The disk beneath their feet slowly began to rise and brought them through an opening in the ceiling. Above them was a large open room of arches and windows. It was beautiful. Had Skye not been there for judgment, she would have really appreciated the craftsmanship.

Lieutenant Guilem stepped back and bowed to the row of cloaked figures. A chill ran across her skin. Skye followed the lieutenant's lead and bowed. Her eyes studied them as they studied her.

"Lieutenant Guilem, who do you present to the court?" An echo of a voice called out.

Skye was unable to pinpoint who spoke among the Khigh.

"This is the human Skye of former planet Earth, apprentice scientist to Kas Liska of Razvedka. She has served two consecutive missions onboard the Evander under their purview."

None of the Khigh moved. "What are the charges?"

Lieutenant Guilem responded automatically. "Performing duties of an Alliance official without proper training or certification."

Skye watched the exchange in silence, looking from the lieutenant to the Khigh as they spoke. The charges didn't sound so bad.

The Khigh spoke as if they could read her thoughts. "Impersonating an Alliance official is punishable by death in the most severe cases."

Shit. Skye could feel perspiration run down her back. She opened her mouth to speak but snapped it shut when she caught the lieutenant's eye. Her breathing quickened. Her heart pounded in her chest.

Lieutenant Guilem continued. "This is in addition to the cases against scientist Kas Liska, and Einar of the Evander."

The cloaked figures were silent. Lieutenant Guilem stood next to Skye once more. The restlessness grew inside Skye while she struggled to keep it leashed and under control. She struggled to maintain a confident poker face. She straightened her posture.

"Human Skye," the Khigh voice said. "Your existence has caused great debate among the Alliance. You are of a species not accepted into the Alliance community, and you do not possess the rights of a citizen.

We reviewed accounts of your interactions with the crew of the Llowei, the Evander, and reports submitted from your work. While it is true that you have not endured the traditional training and certification required for most apprentice candidates, you have not been offered the opportunity or guidance to do so.

It is the judgment of this court that your actions have been ethical and without intent of harm to the Alliance. The reports from your colleagues show development of skill, and praise. You have been placed under probation and will be required to demonstrate your aptitude. Your fate is dependent on your future development. Do you have anything to say?"

Skye took a deep breath and stilled her nerves. "Yes, thank you. I'm trying my best to earn the title I've been given. I'm not afraid of hard work, and I believe I can offer a unique perspective. I would like to know what my future, the future of my crew, and the future of my species looks like under these directives."

"You will be under the careful observation of the Alliance. Sentencing of the crew of the Evander has not yet been determined. There will be a trial study to ensure the validity of the collective reports. If the trial is passed, you will receive the certification you lack," the Khigh echoed. "We cannot give you accurate predictions of the future. There are too many variables."

Skye nodded. With their silence, Lieutenant Guilem bowed, and the platform began to drift downward to the tunnels. They walked in silence. In her room, the lieutenant removed the carbon cuffs. She breathed deeply. Relief washed some of the tension out of her shoulders when she saw her slate where she left it.

Lieutenant Guilem stood in the doorway, watching her settle in. Skye stilled and met his eye, slowly sitting at the table.

"You are quiet for a human," he said, "and you retain your composure well."

Skye let the comment hang in the air. "Have you met many humans?"

He smirked. "I have met several."

Her heart began to race again. "Can you tell me about them?"

He stepped over to the seating area and bent to sit, then paused. "May I?"

Skye cautiously eyed the stone man. "Of course."

He sat and resumed their staring contest, choosing his words.

"There have been several humans recovered across the Alliance – some remain in stasis, some are alert, most are afraid. They often respond with anger and violence. They try to escape. They do not respond well to captivity or isolation. You are different."

She waited a moment before speaking. "No, I'm not. Not really," she thought carefully about how much she wanted to say. "I was afraid when I woke, and I tried to hide. I didn't believe or trust anyone at first. I looked for a way to escape. Had someone tried to restrain me or attack me, I would have responded with violence. I was angry when I finally believed my planet was gone." She studied her intertwined fingers resting on the table. "I still am."

After a moment of assessment, Skye sighed and closed her eyes. She rolled her shoulders and cracked her neck.

"There is much to learn about your species," Lieutenant Guilem said.

"And we are still learning too – about you, about the Alliance, and how we fit into this new life," she lowered her eyes, "and how we came to be here."

"I hear you have been diligent in your studies. It shows in your reports," he slowly got up from the bench, "even found an unlikely tutor."

"You mean Jedre."

"Yes. I found that news surprising at first. But I suppose it makes sense, in a way. You have some things in common."

"Like what?"

He smiled fondly. "Jedre would be an excellent subject of report. A challenge that none in the Alliance have conquered."

"That doesn't really feel right. Besides, I may have already ruined my chances of learning anything about Jedre."

Lieutenant Guilem ducked his head as he exited the room. "I look forward to your future reports, apprentice Skye."

THIRTY

Skye woke with her cheek lying in a puddle of drool. She wiped the spit from her face and looked around sleepily. Murmured voices outside her door caught her attention. She stood as the door opened, and three Alliance officers entered her chamber. Their suits covered them head to toe, much like the one she wore on Shehur. Tinted shields covered their faces. Her hair stood on end as adrenaline fueled her panic response.

Skye's arms hung loosely at her sides, her feet ready to run. "How can I help you?"

The closest officer spoke with a neutral tone. "Human Skye, you are summoned to stand trial with the crew of the Evander. We will provide your escort."

Skye relaxed an inch. "Where is Lieutenant Guilem?"

A deeper voice answered from one of the officers closer to the door. "His whereabouts are not our concern, nor yours."

The closest officer gestured to Skye and tapped a pocket on her vest. "Hold out your wrists, please."

Skye complied. As before, her wrists bound in carbon cuffs for the walk to court. They moved quickly, guiding her to the disc elevator. When it reached the court platform, they ushered her to seating, rather than the floor.

The courtroom was full today. Officers lined tight ranks of people bound in cuffs. Relief and worry tugged her heart when she laid eyes on Einar and the crew. They stood together, seemingly at ease. She thought Kuza might even be sleeping.

As her gaze drifted past the masked officers, she choked on a breath. Not only did she see Joey and Davin, but the faces of many other humans she'd never met. Her heart thumped against her rib cage. A few eyes met hers and grinned in solidarity. Others wore looks of worry or scorn.

Like before, the nine identical Khigh didn't move or speak. Now, an identical bench mirrored the Khigh and accommodated another slew of officials. Where the Khigh were the same, the others were vastly different. Lieutenant Guilem sat amongst them. His stony demeanor revealed nothing but a poker face as good as her own, if not better. Actually, she conceded, definitely better.

Her gaze rested on each individual. None seemed to mind her ogling except one. He wore a military jacket tacked with emblems. The scorn on his face radiated hatred and disdain. Skye felt the heat creep up her neck and prayed her face was not as red as it felt. His contemptuous smirk suggested otherwise. His eyes met those of his neighbor, spreading his disdain like a plague. Now two creatures bore the hatred of burning stars. She took a deep, steady breath.

Skye followed along as the trials started. She assumed that many of the humans present would not be able to understand. Her mind wandered, fabricating different scenarios for her human compatriots. Speculating about their treatment and wondering if anyone else worked like she did or had nanotech.

The Khigh called forth crews, one after another. The same charges were issued: violating council directives, illegal possession of a quarantined species, and unapproved deviation from assignments. The crew members had the opportunity to speak or remain silent. Most chose to stay quiet.

As the trials progressed, Skye noted the severity increase. The initial crews, small in size and harboring few humans, received sentences of probationary trials or status revocation. As the number of humans grew, so did the punishment. Awake humans – regardless of quantity – increased the penalty. Unsanctioned studies on humans increased the penalty. Illegal sale of humans or human parts almost always ended with life sentencing.

Skye nearly vomited. She could tell by the reactions of the other humans, not many of them had nanotech. She both envied and pitied them.

A sultry figure in a bright green dress walked on the platform. It complimented the pink blush of her skin and the blonde curls that cascaded over one shoulder. Skye's head tilted slightly with the presence of the woman. She stood proud and confident, pleased to be presented to the court, unlike all who'd previously been called there. Skye's stomach churned with unease.

"Who presents to the court?" The Khigh voice echoed.

"Mara of Mencuri and the green tower of Ziet, lead researcher of current approved Earthen species studies," she grinned like a cheshire cat.

"We've reviewed your appeal to the court. Your request for the acquisition of the humans in stasis has been conditionally approved," the unmoving Khigh said, dismissing the woman.

Mara sashayed off the court floor. Skye didn't understand, but chills spread over her skin. The woman cast a glance and a smirk at Char as she passed.

Char paled. It clicked for Skye – they knew each other – and this was not a good thing. Char's panic flared panic in Skye. For a brief moment, their eyes met. The fear communicated clearly before Char turned away.

"Crew of the Evander," the Khigh echoed.

Skye swallowed hard. Einar, Kas, Jedre, Char, Zaima, and Kuza lined up shoulder to shoulder. She moved to join them, but a tight grip on her upper arm stopped her. Her shoulder nearly displaced as her body lifted and jerked back.

"Stay right here," the officer warned in a low voice.

Skye held her arm tight and wrinkled her face. "But they're my crew."

"Be silent," he ordered.

Her heart sank as the Khigh began. "Crew of the Evander, you have been charged with violating council directives, illegal possession of a quarantined species, unapproved deviation from assignment, and unapproved human studies. How do you plead?"

"Incomplete," said Einar.

The Vanzkelgan dignitary sneered from the bench. "That is not an option."

The Khigh resumed after an uncomfortable pause. "Explain, Commander Einar."

Einar bowed. "My crew, as we stand, is not complete, my Khigh."

The Khigh did not speak to one another, but as the silence permeated the room, Skye had no doubt they were communicating. She leaned toward the floor. An abrupt jerk on her arm reminded her of the officer at her side.

"Bring the scientist's apprentice to the floor," the Khigh demanded.

Skye looked at the officers. They hesitated only briefly. The one on her right ushered her down after the other's grip reluctantly withdrew from her arm. They passed through a barrier that blacked out the viewing area. Skye could no longer see the humans. Anxiety gripped her throat as she took her place with the Evander.

The cold, deafening platform caused her muscles to tighten and seize. Looking up at the Khigh and the fierce array of officials, Skye struggled to remain still and confident. She looked at her crew, who met her gaze with a nod or a smile. She nodded in return. Zaima caught her eye, straightened her posture, and returned focus to the council. Skye mimicked the movement. The silence continued.

"Crew of the Evander, by unceremoniously inducting a human

to your crew, you bring complications to the Alliance. Scientist Kas Liska, we reviewed your appeal. It is not sufficient to relieve your crew of the offenses, but we will honor subset 42a of the request. You plead guilty to the offenses. Your compounded sentence will be carried out at the completion of a probationary observational trial. Should you succeed, the Evander and its crew will retain their titles. Requested sanction of the observational studies of the acquired humans on the Evander is conditionally approved."

Skye's wide eyes drifted to Kas. Except for a guilty side glance, his eyes remained trained ahead. A deep bellowing horn resounded through the court. The judges stood and faced the ornate, elevated pedestal behind their bench.

A booming voice rang out, piercing Skye's ears and mind. "All hail Premier Entu of the Interstellar Alliance, supreme and all-seeing unifier of cosmos, defender of the Galactic Core and its territories."

Skye watched in awe as the walls parted. Mercurial silver blades swirled around his large, muscular form. He descended to the platform in mid-stride and greeted the court with outstretched arms. The platform created an ornate chair behind the Premier as he sat without hesitation.

A thunk to her head stole Skye's attention. Jedre snarled and nodded his head forward. She realized that everyone had their heads bowed. She flushed and followed suit. As much as she tried to control it, her eyes disobediently stole glances at the premier.

He surveyed the court and fluttered his hand. "Proceed."

The Khigh addressed the Evander crew. "The probationary trial is set. Commence your next observational study on the planet Lohr in the Soturi region."

"Have the humans joined the Alliance?" Premier Entu grinned, the question poised in the air like a poisonous dagger.

The Khigh responded flatly. "No official declaration has been made regarding the human species -"

He grinned widely, getting back up from his seat. "There are so many humans in attendance today. Is this all of them?"

"All of the recovered, awake humans, not occupied in sanctioned studies, are present. The recovered humans in stasis are stored for transport."

His eyes set on her like a hawk with prey in sight. The Premier gestured a hand toward Skye. "There is a human among that crew, is there not?"

"There is," the unmoving Khigh responded.

"Human," Premier Entu's voice boomed. The ornate pedestal reformed into a staircase as he descended to the floor. The split bench of officials seamlessly made way for the Premier.

The silence of the room enhanced the sound of blood pulsing in Skye's ears. Danger radiated from the enormous being, gracefully walking toward her. His uniform floated in the air, trailing behind him with impossible physics.

Skye stood to her full height and raised her chin to meet his gaze. Her pulse quickened as he didn't show any sign of slowing down. She forced herself not to respond, remaining still as a statue. If he didn't stop, he'd have to walk right through her.

But he stopped – a mere meter from her face. "Have the humans joined the Alliance?"

She felt the threat and weight of the question. Her mind was white with panic, but her tongue was quick. "I do not speak for the whole of my species."

His eyes narrowed, but the smug smile never left his face. "Well then, who speaks for the humans?"

With a wave of his hand, the barrier receded, revealing the captive human audience. Skye resisted looking back and forced herself to keep her eyes on the Premier. It felt like bait.

"No one?" He scoffed at the murmur. He stepped closer to her. The crew of the Evander slid to the outskirts of the platform, leaving just the two of them. His floating garment encompassed her, shifting quickly to a cage of spikes.

Skye felt the tension from her crew, the humans watching, and the bench of judges. She felt the air of intimidation and bloodthirst from the creature before her. An eerie calm settled over her as she met his eyes, her face void of emotion.

"We had a tradition on Earth," Skye said, half-expecting immediate death for speaking. "Those sentenced to die were given last wishes," she maintained eye contact, not saying another word.

The corner of his smug grin twitched upward. A spike slipped under her chin, tipping it up. He grinned as the cold touch made her flinch. "Go on."

"I do not speak for the human race. I can only give you my thoughts and final wishes, something that was not afforded to the rest of my people," she paused. "I request for the displaced refugees of my planet to be granted full rights as Alliance members, and a new home planet be found or forged as reparations for the damages done by the Vanzkelgans. I wish to continue my work and education as an apprentice scientist, and complete my unresolved study of the enatomo."

His features reflected in the blades as they neared her skin. "Is that all?"

Her pulse raced as survival instincts screamed from every cell. Her brain racked for a better answer than the one on the tip of her tongue.

"Yes, that is all," she swallowed hard.

BOOM. The ground quaked. Skye fell to the ground, surprised to be alone and not impaled. The Premier was back on his pedestal. How he moved so quickly, she didn't know or understand. The council officials scattered. The Khigh disappeared. Jedre lifted Skye to her feet.

"What's going on?" Skye said, her voice and feet wobbly.

"Rebels are attacking, "Jedre dragged her.

Skye's recoiled in horror. "Humans?"

He nodded, "and Vanzkelgans."

"What?" She breathed, suddenly short of air.

"Your people are at war," he said, "or didn't you know?"

Disks shuttled herds of people into shipping pods. Skye could not keep track of the flying ships, flying discs, flying people. She covered her head and ran with Jedre. They dropped into the tunnel system.

"Why are we underground? We're going to get buried!" She yelled frantically.

"The tunnels are fortified. They will hold while we get to the Evander." Jedre dragged her along.

Explosions showered them with dust and gravel.

"Jedre!" She cried.

"We're almost ther," he said.

Skye saw the exit. The bright suns of Harta scorched her eyes. But she never saw the blast that knocked them from their feet. She stared at the sky, her ears ringing, her body numb to the coming pain. Her mind questioned reality as space ships battled overhead.

THIRTY-ONE

The mask of an officer hovered in her vision, shading the harsh light. Her arm slung over his broad shoulders as he lifted her numb body. She blinked through the panic while being carried away. Her feet struggled to find purchase on the ground.

The pressure of the blasts and showers of debris registered the warzone in her fogged mind. The ringing in her ears irritated the headache behind her eyes. Her hands clasped the sides of her head. It failed to help.

Faint words. Faint words grew into shouts and orders, engines, and fiery blasts. Skye was thrown behind a large crate and covered with a body. Dust and heavy rock rained over them. She coughed and sputtered. Her lungs screamed for air, rejecting the filth that filled them. The weight on top of her crushed her torso until her uneven vision gave out.

She woke with a mask over her face. When she began to move, a strong arm wrapped around her torso and held her tight. She desperately clawed at her face covering, though removing it did little to help her breathe.

Her eyes focused on the officer. His suit belonged to the Alliance, but his face was completely human. Despite introverted and asexual tendencies, Skye appreciated a handsome human being. His phenomenal cheekbones descended to perfectly kissable lips. The peppered stubble covered his strong jawline and stunned Skye with its absurdity. What human had time to shave during an intergalactic conflict, let alone manscape?

Skye openly stared at him. "Who are you?"

He flashed a white smile. "Not right now, love. We gotta get to the ship."

While he continued to monitor for an opportunity to move, his words sunk in and dredged foggy memories. Skye struggled against the stupidly strong arm wrapped tightly around her waist. She pried at his fingers, trying to peel one back.

"Let me go," she said.

He flashed his gun, then quickly withdrew it. "Stop fighting me. I have enough enemies to fight off right now, I don't need you fighting me too."

"We're not friends," Skye said.

His eyes searched for hers until they met. "We're not enemies."

She bared her teeth at him and struggled against his grip.

He shook her. "We are not enemies. You are their pet – a lab rat. They are studying you just as they do everything they come across. You are not a member of their crew!"

Skye cursed as heat flushed her skin. Her nostrils flared. "What I do is none of your concern."

"Of course it is!" he said. "We're the last of our species. We have a responsibility to each other."

She stopped for a moment while bile rose in her throat, fueling her struggle.

"Let me go!" she roared.

His grip faltered. Much to his surprise and panic, she burst free.

"For fuck sake!" He scrambled to grab her again.

Adrenaline pumped through her veins as she fled. She zig-zagged out of his reach, jumping over crates and swerving around tables.

Shots fired behind them, whizzing by. A scorch mark marred a storage container in front of her. She flinched and leapt the other way, hoping not to meet the same fate.

A howl of pain over her shoulder startled her attention. Without many options, she ducked behind a barrel. Shielding her head from a succession of blasts and falling debris, she peeked around the corner.

The man lay next to a crate. He pushed himself upright with great effort. His skin was pale and sweating. He grimaced with labored breath. The stomping of feet drew his gunfire, causing the Alliance patrol to scatter and take cover. Skye caught a glance of the shoulder grazed by the cautery cannon. The angry red skin blistered under the charred remnants of his shirt. She winced.

He touched his ear and tucked his head against his shoulder. Skye strained to hear him, but he was definitely talking with someone.

"Leave me here. I won't be able to make it back with –" Shots resumed around their hiding positions. Sky covered her head to block blast debris. "– have to make it. Don't argue, just make sure you get everyone there."

He was still firing back as he argued. "We still have people to save. Stay on mission. Stay focused!"

A shot from the Alliance hit a barrel, releasing pungent gases. Skye felt dizzy. Her vision blurred, and her head hit the ground hard. The last thing she heard was him saying, "See you on the other side."

She wasn't sure if it was meant for her or whoever he had been talking to. He was looking right at her when he slumped over, and his weapon clattered on the ground.

THIRTY-TWO

For the second time this year, Skye woke up in the medical bay of a space ship. She still thought in Earth time, which was arbitrary and irrelevant now. The thought of more lessons from Kas or Jedre made her groan and burrow deeper in bed. While not the comfiest thing she'd ever slept on, the med bed was also not the worst. Her face nuzzled into the soft, thin sheets.

"Welcome back, Skye," Char said. "Don't try to get up yet. You've been unconscious for a shift."

I need to learn Jodra time if I'm going to stay here, she thought.

Char laughed. "That would be helpful for future reference."

Her vision swirled, bringing a wave of nausea to her throat. "What?" Skye said, dizzy.

Char repeated. "Learning Jodra time."

Skye tensed as a chill ran across her skin – hair-standing, goosebumps and all. Her mind lagged to comprehend. "You just read my thoughts?" Her raspy voice tasted bitter of morning breath.

"Calm down, Skye. You're elevating your heart rate. If you keep escalating the machines, they will administer you a sedative."

Skye continued to panic, then felt incredibly drowsy. Her head hit the padded table before rolling to one side.

"Oh, like that," Char bent closer to Skye's face before her eyes closed. "I'll see you when you wake again, and I'll explain."

Her muscles felt strained and stiff but well rested when she woke, again. No more wires or tubes surrounded her bed. An alarm chirped every minute or so. Char poked her head around a stiff, white curtain. Skye jumped at the sudden movement.

Char smiled. "Hello, Skye. Welcome back."

"Hello, Char."

"How do you feel?"

"Pretty good," Skye watched the medic with new curiosity.

Char's head cocked to the side as she laughed. "Well, you are a beautiful human specimen, but that's not the answer I was expecting." She checked the computer. "You only received a small dose of sedative. Huh. How do your bones and muscles and skin feel?"

Skye chuckled sleepily and stretched her back and arms. "My bones and skin feel good. My muscles feel a little stiff. Overall, good."

"Is your mind adept to process a basic explanation of the med bay equipment?"

Skye smiled slowly. "Yes, Char."

"Oh, good. Before you lost consciousness, again, I told you I would explain ... what happened earlier." Skye nodded, satisfying Char to continue. "You were hooked up to a cortex processor. It essentially reads and interprets brain waves. So, yes I could 'read your mind'" She laughed at the phrase. "But I have trained extensively to read the equipment. I actually wrote a dissertation on the function of the tech in pain management of various species and established the Alliance pain scale." She beamed and gestured extensively with her hands. "It's not as if I could read your thoughts without it, nor could anyone without sufficient knowledge of cortex processor tech."

Skye took a deep and purposefully even breath. "That tech could be useful... in many situations."

Char watched Skye blankly, then recoiled in horror, turning a shade of angry that suggested deep offense. "I would never!" Char sputtered. "Skye! This is exclusively medic tech!"

Skye, startled out of her relaxed state, regained focus and tilted her head forward to make eye contact. "Char, I was not questioning you. I only thought that it could be dangerous in the wrong hands. I doubt everyone across the territories are as honorable as you."

Char huffed and gestured thoughtfully as she calmed down. "Oh, yes. Well, okay. I see what you're saying now. Yes, that could be true."

"It's really never dawned on you?" Skye said skeptically.

"You humans are such suspicious creatures. The Alliance prides itself on transparency and a code of honor, Skye. You will learn this."

"We just got out of court, Char. A court full of disobedient citizens and non-citizens. Do you honestly want me to believe there aren't any secrets in the Alliance? Let alone a black market."

Char huffed. "You'll see. Now, wait right here while I finish these scans. Then, you'll be good to go."

Skye took a moment to look around and saw a human man in stasis. She froze and felt the panic creep up her chest, thankful the sedating device wasn't hooked up.

"What is he doing here?"

Char followed her line of sight. "We're awaiting Jodra Core transport. You were both damaged in the firefight. I told them they could have killed you," she squeaked, "but apparently they deemed it a necessary risk if it meant the capture or death of this human."

"So, who is this guy?" Skye said, noting Char's flabbergasted response. "Don't look at me like that."

Char blushed and composed herself. "I just assumed that you of all people would know. Do you think the other humans don't know either?" She looked like she just figured out the juiciest bit of gossip in all of Jodra.

"You're going to have to fill me in. I don't read minds," Skye said, deadpan.

"Funny," Char gave her a pointed look. She pointed to the man in iso. "I thought his face was a bit different than I remembered. I'm glad I'm not the only one. We've met him before. He tried to blow up our ship!" While Char focused on the scans, the tightness in her expression relayed her true feelings. "That human, Rhys, he is the most wanted man across the Alliance. He's the leader of the rebellion. Well, the human rebellion, at least. There are a few right now."

"The human rebellion," Skye repeated quietly. The weight of war unsettled her stomach. She'd never experienced it firsthand on Earth – she was too young – but she'd lost several friends. "Is the Alliance at war often?"

"War?" Char repeated, aghast. "Heavens, no. The Alliance was created out of the last war and constantly strives to maintain peace. Rebel groups may emerge," she hesitated, "then their issues are resolved. There is no war within the Alliance, Skye. I'll send you over some reports..." Char eyed her sympathetically. "In the meantime, you are to go to the canteen to get dinner. I have you on a strict 3 shift regimen to correct your health. The schedule is programmed into your band. Please make an effort to follow it."

The Jodra Core attached and prepped for prisoner transport. Skye made an effort to mind her business and keep to Char's schedule, but the movement caught her attention. His shoulder looked semi-healed, but not completely. Lieutenant Guilem and several officers led him away, wrists bound in carbon cuffs.

He resisted their pull. Of course, he wouldn't make it easy. She kept her distance, but he saw her anyway. He shook his head and scoffed when their eyes met. She walked closer as they dragged him to the access port and waited for the seals to decompress.

"Good evening, Lieutenant," Skye said. "Good evening Halden."

Lieutenant Guilem nodded an acknowledgment. "Good evening, Skye."

Halden beamed and recoiled at the attention. "Hello Skye."

The prisoner cast a dark glance over his shoulder. He jostled under their grip. "You know, you'll never be one of them."

Her eyebrow raised before her poker face set in, void of expression. Her icy stare responded to his challenge. "I know exactly who I am, and I make my own decisions. I've been doing it long before you came along."

His grin dropped momentarily while he shook his head. "You have Stockholm syndrome. These monsters have you brainwashed. There are only so many humans left. We need to stick together. We need to rescue each other because no one else is coming."

Skye's back straightened. Her chin lifted as she spoke. "You're out of your mind if you think I'd trust you just because you're human. These *monsters*, as you call them, have done more for me than any human. They're my crew. Rhys, if that's even your real name, I don't know you, and I sure as hell don't trust your intentions."

The officers dragged him across the barrier to the custody of the destroyer. Lieutenant Guilem watched the exchange, silently standing guard.

A curious smirk pulled unnaturally at one side of his mouth. "They call me Rhys," he narrowed his eyes, cocking his head to the side with a crack, "but you can call me Silas."

The locking mechanisms disengaged and released the doors. They waited in the transition room as the series of doors and decontamination procedures ran through the protocols. The ships disengaged.

Skye stood on the deck of the Evander and watched the destroyer disappear into hyperspace. His words, their conversations, played in her mind. She chided herself for entertaining the thoughts. But the seeds of self-doubt were planted. She could feel dark tendrils of uncertainty spread like kudzu vines.

Her jaw and fists clenched. She hated him for it. She doubted the truth in the words, even though she thought them herself at times. She found herself staring into the vast space, lost in thought.

"He's wrong, you know."

Skye jumped at the intrusion of her quiet.

Jedre laughed. It was a genuine laugh. One she rarely elicited from the large man.

Skye frowned. "Is he though?"

"Yes. He is wrong. And he is especially wrong about you." He leaned against the wall of the ship and crossed his arms.

Skye grinned, recalling their last conversation with sadness. "You don't even like me."

"Eh, I have a general distaste for humans." He paused and curled his upper lip. "I have a general distaste for most beings. My point is, I don't have to like you to recognize that you are a member of this ship. You have earned your place in a very short period of time. If anything, I'd say he's jealous."

"Thanks, Jedre," she said, looking out the window a moment more before she turned to him. "You know, it's a little creepy when you're this nice. I'm not used to it."

Jedre smirked and pushed off the wall. "Don't be a dick, Skye."

She blushed as the translation registered, her mouth forming an oh. They would need to amend the nanotech to recognize the nuances of human slang. She pulled out her slate and took note. It was time to schedule that conversation with Kas.

ACKNOWLEDGMENTS

There are so many people who helped and encouraged me along the way. First, I'd like to thank my husband for his unending support. It would never have seen the light of day otherwise.

Thank you to my beta readers: Michelle Ramey, Natalie Ramey, Quincy Thaikattil-Lawrence, Abigail Miller and Annabella May.

And thank you to my editor: Laura Owenby, from Red Pen Reviews.

Special shout out to sepulchritude and contributors of Space Australia of Tumblr

www.ingramcontent.com/pod-product-compliance
Lightning Source LLC
Chambersburg PA
CBHW060557310726
48982CB00008B/1149/J
* 9 7 8 1 7 3 5 4 1 6 1 2 0 *